Could It Be

MAGIC

The Land of Enchantment #3

KATHLENA L. CONTRERAS

Flying Tiger Press

flyingtigerpress.com

Cover design by Kathlena L. Contreras

Cover art "The Sandias: Albuquerque's Icon"
© 2007 Glenn F. Hohnstreiter

conrado c/o Shutterstock

Acknowledgements

Thanks to my biggest fan, best booster and my own romantic hero, Bob. Also to Lara LaVonne Jordan and Laura Phillps Carlson. Thanks so much for your sharp eyes, thoughtful comments and friendship. It wouldn't be the same without you.

Preface

I know it's strange to start a novel with a short story, but the events in the short story, "This Magic Moment," come first. So just consider it a really long prologue, and a number of references in the novel will make more sense.

This Magic Moment

a Land of Enchantment short story

Amethyst Rey stared at what lay inside the little box on the linen tablecloth.

A ring. White gold—or platinum. Candlelight glittered on the spray of diamonds surrounding a stone the size of her little fingernail. It was a purple so deep and rich it looked fake.

An amethyst. Of course. And she somehow knew it wasn't fake.

The murmur of other diners in suits and little black dresses wove in and out of discreet piano music. Amethyst's concession to dressing up consisted of a silk boatneck top, broomstick skirt in shades of indigo, purple and violet and a silver concho belt.

She concentrated on keeping her voice low and reasonable. "You have got to be kidding me."

Across the table from her, Jas Harker wore an ever-so-earnest look. "Never."

She should've known something was up: dinner at Blue Coyote in Santa Fe, Jas dressed in a sport coat and opened-collared shirt, opening the door of his emerald-green Infiniti IPL convertible. Good-looking as always with his black hair freshly barbered into stylish disarray, those deep, dark eyes, the mismatched brows, one with a little quirk to it.

She shook her head. So much charm...so little reliability.

"What are you up to now?" she said.

He carefully pushed his dessert plate aside and folded pale, clever fingers in front of him. "I want you to marry me."

Amethyst leaned an elbow on the table. Candlelight traced a glass cut on the side of her thumb—occupational hazard for a stained glass artist. "I got that part. What I'm wondering is what else you want."

"What else do you think I want?"

With Jas, there was always something else. But since she'd been enjoying a very nice night out with him, she probably shouldn't mention that.

"Maybe one binding isn't enough," she said. "Maybe now you want the legal kind."

He sighed and took a sip of wine. "A man usually asks a woman to marry him because he loves her."

"Except you're not a man."

He leaned close and whispered, "Try me."

She held her ground. "A professional collaboration seems to be working pretty well. Anything closer..." She turned sideways and crossed her legs. "Um, no."

His mouth ticked up on one side. "Ah-ha. That's what this is about. 'Amethyst, insecure in her abilities, rejects a degree of closeness that might reveal her mediocrity.'"

Her face went hot. "Mediocrity? *Mediocrity?*"

He wore an innocent look. "Am I wrong about that?"

She spluttered and swept a hand around her. The restaurant disappeared. Piñon pines and juniper trees replaced the other diners. Instead of faux-painted walls, a night sky with stars like slivers of glass surrounded them. Crickets' music took the place of the tinkling piano.

"Nice." Jas grinned and drew a finger along the candle flame. It turned a rich rose color and twined patterns upward in the darkness. "So much more intimate."

"That wasn't—I didn't—" She fumbled at the magic. Nothing happened. She tried again.

He caught her hand. "Here. Let me."

The restaurant blinked back in. The ring was on her finger, too.

Amethyst yanked it off and plunked it back into its box.

He watched with amused tolerance, the kind of look one would use with a puppy's silly antics. "So you aren't insecure."

"No!"

"Are you sure?"

"Yes!"

He leaned back, twirled the stem of his glass between his fingers. "So. Are you up to a challenge?"

She folded her arms. "Name it."

"How about a little contest of wizardry?"

"Let me guess. You win, I marry you."

"Exactly the stakes I had in mind."

She snorted a laugh. "I don't think so."

"Then you *don't* trust your powers."

Amethyst gave him a sweet smile, tipped her head to one side and zapped him into the middle of the parking lot. One Brooks Brothers shoe remained underneath the table.

For good measure, she put on a curse that would make the sole come off the first time it was exposed to water.

Melodie set down her tea. It hit the coffee table with a thunk and a jingle of ice. "You did *what?*"

Amethyst pulled her fingers through her hair. "I know. But I was mad."

What were best friends for, if not to point out massive stupidity?

"And so you agreed to marry the man if he can best you in wizardry." Melodie angled into her end of the couch and folded her arms. "Didn't it once, maybe, *vaguely* occur to you that he might be setting you up?"

"Well...maybe after I got back to Albuquerque." She stirred the ice in her glass, avoiding Melodie's eyes. Colors from the stained glass panel on the wall behind her reflected in the ice, turning them into cubes of green, gold, vivid sky-blue.

"And then?"

Amethyst sighed. "When I got home, I couldn't find my way to the front door."

Melodie burst out with a laugh. "What do you mean?

Your front walk is straight and ten feet long."

"Ever heard the saying, 'He led me down the garden path'? That's what happened. I wandered that path for fifteen minutes before I could break the illusion." Amethyst made a face. "Complete with sphinx moths, night hawks and evening primrose."

"I guess I shouldn't say anything about it sounding pretty."

"Not," Amethyst said, "under the circumstances."

"You'll just have to tell Jas the bet's off, Wiz." That was the nickname Melodie had given her in their UNM days. Short for 'whiz kid.' "If you're gonna marry him, it'll have to be for the usual reasons."

"Bad ones?"

"Have I ever mentioned that cynics are annoying?"

"We're talking about Jas here."

"Point taken," Melodie said. "But still. I don't think this is an arms race you want to join."

"The only thing is, I already have." Amethyst shifted in her seat. "When he went home, he didn't *have* a front door."

Amethyst sent a questing thread of magic through her front door. The wards and guards she'd layered and latticed the house with glowed electric blue and sizzling yellow to her wizard's eye. The front yard looked perfectly normal in the morning sunlight, with its sweep of gravel made to look like a dry streambed, grey-green chamisa and purple-flowering Russian sage. Her Subaru sat on the driveway, unscathed. No lurking spells she could detect.

She braced herself and cracked open the door. Nothing rushed in but a breeze smelling of the lavender, rosemary and wormwood lining her front walk. She took a breath, opened the door and stepped out.

Nothing. God, it was like being a mob informant. You knew the hit was coming, just not when. Or where, or how.

She dashed down the front walk (it remained straight and about ten feet long), across the driveway and to the mailboxes. She jabbed the key in the lock, scooped out the mail, bolted back into the house and slammed the door. At the kitchen counter, she slitted open envelopes. One held what looked like letterhead. She unfolded it—

And dropped it on the counter.

Magus Corporation. Jas's company. In Jas's heavy, backslanted hand, it read, *Touché. Are you ready for Round Two? Excellent wards, by the way. Almost impervious.*

She touched a thought to the letter. Flame sheeted across it, leaving a black curl of ash and a scent of hot copper. She flicked the burnt paper with more magic and it vanished.

Amethyst rubbed her arms. *Almost* impervious. What did that mean? Pointing out that he'd been able to breach her defenses with something as simple as a letter? She sniffed for spells, something she might have brought inside with it. Still nothing.

"Okay, Jas," she said to the air. "I get it. You're trying to psych me out, aren't you? Well, it's not gonna work."

She stomped down the hall, through her bedroom and into the bathroom. Turned on the shower. Her sweats halfway down her hips, she hesitated. Her wards still pulsed and glowed, protecting against, among other things, wandering wizards' eyes. Gritting her teeth, she undressed the rest of the way, turned on the water and stepped into the spray.

The scent of roses surrounded her when she ducked under the showerhead to rinse her hair. She cracked open an eye.

Rose petals, red, creamy white, yellow, pale lavender, fluttered all around her. The shower floor was a confetti-pile of petals. She yelled and jumped out, suds trailing down her shoulders and arms.

Hugging a towel around her, she cursed and shivered. *Almost impervious*—water had to get through the wards. Electricity. *Air*, for godsake. Which meant one of two things.

Either she was so screwed…or she was going to have to get out there and fight back.

Melodie looked up from her laptop. "At least you don't look like a Rastafarian on a bad hair day anymore."

Amethyst plunked down in a chair and toweled her hair. All around her, hard drives, motherboards, flowcharts and printouts of code battled for territory with Melodie's Beanie Baby collection.

"Thanks for letting me use your shower." *All* the taps at home had been spouting rose petals.

Melodie closed her computer screen and folded her hands under her chin. "Roses," she sighed. "How romantic. How can you resist?"

"Like this," Amethyst said. She fished her phone out of her purse and punched the icon with Jas' smiling face.

He answered on the second ring. "Did you get the flowers?"

"Lovely." She scratched her scalp. A five-mile drive down Lomas Boulevard to Melodie's University-area home had given the shampoo plenty of time to dry. Her head still itched. "But you know, I've been thinking about this marriage business. You don't even know what it's like to live with me. Maybe I squeeze the toothpaste tube in the middle and put the toilet paper roll on the wrong way. For all you know I hang my clothes over the backs of chairs, leave the dirty dishes in the sink and watch *Green Acres* reruns. What if I like parties with loud salsa music?"

Melodie's brows went up at that.

"I'm relatively certain this is the first time you entertained the notion of hosting a loud party," Jas said. "And if you did have one, I suspect between the two of us, we could come up with a spell to contain the noise."

"I sure hope so. Because you never know when you might need it." She grinned and ended the call. "Hey, think Marl can spare you for a girl's night out? Say, eleven-thirty or so?"

"Girl's *late* night out. What do you have in mind?"

"The premier of a new reality TV program. It's called

'The Jas Harker Show.' I think I can promise it'll be worth staying up for."

The coffee table was all set with popcorn, crackers and a jalapeño cheese ball, veggies and dip. A couple of glasses of Yellow Tail shiraz caught and splintered the light into rubies and garnets.

Melodie smeared cheese on a cracker and propped her socked feet on a corner of the table. "So what're you going to do? I'm assuming Jas's house is as spelled up as yours is."

Amethyst folded her hands over her middle. "Spell work is like hacking. There are always vulnerabilities to exploit."

"Yeah, and Jas owns a computer security company. I think that makes him a little harder to hack—however you want to do it."

Amethyst smiled. "But not impossible. Watch."

She flicked on the TV. In this case, since she was using the 44-inch screen as a scrying medium, she didn't use the remote. An image of Jas's home in Albuquerque's foothills shimmered to life, modern angles of glass and stacked sandstone just visible above an adobe wall and native landscaping. The Sandia Mountains hulked behind, a looming shadow of five thousand-plus feet of granite boulders and scrubby high-desert vegetation against a black-velvet sky. The neighboring homes, with their flat pueblo-style roofs, were more conventionally

Southwestern. This late, most windows were dark.

"I debated the type of music to use," Amethyst said. "I like salsa, but it just doesn't have that certain *je ne se quoi*, the sort of thing to really…shall we say, wake things up in the neighborhood. So I settled on some Ice T. Lots of good, explicit lyrics."

"Oh, no," Melodie breathed with convincing horror.

Amethyst frowned at the TV screen. The picture panned and zoomed in on a cluster of rocks at the base of an Apache plume bush several houses distant. "That's where I stashed the MP3 player. Straight illusion would've been the most robust, but would have taken a lot of maintenance." She tossed a handful of popcorn into her mouth and settled back into the sofa cushions. "Ready?"

Gangsta rap blared out over her speakers. *Boom-chugga-boom*, complete with subwoofer to really make the windows quiver. She quickly dialed it down.

"That's what the neighbors are hearing right about now," she explained. "The MP3 player takes care of the actual—well, for lack of a better term, *music*. I'm just amping it up with magic. And since it only seems like it's coming from Jas's house, his protection spells don't interfere with it."

"Uh-oh," Melodie said. "Looks like Jas hears it. All the lights just came on in his house."

Amethyst grinned. "That's the beauty of the whole thing. He's blissfully snoozing away and can't hear a thing. The lights are illusion. And see all those cars parked on the street and hear those happy party sounds? Those are illusion, too. But the neighbors, I see, hear it just fine."

Lights were coming on in other houses. Amethyst zoomed in on one. A trim middle-aged man came outside, belting his robe with sharp little tugs. He glared at Jas's house and stomped back into his own.

"Now," Amethyst said. "A little patience."

They sipped wine, ate snacks and gasped at the lyrics coming over the speakers. An APD cruiser eventually appeared on screen, pulled over at the curb in front of Jas's house.

Amethyst gave a wicked grin and snapped off music, lights and party noises. The cop got out of his car, walked up to the courtyard gate and rang the bell.

"Now for the good part," she said.

Jas came to the gate in his own robe and slippers. The cop explained the visit. Jas displayed admirable bafflement, gestured at his house, all dark except for entry lights. Amethyst and Melodie laughed and threw popcorn at Jas' image on the TV. The cop got back in his car and Jas went back into his house. Amethyst turned everything back on again.

The cops showed up twice more. The last time, angry neighbors, tousle-haired trial lawyers and neurologists in their jammies and bathrobes, joined the fray. Amethyst left the illusion running then. The red and blue lights of three cop cars strobed across real adobe walls and illusory Jags, Beemers, Audis and Lexuses (or was that Lexi?). Cops muscled past Jas into his courtyard, visions of coke-sniffing, Ecstasy-dropping party-goers no doubt dancing in their heads.

"Oh, God, Wiz," Melodie choked between giggles.

"You're doomed. You'll have to change your name and move out of state."

Amethyst crossed her ankles, swirled her wine and gave a smug, one-sided smile. "At least he won't want to marry me now."

Amethyst's phone rang. She rolled over in bed and picked it up.

"Violita!" Her mother's nickname for her. Her mother's voice, in fact. "I'm so happy for you!"

"Huh?" Amethyst said. She squinted at the clock. Nine thirty-seven. Too early. She'd still been tormenting Jas past two last night.

"Jasper just called and spoke to your papa. You never told us!"

"Uh…told you what?"

"You have to have the wedding at Saint Francis church. You can wear my dress. We'll have it fitted to you. Auntie Cecelia can do the flowers—she owns Flores de Taos, remember? I'm so proud! I can't wait to tell Maria and Inez. Have you told Alejandro Junior yet? I know he hasn't thought very well of Jasper, but he'll change his mind when he knows how you feel. Oh, *mija*! So rich! So handsome! Such a lucky, lucky girl! I'm putting Papa on now."

Dad's voice came on the phone. "Your mom said it all, Thistle. As long as you're happy, so are we."

Amethyst sat up, fully awake now. "Jas told you we're

getting married?" Amazing how calm her voice sounded.

"Actually, he asked for my blessing," Dad said. "I guess he must be a little old-fashioned."

"Such a gentleman!" Mama said in the background. "So polite!"

Amethyst felt her blood pressure going up. Her pulse pounded in lips and throat and fingertips. "Did you give it to him?"

"Well...yes." Dad hesitated. "Should I not have?"

She gripped the phone so hard the plastic creaked. Magic boiled under her skin. She wrestled it down with an effort. "I think he might be a bit premature."

Dad was silent a moment. "Look, Thistle. If he's—"

"Don't worry about it, Dad," she interrupted "It's just a miscommunication. I'll get it straightened out. Just do me one favor? Don't let Mama call the family. Please."

She set down the phone and spent some time just breathing. It didn't help. She got up, jammed her legs into jeans and yanked on a black shirt with a mean-looking Ford Mustang. Keys fisted, she headed for her car.

In the Magus Building lobby, her feet rapped a quick beat on the floor of water-smoothed pebbles. Voices echoed in the two-story-high space. She paused at the fountain, a ten-foot-high boulder of glossy black granite shot through with stained-glass colors.

"Don't watch, Talys," she told the fountain. "You're not gonna like what happens next."

Before he could answer, she strode to the security desk.

She concentrated on being polite to the young man

there. "Amethyst Rey," she said. "Here to see Mr. Harker."

Politeness was easier with a minimum of words.

"Is he expecting you?"

Amethyst smiled. "I imagine so."

He spoke to his computer a moment. "Go right on up, Ms. Rey."

She kept the smile plastered on her face. "Thank you."

She rode the elevator to the top floor. Jas' assistant escorted her into his office and shut the door behind her.

Jas stood and came around his desk, arms outstretched. "Amethyst! How are you this morning?"

She flung up a ward so strong it bounced him back against his desk. "You *called* my *mother?*" Fists clenched, she took an aggressive step toward him. "Magic, you said! You said we were using magic!"

He straightened his tie and shrugged. "You were the one who brought ordinary folk into it, with the police." His lips thinned a little. "And my neighbors."

"You *told* my *mother* we're getting *married!* Do you have any idea what my life will be like now? Do you?"

"You could always do what I did with my neighbors—persuade her it was only a dream."

"I can't use magic on her. She's my mother!" Her blood pressure was going up again. She must've been turning red, because he made patting gestures.

"Calm down, Amethyst. You know as well as I do what happens when a wizard gets too angry."

"Yeah," she said. "This!"

She swept an arm around the room. The desk flowed

and hunched, the legs thickened, a thick protuberance sprouted from one end. The wood turned to muscle, skin, hair, the black scimitars of claws. A bear's blocky head and short ears appeared. It reared on its hind legs and roared.

"Amethyst!" Jas shouted and ducked the swipe of a huge paw.

The chairs changed, too, taking the shape of pronghorn antelope with lyre-like antlers. The pictures on the walls became hawks, ravens, owls. Fingers of frost crackled across the windows as she pulled energy out of the air to add mass to the furniture for the transformation. The computer changed to a skunk that promptly raised its tail and scuttled for the door. Amethyst sent a pulse of magic that whipped it open.

"What are you doing?" Jas shouted. A covey of scaled quail that had been a stack of papers exploded into the air and buffeted past his head. Three pronghorns bounded out the door. The bear dropped to all fours and lumbered after them. Screams and shouts came from outside.

"I," Amethyst said, "am leaving. Have a good day."

She walked out the door. A roadrunner sprinted past her. Office doors slammed. A man with a cup of coffee in hand backed quickly to avoid the skunk. Jas' assistant, arms over head and on the floor by her desk, shrieked while ravens croaked and tore at her breakfast pastry.

At the elevator, Amethyst gestured. The doors whisked open like the turbolift on the starship Enterprise. Beyond lay quivering cables and empty elevator shaft. No big deal. She stepped across the threshold onto nothing. On the other side of the reception area, Jas stood in his office door, tie askew, black hair wild. He waved his hands, both casting spells and warding off the owl that beat at him with its wings.

He shouted at her again. She gave a cheerful little wave and descended into dim air that smelled of lubricant.

Jas would be busy a while. She'd done straight transformation—big medicine, and a lot harder to undo than illusion. The shaft echoed with the clatters and clangs of the elevator car coming up. She stepped onto the narrow shelf of a landing and waited. The car slid up to her level. She flicked the doors open again. The programmers and techs and office assistants inside goggled.

"Hi," she said. She stepped in and pushed the lobby button. The elevator, which had been going up, went down.

If Jas decided—and could manage—to lock down the building, she'd have a time getting out, wizardry or no wizardry. But the tall lobby door swung open on the bright morning. She walked along aisles of cars, swinging her arms and humming Tom Petty's "I Won't Back Down."

Behind her, Jas's voice called her name again.

Damn. He was steaming toward her across the parking lot. No elevator for him—he could just zap himself through his own protective spells. What the hell had he done about the rampaging office furniture? She ran the last few yards to her Subaru and slid inside. She might've zapped herself away, but that was more big medicine too soon after the last big medicine.

She fired up the Subaru and went squealing out of the lot onto the tree-lined curve of America's Parkway. She glanced in the rearview mirror. An emerald-green Infiniti bounced down the driveway after her. She cursed—and tossed a curse behind her. His car would be warded, too, but as a practical matter, he couldn't ward his surroundings while moving. So she liquefied the tar in the asphalt. The Infiniti fishtailed and fell back.

She grinned. So much for rear wheel drive. She made a right onto Louisiana and headed for the freeway.

Jas's car appeared beside her on the onramp—*poof*, out of thin air. The displaced air made a crack of thunder. He might not have all-wheel drive, but he had more horses under the hood than she did. He poured 'em on and zipped ahead, crowded her out where the lanes merged.

She pulled up force between the cars, a kind of cross between shield and ward, and nudged the wheel, pushing back. They jockeyed like NASCAR drivers in the straightaway, then he cast some kind of barrier that made the air thicken, turn into gel that bogged her down. She turned the vents in the car to recirculate and flung rippling, purple fire ahead. She punched through to freedom, trailing streamers of indigo flame behind.

She peeled around the curve before the San Mateo exit doing 80, Jas in front, trying to slow her down. The lanes multiplied. An open patch of freeway appeared ahead.

She called up a dust devil, sent it spinning along the concrete-lined arroyo that ran beside I-40. Tumbleweeds, trash and dirt went airborne, spinning in a greyish-brown tower. Amethyst called it onto the freeway, right on top of Jas. His taillights flared red in the murk, dived for the shoulder.

Conjuring a doppelganger, she drew camouflage over herself and eased off onto the shoulder. Jas must've sucked the energy out of the devil—it tattered away, dropping tumbleweeds like discarded toys. Ahead, her doppelganger streaked away, past Jas through patchy dust. He powered back into traffic after it.

"Buh-bye, Jas," she said.

The double would go for a while, but it wouldn't spray magic like sparks from a Catherine wheel. He'd probably figure it out the first spell he launched at it.

Cars whizzed past. Brake lights popped on. She shifted into Drive and checked her rearview mirror.

Traffic filled every lane. Illusion? Or had her monster dust-devil spooked the other drivers? She flipped on her turn signal and waited for a break.

A car pulled out of the pack and rolled along the shoulder. A green car. It stopped behind her. Jas got out.

Amethyst leaned her head on the steering wheel and ground her teeth, then flung open the door and climbed out.

Jas wore his most irritating superior-wizard smirk. "Tired yet? Hungry? Want to go somewhere for a bite?"

She was hungry—roaringly hungry, the kind of hunger you only got from doing major wizardry.

"Don't taunt me, Jas. I'm not in the mood for it."

He leaned an elbow on her car's roof. "Ah. Is that because you've finally decided you're overmatched?"

Okay. That's it. She worked a communication spell, the sort of thing wizards used to send messages in the days before radio transmitters and the Internet.

Traffic had slowed, now only rolling past. She turned to face it.

"Hello, everyone. This is Jas Harker, computer security magnate." Amethyst swept a hand toward Jas. "You might guess that, given his position, Mr. Harker is a man used to getting what he wants," she said as if playing to an audience—which she was.

On every car radio on the freeway, her voice would emanate. On every GPS or seatback DVD screen, the image of her and Jas would be displayed. For those poor, benighted souls who owned neither, rearview and vanity mirrors would be briefly transformed into displays. Jas frowned and glanced at the nearby cars. A couple of heads had already turned.

"The sort of man who doesn't understand the meaning of the word 'no,'" she went on.

"All right, Amethyst," Jas said. "That's enough."

She ignored him. "This is a great asset in the business world. Not so much in personal relations. Especially when the 'no' in question is in answer to a proposal of marriage. I've tried saying no in every shape, form and manner, yet still Mr. Harker, this paragon of corporate America, persists. So let me try one more time."

Jas's face was a shade of crimson she'd never seen on him before.

She drew breath and shouted, "*No!* I don't want to marry you! Is it clear now?"

All up and down the freeway, six lanes of crawling vehicles, horns honked. A semi truck trundling along the eastbound lanes blew its air horn and flashed its lights.

All traces of Jas's smug smile were gone. "You sent that out? How far did it go?"

"As far and wide as I could send it."

He folded his arms, took a step back, nodded once. "All right. I cede the field. I thought I was trying to convince you that I was serious. I see I should have realized you were."

He turned and got back into his car. Traffic crept by. A man in a Ford pickup braked, motioning Jas in ahead of him.

Jas pulled into the opening and coasted past Amethyst without a glance.

"Then why are you so upset?" Melodie said. She set a mug of chamomile tea on the table in front of Amethyst.

"I don't know!" Amethyst said. "I won the contest. I got what I wanted. But the look on his face when he realized what I'd done, the way he wouldn't even look at me when he drove off—" She swallowed hard.

"Drink your tea," Melodie said.

Amethyst put her hands around the mug, but there was no way that tea would go down the pinhole of her throat.

Melodie sat back and sipped her own tea. "Have you talked to him since?"

Amethyst could only manage a shake of the head.

Melodie studied her a little longer. Finally, she stood up and put her arms around her. "I know I'm going to regret saying this, but maybe you should."

A methyst wet her lips, took a breath and rang the bell. Through the gate's rustic boards, slices of courtyard were visible—flagstone path, cherry sage and New Mexico olive, tall double front doors.

"Yes?" Jas's voice came from the intercom speaker.

"It's me. Amethyst." It was superfluous—he had to know already. If he hadn't taken a look with wizard's senses, there was his surveillance system. "Do you have a minute?"

Silence from the intercom. Then, "Come in. The front door's open."

The lock clicked. She shifted the package under her arm, pushed open the gate and advanced. The front doors were nine-foot slabs of birch. She pushed on one brushed nickel handle. The door swung open noiselessly on pivots instead of hinges.

Jas met her in the foyer. He looked cool in chino shorts and deck shoes.

She held out the package. "This is for you."

He took it like a postal worker would a box without a return address.

She prickled all over with shame. "I came to tell you I'm sorry. It was wrong, what I did. It was…mean…" She ran down. It sounded lame. Inadequate. "I just wanted to tell you." She turned to leave.

"Amethyst, wait." He gestured an invitation. "Why don't you come in and sit down."

It crossed her mind to decline, then she ducked her head. "Thanks."

She followed him into the living room. Tall windows looked out over Albuquerque, across the Rio Grande Valley, all the way to the truncated cone of Mount Taylor, soft and blue on the horizon. He offered her a seat on a caramel-colored leather sofa, then sat at the opposite end.

He unwrapped the package. It was a stained glass window hanging—a crimson rose against desert terra cottas and tans, blue wispy opalescent glass that looked like a sky laced with mare's tails. He held it on his knee and gazed at it a long time.

"It's beautiful." He finally looked up. "But you didn't have to do this."

She made a small, unhappy gesture. "It's not enough." She hesitated, then rushed on. "I didn't want to leave things the way they were—after what I did. I—I—I—" She couldn't go on.

"You...?"

She wrestled with a number of embarrassing admissions. "I'd be sorry never to see you again."

"So would I," he said then held her with that dark gaze of his. "What do we do now?"

"Um." She traced a seam in the couch cushion. "Maybe, if you want to, we can still be friends."

"Mmm." He shook his head. "You know I'd like more than that."

Something in her middle couldn't decide if it wanted to jump up or cringe. "But you know, Jas, that's the problem. You had your chance. I don't hate you anymore, but I don't know if I can ever love you. And even if I could, you're skipping some steps in the process. We'd have to date, first. See where things go."

He leaned back. "We have been dating."

"Working on spells together with the occasional meal out are not dates."

"And those times you've been here, at my home? And I've been to yours?"

She would *not* get annoyed. She owed him that much. "Did we ever snuggle on the couch and watch *Persuasion*? Have I ever made you a home-cooked meal or a cake on your birthday?"

"Our relationship is more interesting than that."

"That's one word for it," she muttered.

"Here's an idea," he said. "Let's split the difference. We'll get engaged."

"If I'm engaged to you," she said with exaggerated patience, "I'm promising to marry you."

"Engagements can be broken. No harm, no foul."

Amethyst folded her arms. "We date first."

"Come on, Amethyst," he coaxed, beckoning.

She glared at him, exasperated.

"All right then," he said with a teasing smile. "How about a little contest?"

৵

Could It Be Magic

CHAPTER 1

The Hunt

She was being hunted.

Amethyst Rey knew it as well as the deer knows when she catches the scent of a mountain lion. She could almost feel the hunter's dark gaze on her, gliding along her neck over the curve of her shoulder, down her arm and wrist to caress her hand where it guided the mouse across the desktop. She imagined she caught a whiff of his aftershave, tangy and musky like the desert after a rain. The air whispering through the ceiling vent might've been his breath on her ear, on the back of her neck.

She gave her ponytail a flip as if dislodging a pesky fly and opened herself to the magic.

Even here in the Magus Building, in the middle of

what was arguably some of the most advanced tech in the state of New Mexico—including the two national labs—the magic shimmered and glowed to her wizard's eye, an ether that surrounded and permeated everything. Without looking up from the lines of code on the screen in front of her, she conjured a ward.

"Is that really necessary?" a man's voice said behind her.

Amethyst jumped and spun in her chair, her heart jackhammering. "Dammit, Jas! Don't *do* that!"

That whiff of aftershave obviously hadn't been her imagination.

Jas leaned against the doorjamb, picture of the business magnate at ease—dress shirt with the sleeves rolled up, sage green tie loosened, black hair gelled in attractive disarray. His eyes, deep and dark as a forest pool on a moonless night, sparkled with amusement under uneven brows—one had a teasing little quirk to it. Those damned crinkles at the corners of his eyes dared her to be annoyed with him.

"Sorry," he said. "I thought you knew I was here."

Charm had its limits. She sat back in her chair and folded her arms. "I knew you were *somewhere*. So did you have a specific reason for spying on me?"

"I wasn't spying on you. I came to ask you out."

"Out," she repeated.

"On a date."

She eyed him. "Isn't it sexual harassment or something when your boss keeps hitting on you?"

"I'm your *boss* now, am I?"

"You know what I mean."

"'Corporate tycoon seizes innocent young woman in his clutches.'" He gave an evil grin and rubbed his hands together. "I like that."

"I don't think I ever claimed to be innocent."

The grin became a seductive smile. "'*Come* for me, Ana,'" he quoted in a husky voice.

Her face went hot. So did some other things. But getting hot and bothered with Jas Harker, wizard, owner of Magus Corporation and world-class conniver wasn't in the cards for the foreseeable future. If ever.

"I can*not* believe you read that stuff," she said. "And here I thought all this time you were a gentleman."

"How about this, then? Come out *with* me."

He never gave up.

"Why the look?" he said. "Dating was your idea. Have you changed your mind?"

She heaved a sigh. "Okay, fine. I'll go out with you. But on two conditions."

"Only two?"

She ignored that. "First, no wining and dining. And no proposals of marriage."

"Ever?" he said, sounding a little dismayed.

She wasn't swayed. "Not unless you enjoy the sound of the word 'no.'"

"You're a hard woman, Amethyst Rey."

"You have no idea."

That teasing light came back into his eyes. "You're making me a hard man."

"You're not helping your cause."

The usual smooth charm returned. "All right," he said. "If the bad-boy attitude doesn't appeal, I'll behave myself. But I have conditions of my own."

"Uh-huh. Let's hear them."

"No standing me up. And no date sabotage."

"Damn." She snapped her fingers. "Headed off at the pass."

"I'm serious. If you agree to go out with me, you have to give it a chance."

She thought about it. He *could* be pretty good company, even if he was a devious conniver. And if she wanted to be perfectly honest with herself, there'd been a time when she would've been thrilled to go out with him.

"Okay, I promise" she said. "How about you?"

"I won't put you under obligation with expensive outings and gifts. As for marriage proposals…" He tilted his head. "Isn't that the point of dating?"

Amethyst opened her mouth to argue, but nothing came out.

✦.✦.✦.✦.✦.✦

"But I don't understand, *mija*," Mama said. "What happened to getting married? First Jasper calls to ask for your papa's blessing, then Papa tells me, 'Don't tell anybody yet, Tonia. Not until Amethyst makes it official.' Well, I've waited a month, and I still haven't heard anything."

Amethyst held in a sigh. So *this* was what was at the bottom of Mama's lunch invitation: *It's been a long time since we've gotten together. I'll be in Albuquerque on Friday. Why don't we meet at the Range?*

The Range was a restaurant with attitude. Overhead, papier mâché cows were strapped to the ceiling fans: flying cows. The seats were capped with imitation tooled leather and upholstered in fabric with cowboys and bucking broncos. The food was some of the best in Albuquerque.

Amethyst took a bite of spinach enchilada. "Jas went about that all backwards, Mama. He asked, and it never occurred to him that I might say no."

Mama's well-shaped brows climbed. "You said *no?*"

Amethyst made a frustrated gesture. "I know. He's charming, he's rich and he's about the best-looking man I know. Most people would be all like, 'Are you crazy?' But I have to feel I can trust a man if I'm going to spend my life with him."

Especially if that life might extend several centuries, as wizards' did.

"Violita," Mama said, somehow managing to scold even while using Amethyst's nickname. "Jasper's stayed with you through thick and thin. Why don't you feel you can trust him?"

"You've seen him in action—you know how he is. He's used to getting his own way."

"Most men are like that. If we let *that* scare us off, no one would ever get married."

Amethyst laughed. "Maybe. But Jas has a tendency to stylishly, charmingly run right over the top of anything and anybody in his way. I guess I don't want to have to battle him to maintain my independence."

"I won't lecture you about marriage being about giving up some independence in exchange for other things," Mama said. "But I think something happened to *make* you not trust him. Because since I've known him, what I've seen is him trying very hard to show you something else."

Amethyst concentrated on the green chile she was spooning over her black beans. "I know he has," she said quietly. "That's why I can call him a friend now."

"Can you tell me what happened?"

"There's no point in making you mad at him now. It was a long time ago, when I first knew him."

"But it was bad enough it still bothers you."

It was, in fact, that bad. When a guy you're beginning to develop feelings for turns out to be a wizard who slaps a binding on you that takes your will and leaves you helpless...

Well, Amethyst had spent most of the last year trying to forgive Jas for that. Dwelling on it didn't get her any closer to that goal.

She shook her head. "Let's just say he wanted something. And led me along to get it."

"Your magic."

Amethyst looked up sharply.

Mama's lips thinned. "That's what that huge vase of flowers was about back then," she said. "I always thought it was strange he didn't just take them to you at the hospital. And then how he wouldn't stay when I told him you'd be home soon."

"Mama," Amethyst said. "How *do* you do that?"

"Maybe I have a little magic, too. It does come from my side of the family."

The waiter came and refilled their glasses. The hum of conversation from other diners gave a comforting sense of privacy. With the topic under discussion, it was best to guarantee privacy.

Amethyst worked a spell of bafflement. Just a little something to make their conversation unintelligible to any eavesdroppers—accidental or otherwise.

"So." Mama said. "Was this marriage proposal just another way to get you for your magic?"

Amethyst almost choked. "Exactly what I asked. But...probably not. At least, I don't think so."

"No?"

"That's what my gig at Magus Corporation is all about. I'm the wizard on staff."

Mama's fork suddenly tinked against her plate. "Violita!" She glanced around.

"Don't worry, Mama. I made sure no one can hear us."

She glanced around once more as if to be sure, then relaxed. "What about the people you work with? They don't know, do they?"

"Of course not," Amethyst said. "As far as everyone except Jas is concerned, I'm only the stained glass artist who moonlights as a consultant."

"And is that how *he* thinks of you?"

"God only knows how he thinks of me. Probably as a challenge. After I took marriage off the table, he was negotiating for an engagement. Jas *lives* for negotiations.

Part of being a corporate magnate, I guess. We ended up compromising. We're going to try dating." At Mama's confused look, she explained, "Our relationship has been a professional one." A collaboration of wizards. But Mama didn't know Jas was also a wizard. "Somewhere along the line, he decided it was a personal one. I had to set him straight on that."

"You make a simple thing very complicated, *mijita*."

"I'm not sure it's me who's making it complicated, but yeah." She sighed. "It is."

CHAPTER 2

Santa Fe

Amethyst's relationship with Jas wasn't, as she'd told Mama, strictly a professional one. But it sure wasn't a romantic one, either. She was morbidly curious to find out what a real, live, official date with him would be like after…whatever it was they had.

She stood in front of her closet, flipping through hangers. Jas had said they were going to Santa Fe for the day, which left a lot of room for clothing options. The disgusting thing was that she was actually agonizing over what to wear.

"What do you think, Caramela?" She glanced over her shoulder at her caramel-colored pit bull, who lay on the bed in the middle of a scattering of skirts and slacks, shells and camisoles and cardigans.

"Do I go with don't-give-a-damn jeans and a sweatshirt?"

Caramela just looked up from where her chin rested on her paws and whapped her tail on the comforter.

"You're right," Amethyst said. "Since I'm agonizing, I must give a damn."

She picked up a silk cami top she'd found on Etsy dyed in garnet and gold and indigo, something that actually looked good on her—well, the polite term would be *athletic*—but in plainer words, her flat-chested figure. Or lack of figure, as she tended to think of it.

"On the other hand," she said to Caramela, "I don't want to make it look like I'm trying to impress him. That would send exactly the wrong message."

She stroked the camisole's cool, vivid silk with the backs of her fingers. It wasn't the kind of thing she got to wear very often.

"Oh, hell," she said and snagged a pair of nice jeans from the mess on the bed.

Jeans would dress the cami down. A black cardigan and boots, and she'd look like she only gave half a damn.

She wasn't much into makeup and hair anyway, so she just put on a little mascara and eyeshadow, caught her dark hair in a beaded barrette she'd found at the Indian Pueblo Cultural Center and called it good.

She was dithering over whether or not she should wear something else after all when the doorbell rang. Caramela launched herself off the bed and thundered down the hall with her smoker's-voice barks. Amethyst took one last, doubtful look at herself in her closet door mirror, sighed and followed Caramela to the front door.

Jas waited outside. His usual charming smile faded. He blinked, looked her up and down and said, "Good morning, Amethyst."

He didn't say it caressingly. Not quite.

"Um, hi," she said. "Come on in. I'll get my coat and

settle Caramela for the day."

Caramela gave Jas a thorough sniffing-over. The stiff wag of her tail said, *Okay, Mom's talking to you, but I still don't trust you.* And she was keeping Jas' attention on her instead of Amethyst. Good dog.

Jas took Amethyst's coat and held it for her.

Damn. Suggestive Jas she could handle. Gentleman Jas was harder to resist. She avoided his eye as she slipped into the coat, then made a business of giving Caramela a goodbye kiss on top of the head and locking the door, even though technically, she really didn't need to lock it. The wards on her house did a much better job of protection than any lock.

Jas' emerald green Infiniti IPL looked as incongruous parked on her cracked driveway as a coach-and-four. At least she'd been able to replace the old garage door and the single-paned aluminum windows with insulated vinyl ones, as well as put in some nice xeric landscaping recently. Now her house looked cute, not just old. Jas circled around to the passenger side and opened the car door.

"Thanks," she muttered, ignoring the fluttering taking place in her middle.

She'd known the man for, what, something like two years now? Minus the year or so she'd spent pretending he didn't exist. You'd think she'd be past falling for his gentlemanly wiles.

He twisted the key and the Infiniti purred like a waking tiger. Turning and hooking an arm around the back of her seat, he backed down the driveway and swung into the street. At the bottom of the hill, he slid the car into a break in traffic on Eubank.

"Not fair," he said. "Wearing something that begs to be touched, when anywhere I touch it will get me in trouble."

She tugged her cardigan closed, trying—and failing—not to think of him stroking the silk of her cami. This was *not* a good beginning.

"I *knew* I should've worn a sweatshirt."

He laughed. "Don't worry, I'll be good."

Although that sidelong, crinkle-eyed smile said exactly the opposite.

Driving along I-40, the silence was positively painful. They passed Uptown, the Magus Building reflecting the mall, the freeway, the surrounding buildings in its 25 stories of green glass.

"So," she said. "Any new magical incursions on the business?"

"No, we are not talking shop today. This is our chance to get to know one another better."

"We *do* know each other better," she muttered.

"In certain contexts."

"Yeah. Crises."

He grinned. "You can always pretend this is one."

That got her to laugh. "Okay, how's this? This is exactly why I hate dating." She waved her hands. "Doing this getting-to-know-you thing without coming across like a complete dweeb."

"There's a way around that. You could marry me."

She folded her arms and glared at him.

"What?" he said, all innocence.

"You know what."

"It wasn't a proposal. Only an observation."

"*Of course* it was."

He gave an enigmatic smile. She would *not* ask what that was all about.

The usual string of slowpokes was absent, so he was able to take the flyover between I-40 and northbound I-25 with enough speed to induce G-forces. Amethyst hung on and enjoyed it.

"Hey," she said. "If you really want to win my heart, you could let me drive this someday."

He threaded through traffic and punched it. The Infiniti gave a muted howl and zipped past the surrounding cars.

"There, you see?" he said. "I've just learned you love fine cars. Was that so bad?"

"Huh. Most guys would consider that an example of dweebishness."

"I'm not 'most guys,' and I don't."

She glanced at him, surprised. It was ridiculous how such a simple statement could spark such a warm, friendly glow.

"Oh," she said. "That's...good."

"I'm encouraged," he said. "You do care what I think of you. I'll press my advantage, then. As soon as we're out of town, I'll pull over and let you drive the rest of the way to Santa Fe."

Daring her to say no, damn him. "Okay. But you'd better know I was exaggerating when I said you'd win my heart."

He slid her another smile. "I have other plans for that."

◆◆◆◆◆◆

Driving at over 100 MPH, it took substantially less than the usual hour-plus to get to Santa Fe. No need to worry about crashes or traffic tickets with a pair of wizards in the car. Wards kept any accidents at bay, a shield of fizzy power foiled radar and cameras, and illusion changed the car's appearance every few minutes. They took turns deciding what it looked like.

Amethyst started with a black 2012 Mustang Mach I.

"Why am I not surprised?" Jas said and followed that up with a jacked-up, tricked-out, fire-engine red Dodge shortbed pickup.

"You know what they say about guys who drive oversized pickup trucks," she said.

He raised his brows in a question.

She smirked. "Never mind."

"Amethyst—" he began, warning.

"Smart Car!" she said and worked the illusion.

It went downhill from there. Jas conjured an illusion of a Ford Pinto, so Amethyst called up an old Volkswagen bus.

She was laughing hard by then.

"Have you ever actually driven one of those?" Jas said. "You might as well make us look like a UFO. The state police will believe that before a Volkswagen bus going over a hundred."

"As if a Pinto could. Besides, you were the one who started it with the minivan. You want to put illusions like that on your car, wait 'til *you're* driving. Better yet, wait 'til you're by yourself."

Sometimes being a wizard could be fun. Being with *another* wizard could even be fun. Although if you'd told her that last year, Amethyst would've said you were crazy.

When she downshifted to climb the grade of La Bajada's basalt cliffs, the section of I-25 that carried traffic out of the Rio Grande Valley and onto the mesas southwest of Santa Fe, Amethyst decided she might've been lying when she told Jas that driving the Infiniti wouldn't win her heart.

She dropped out of hyperdrive not long after they passed the Santa Fe Relief Route a few miles outside of town.

"I see you enjoyed that," Jas said.

"I did," she said and sighed. "Thank you."

Keeping to the 65 MPH speed limit felt like driving with the brakes locked up.

"Did you have any destinations in mind?" she said. "Or do I get a vote?"

Jas waved a hand. "You're in the driver's seat. What do you want to see?"

"I got to drive a fast car fast. Now I want…" Amethyst closed her eyes, relying on the car's wards for a moment. "Chocolate."

He made a noise in his throat. "First the silk top, now you use a voice like that," he said. "I never took you for the vengeful type."

She grinned and took the St. Francis exit.

Santa Fe Style was part of the building code here. Flat-roofed buildings with earth-toned stucco exteriors to match the historic adobe architecture lined the streets, whether it was a McDonalds or a Whole Foods or a government complex. Northern New Mexico style popped up for variety, with pitched metal roofs instead of flat ones.

Santa Fe wasn't an easy town to get around in. The streets went every which way, and the closer you got to the Plaza, the narrower and more unpredictable they became, like the donkey trails they'd once been. It was an *old* town.

She wended her way along Paseo de Peralta to a small, pueblo-style building with turquoise trim and parked.

"Kakawa Chocolate House." She unbuckled her seatbelt. "I can get my own door."

She snagged her purse from the passenger floorboard and got out of the car.

Jas climbed out, too. "My keys?"

She cocked her head. "I'm thinking of kidnapping your car." His eyes got a wicked glitter and he opened his mouth to say something, but she held up a hand. "Do not say I could drive it all I wanted if I married you."

"I was going to say I'd buy you one of your own if you married me."

"Not. Another. Word." She tossed him the keys across the roof. "And this is my treat."

That was the nice thing about working for Magus Corporation. It paid its consultants really, really well. She no longer had to pinch pennies until they screamed for mercy.

The aroma of chocolate enfolded them when they stepped into the shop. Small, round, leather-topped tables dotted a low-ceilinged dining area. At the end of the room stood a large case full of chocolate truffles. A small kitchen stretched behind it. As usual, most of the tables were occupied and a line of people three deep waited to order.

Jas stood looking up at the chalkboard menu. "What do you recommend?"

"Hmm." She studied the menu, trying to keep the idea that was forming from showing on her face. "Well, you can't come to Kakawa without getting a hot chocolate. You might want to give the Aztec Warrior a try."

He nodded. "I'll get us a table."

She smiled and thanked him, then placed the order.

Amethyst brought the tray of tiny cups of chocolate elixir to the table and placed Jas' cup of Aztec Warrior in front of him. Taking her own cup of caramely Tzul, she took a sip. Jas sipped at his cup.

His eyes went wide.

She put on a concerned face. It was all she could do to keep it there. "What's the matter?"

He put down his cup. "Amethyst!"

"What?" she said but ruined the effect by dissolving into laughter.

"That's stronger than espresso!"

"What, you were expecting Swiss Miss? Oh, well, I'll drink it if you can't."

He picked up his cup, met her eyes across the rim and

drank.

"I always add a little sugar to mine," she said, deadpan.

He swallowed, cleared his throat and said in a strained voice, "I'll bet you do."

"I'll get us some ice cream when we're finished. I don't know about you, but I'm hungry."

"I'll choose my own flavor, if you don't mind." He took a tiny sip of chocolate. "I don't trust you any longer."

"That's because you know me better now."

He made a disgusted noise, but his eyes were sparkling.

✧.✧.✧.✧.✧.✧

As long as Amethyst didn't let herself remember that this was a date, she was having fun. Jas was enjoyable company—once he got past the offhand marriage proposals.

After Kakawa, they hit the Canyon Road galleries. Jas had told her when they first met that art was his hobby. She would've decided that was all part of his plot to lure a certain stained glass artist into his clutches, except for the art displayed all over the Magus Building, from the sculptures in the lobby to the paintings on the walls to the pottery in his office.

As they walked up the narrow sidewalks of Canyon Road, Jas pointed out various old adobe buildings. This one had been the ceramicist Frank Applegate's home, that one the home of Olive Rush, the illustrator and muralist.

Another had been bought and remodeled by the architect Alice Clark Myers. Amethyst, who had an MA in Fine Arts, was a little chagrined that she didn't know a lot of the names he mentioned.

They visited galleries, then Amethyst led him along an alley to the wind sculpture garden.

They walked along gravel paths that wound among wind sculptures of every size and shape. Welded metal helixes spun, double flowers whirled, tulips twirled. Amethyst wandered among them, stopping to admire the shape and motion. One of these days, she'd have enough money to buy a small one for her backyard.

"You, my dear Amethyst," Jas said, "have expensive taste."

She winced. Maybe she shouldn't have been quite so enthusiastic. Next would come the inevitable, *If you marry me...*

"Me?" she said. "I just admire the craftsmanship. Can you imagine what it must take to balance these things?"

"Ah," was all he said. "Ready for some lunch?"

She was surprised at the spurt of gratitude that went through her that he *hadn't* dropped the marriage bomb.

No trip to Santa Fe was complete without a visit to the Plaza. Jas helped her on with her coat when they got out of the car. If she wanted to be perfectly honest with herself, she enjoyed the attention a lot more than she should.

As a friend, he was fine. He actually made a good, reliable one, and there was just enough distance for comfort. But she couldn't, *couldn't* afford to let him past her defenses again. It had hurt too much for far too long, realizing that all the attention he'd lavished on her in the beginning had only been to beguile her, to persuade her to lower her guard. He'd expressed remorse for that damned binding. He flat out told her he'd made a mistake. But—

Maybe the problem was her. He'd caught her by surprise and betrayed her, and maybe no matter what he did, she'd never trust him again. Still, she liked him. She had from the start. Sometimes she wondered if she more than liked him. But—

Always *but*. That was the problem.

"What's that face?" Jas said. "You look like you're gnawing on a particularly unpleasant problem."

She came back to the present with a start. Tourists crowded the sidewalks surrounding the Plaza. A police officer with a Belgian Malinois stood between two parked cars talking to a couple and their young son. Half a block up, a busker played an accordion.

"Jas—"

"What is it?"

He stopped and steered her into an alcove leading to an African art shop. Behind the plate glass, masks and sculptures stared open-mouthed at them.

"This isn't—" *going to work.* She couldn't get the rest out.

Shielding her from the flow of people along the sidewalk behind him, he studied her. "Are you not enjoying yourself? Would you rather do something else?"

"No," she said. "No, I'm having a great time."

"Since you don't look happy about it, I assume there's

another problem."

She glanced away.

He moved closer, slid his hand up her arm. "There's nothing wrong with having a good time, Amethyst. Just enjoy this day. It's enough."

He could be right. Maybe it was enough to just have fun, even if it was with slippery, shifty Jas.

Finally, she puffed out a breath. "Okay."

"All right now?"

She nodded.

He stepped out onto the sidewalk again, drawing her with him. They continued toward the Plaza.

Still troubled, she glanced at Jas. "Are you laughing at me?"

"Good God, no. I'd never dare."

"Then what're you so tickled about?"

The smile that had been playing at the corners of his mouth sat down and made itself comfortable there. "I'll let you work it out for yourself."

"That's not nice."

"It might not be nice," he said. "But at the moment, it's safer."

She frowned at him, but oddly enough, the conflict that had been churning in her ebbed.

At 7,000 feet altitude, Santa Fe was quite a bit colder than mile-high Albuquerque. Though the day was lovely, with the Plaza's bare trees weaving a filigree tracery against a snapping, humming blue sky, Amethyst snugged her coat around her. The vendors at the Indian Market along the front of the Palace of the Governors sat bundled in scarves and puffy insulated jackets.

Jas right behind her, she wove in and out of the throngs of tourists inspecting blanket after blanket covered with silver and turquoise jewelry, Pueblo pottery, fancy beadwork. She stopped to buy a pair of inlaid turquoise hoop earrings from a Navajo silversmith, then they continued on up Palace Avenue, past old adobe buildings with courtyards beyond open gates.

One of those courtyards was the entrance to The Shed, one of Amethyst's go-to New Mexican restaurants when in Santa Fe. It was also the go-to restaurant for about half the tourists there. People filled the brick-paved courtyard under a ramada netted with now-bare wisteria vines.

Amethyst groaned. "We should've put our names on the waiting list before we walked around the Plaza."

"It might not be as bad as it looks," Jas said. "Let me go check."

He sidled through the waiting groups and disappeared through the door. A moment later, he reappeared.

"Ten or fifteen minutes," he said.

Amethyst's brows climbed. "A crowd like this, on a weekend? Usually it's an hour, hour and a half."

He only shrugged.

Sure enough, the red lights on the pager he held started blinking a few minutes later. The waiter ushered them to a cozy table at the back of the restaurant. After Jas pulled out her chair then took his own seat across the table, the waiter hovered, unusually attentive.

She took her menu, giving Jas a suspicious look over

the top. She ordered a white sparkling wine, Jas a Sangre de Cristo margarita.

When the waiter left to fill their drink orders, she leaned across the table. "What did you do?" She waggled her fingers, miming casting a spell.

"Don't worry, nothing like that." He raised his menu to study it.

He'd sure done *something.* The manager, a trim, middle-aged Spanish woman, brought an order of chips, salsa and guacamole 'on the house.' Their drinks were on the house, too.

Amethyst stared at the tray of red, white and blue tortilla chips in consternation, then gave in and scooped up a bite of creamy, spicy guacamole.

On the one hand, it was all very flattering. On the other…

Well, she couldn't think what was on the other hand. Just that she had a strong hunch Jas had slipped someone a Benjamin at some point.

He sipped his margarita, licked a few crumbs of salt from his upper lip. A sudden, disconcerting thought of doing that for him intruded.

Not going there, she told herself. *No way, never, ever, ever. Don't even think it.*

She kept her mind firmly on lunch after that.

"My treat this time," he said when the check came. Fortunately, he paid with a card, so she didn't have to see how big a tip he left. Judging from the warm smiles and heartfelt thank-you's the staff offered on the way out, it was a big one.

On the brick-paved sidewalk out front, Jas took her hand.

"Let me show you something," he said.

It seemed like an appropriate moment for a smart remark, but something about the way he said it kept her quiet.

He drew her up the street and around a corner. A parking lot took up much of one block, and a little farther on was the back of a building that looked like it had been built in the 1940s or '50s. He turned another corner, this one lined with newer buildings. Tucked between two of them was an adobe wall with a green-painted gate. He touched the latch. The magic stirred and the gate swung open under his hand.

A courtyard like so many of the old adobe houses boasted opened ahead. A huge tree stump about four or five feet high rose in the middle of a stretch of gravel. Winter-killed hollyhocks stood in front of the mullioned windows and doors with raised sills that opened onto the courtyard. It would've been sad and forlorn if not for the rosemary filling the stump's rotted-out center and spilling down the trunk. And the faint, ringing tickle of spells of protection and preservation.

Rosemary for remembrance. The phrase popped unbidden into her mind.

Jas still held her hand, warm against the winter air. "This was my home, once."

She turned to him, surprised. He was looking up into the vanished branches of the tree.

"When I hosted parties, I had pierced tin lanterns

hung in this tree," he said. "There were hollyhocks then, too, and a goldfish pond over there, in the corner—no koi back in those days. Everyone came—the governor, artists, local landowners."

All she knew about his past was that he'd come to New Mexico in the 1920s. She perked up, bubbling with curiosity.

"What kind of business were you in then?"

"I backed some mines," he said. "I still do. But most people knew me as a patron of the arts, a man who'd made his fortune in the stock market and had spare cash to spread around. I put it about that I'd left a disinterested wife behind back east—that kept the women from expecting marriage."

Kept the women from expecting marriage? Hmm.

"Do you have kids?" she said. Damn. Most kids born in the '20s would probably be dead by now. "Um, grandkids." Even the grandkids would be old.

He shook his head. "After I realized someone was hunting wizards, I made sure I didn't have any more children. I'd already lost a son to that—" He swallowed what clearly would've been a curse word. "I didn't intend to lose any more."

"Oh." It came out in a whisper.

When she was thirteen, she'd lost her Nani, her great-grandmother, to the same predator. The only good thing was that the wizard who'd drained other wizards of their power would never hunt again.

A new thought occurred to her. "If you were living here, in Sante Fe... You might've known my great-grandmother. Or heard of her?"

He plucked a seed husk from one of the withered hollyhocks. "I knew someone up north was using magic. I could sense it, the way I sensed it when you first started using it." He quirked a rueful smile. "But an Anglo poking around, asking questions in Spanish villages… Let's just say I got more than my fair share of shrugs and *Yo no sé.*"

"You'd probably get the same thing now. You should've said you had consumption or something. They might've been less suspicious of an Anglo looking for a *curandera*. Lots did."

"I would have, if I'd known I was looking for a healer." He crumbled the hollyhock pod between his fingers. "Even if I'd known I was looking for a woman. Women's power tends to express itself in healing and making things grow. Sometimes in foreknowledge. Our sort of wizardry is unusual in a woman."

Ah-ha, she thought uncharitably. The marriage proposals were making more and more sense. Turning so he couldn't see her face, she blew on the fingers of her free hand as if cold—which she actually was.

He placed his hand on the small of her back. "Come on. It's too cold to stand still for long."

He walked with her out of the courtyard, locked the gate behind them once more.

She didn't want to continue along the turn her thoughts had taken. Plus she wasn't sure she could keep them off her face. Questions seemed the best distraction.

"It sounds like you had a good life here. Important rich guy surrounded by boho women who weren't expecting anything permanent. Why leave Santa Fe?"

He shrugged. "It was time to move on. Time to reinvent myself again."

He sounded so lonely and resigned. Living for centuries sounded pretty good until she thought about the reality of it.

Without deciding to, she took his hand and squeezed it. He glanced aside at her in surprise, then gave a quick squeeze in return.

"So you died." She made air quotes.

"Aneurysm," he said. "I drifted for a few years. When it became apparent that computers were going to be important, I started putting out feelers. I met a young fellow named Bill Gates when he opened a small business called Microsoft in Albuquerque."

She stopped in the middle of the sidewalk. Since they hadn't reached the Plaza yet, she didn't have to worry about creating a traffic jam.

"Holy crap. You know *Bill Gates?*"

"I've finally impressed you. You've made my day."

She rolled her eyes. "But that was in the Seventies, wasn't it? If you were talking to Bill Gates then, by now you'd have to seem, what? Seventy-something years old?"

That was a weird thought. To all outward appearances, Jas looked somewhere in his mid- to late-thirties.

"My grandfather..." He made the air quotes this time. "...was the one who had dealings with Microsoft. I inherited the estate and started Magus Corporation."

She started walking again. "For a guy who hasn't had

kids in the last hundred years or so, there must've been an awful lot of logistics involved to make that work."

"There were."

"This longevity stuff is going to be a real pain in the butt, isn't it? Trying to make it seem like I age and die like everybody else."

He sputtered a surprised laugh. "Most people wouldn't think of it that way, but yes. It can be. Especially since the advent of computers."

"Geesh."

"Not to worry, though. I have an in with a computer firm that has access to databases all over the world."

She walked beside him in silence a while. "When did that become a comforting thought?"

He took her hand again. "That's something else I'll let you work out for yourself."

✦✦✦✦✦✦

It wasn't late when Jas pulled off the freeway and turned onto Eubank, but this time of year, it was already getting dark. Amethyst watched the taillights in front of them. They passed the Owl Café, circles of red neon outlining the eyes of the owl on the building's roof, then the pet store on the corner with the huge chameleon crawling across the top of the sign. The next turn Flint, her street, then he'd pull up to her house, and then—

Her mouth went dry. She hadn't thought about this part of the date.

She would *not* be nervous. She was thirty years old, for godsake. It wasn't like any of this was a mystery.

And maybe that was exactly the problem.

The Infiniti purred up the little hill on Flint and finally swung into her driveway. Jas turned off the key. The headlights winked out and the engine fell silent.

She fought the impulse to snatch up her coat and purse and bolt for the front door. Unfortunately, trying to be cool and casual about it also gave Jas time to get out and come around to her side of the car.

She climbed out, hooking her purse over her shoulder and hugging her coat to her chest.

Putting on a smile she fervently hoped looked sincere, she said, "Thanks, Jas. It was a great day. I had fun."

He took her elbow and walked her to the door. Damn.

"My pleasure. I hope we'll be doing it again soon."

They stopped on the porch. She started to reach for her purse, for the keys inside. Jas' hand slid up her arm. His other hand rose, maybe to go around her, maybe to cup her face.

Her mouth was still dry, and now her heart lurched into overdrive. Real fear sank cold claws into her chest, clamped its jaws on her throat. Every instinct screamed to grab the magic and fling up a shield, a fending, anything.

She took half a step back, caught herself, then held up her forefingers in a cross, making a joke of it. "Uh-uh. Not after what you did the last time you kissed me."

When he'd put that binding on her. When all she could do was stand unresisting in his arms, unable to even think of breaking free—

In the glow of the porch light, his dark eyes were serious. "Never again, Amethyst," he said quietly.

Shivers ran through her. Even her breath shook. God. How humiliating. She swallowed, breathed deep, catching the desert scent of his cologne.

"I know." She touched his hand where he'd dropped it to his side once more. "The problem is convincing the emotional brain. Just...not yet. Okay?"

He nodded. "Rain check?"

Her pulse was still pounding in throat and lips and fingertips, though it was beginning to slow. "Well, it's on backorder. I'm not sure how long it'll take to come in."

He laughed softly. "I'll wait," he said and touched her cheek.

Thank *god* she didn't flinch.

CHAPTER 3

Kiss Me

"You're pretty quiet, Wiz," Melodie Odham said. "Something tells me things didn't go well yesterday."

Melodie had been Amethyst's best friend since their days in UNM's Information Technology program, before she'd left computers for stained glass. That was when Melodie had nicknamed her 'Wiz', short for 'whiz kid'. Neither of them knew then how appropriate it was…and not for Amethyst's aptitude with computers.

"Actually," Amethyst said, "it did go well. I got to drive his car. We had lunch at The Shed. Jas took me to see his old house when he lived in Santa Fe."

"Uh-huh," Melodie said. "And you're slouching along the trail with your hands in your coat pockets and your head down because you're giddy with joy."

She was, in fact, doing exactly that. Not even enjoying the glint of sunlight on the Rio Grande River, the huge cottonwoods of the bosque all around them, brown leaves clinging to their branches silhouetted against another perfect blue New Mexico sky. Ignoring poor Caramela, who'd picked up a stick and was prancing happily along with it.

"Okay," she said. "It went well until we got back to my house."

Melodie perked up.

"He walked me to the door. He started to kiss me." She walked several steps, her footsteps almost silent on the soft earth of the trail. "Mel, I panicked."

"You what? Why—? Oh. *Oh.*" Melodie frowned, puzzled. "Are you saying you haven't kissed him since—then?"

Melodie knew about the binding Jas had laid on her—and exactly how he'd gone about doing it. She was the only person who did.

Amethyst nodded.

"My god, Wiz," Melodie burst out. "He's kissed you exactly once? And that's it? Nothing else? The man asked you to marry him!"

She threw up the hand not holding Caramela's leash. "I know, huh? Why do you think I told him no?"

"Because he's Jas Harker?"

Amethyst grinned. "Besides that. Things have to be done in the proper order, I tell him. Now he leans in for a kiss and it's all I can do to keep from throwing the whammy on him and running inside and locking myself in the house. It was the most humiliating moment of my life."

"You've had several most-humiliating moments in your life. Usually to do with men."

"Acting like a dork on a date is one thing. Turning

into a quivering knot of sheer terror when your date tries to kiss you is a whole new level of humiliation."

Melodie gave her a sharp look. "You're not exaggerating, are you?"

"I wish."

A flock of waterfowl on the river made faint music. Overhead, ravens croaked, dive-bombing a bald eagle on a cottonwood branch. The eagle looked pretty unconcerned about the whole thing, gazing around as if no such harassment was taking place.

"Well, what'd he do when it happened?" Melodie said.

"Promptly backed off. Then said he could wait."

Melodie's eyes went wide. "Whoa. That's serious stuff. What are you going to do?"

"I don't know, Mel. I can handle Jas when he's being Mr. Pushy CEO. When he's being considerate…" She sighed. "Not so much."

"There's something I'm not understanding here. I thought you wanted to put him off the whole let's-take-this-to-the-next-level plan. What you describe would definitely qualify. So what's the problem?"

"I don't know!"

At the tone of her voice, Caramela dropped her stick and nosed Amethyst's hand. She reached down and stroked the dog to soothe her.

"Okay, I lied," Amethyst said. "I do know. The thing is, I don't want to be one of those women twisted up in a seriously unhealthy relationship."

"With a man you can't even bring yourself to kiss,

because the last time you kissed him, he put the whammy on *you*."

"That's the part that falls under the 'seriously unhealthy' heading."

"Okay, I get that. I also get why you'd react the way you did."

Welded iron jetty jacks with rusty steel cable strung between for erosion control crossed the trail, looking like relics from some World War II battlefield. Amethyst and Caramela ducked under the cable between a tangle of dead vegetation, waited for Melodie to follow then continued on.

"Look," Melodie resumed. "You know I'm no big fan of Jas Harker after what he did. Obviously he's done some convincing between then and now for you to be friendly with him. I'll respect that and not badmouth him. Anyway, it's obvious you're still attracted to him."

Amethyst scowled

Melodie waved a hand. "Truth hurts, huh? Anyway, I think the problem is that the way you reacted caught you by surprise."

"I was nervous about how I should handle the whole good-night scenario," Amethyst said. "I sure didn't expect to have a meltdown on the front porch."

Melodie nodded. "Then I guess you have to decide which is stronger. The attraction? Or the fear?" She gave Amethyst a frown. "And if it turns out the fear *is* the attraction, I'll tell you right now, I'm going to stage an intervention. Because even if it's none of my damn business, I'm not about to let my BFF get tangled up in that kind of crap without trying to do something about it."

"Trust me," Amethyst said. "I don't find fear the least bit attractive."

✿✿✿✿✿✿

The moment Amethyst had been dreading arrived: her phone rang. She didn't even need to pick it up to know who it was. The fast techno ringtone told her that.

She squeezed her eyes closed. The ringtone kept playing.

She let out a long breath and thumbed on the phone without looking at his charming smile in the picture on the screen. "Hi, Jas."

"Amethyst," he said. "Are you busy?"

She sat in her front bedroom-slash-home office-slash-workshop, her computer armoire open and her laptop running. On her worktable under the window, cut pieces of stained glass in gold and opalescent white and ice blue waited for the grinder out in the garage.

Drumming her fingers on her desktop, she contemplated the spreadsheet on the screen. Did she want to be can't-stop-now busy?

No, avoiding it wouldn't make it any easier. Might was well just get it over with.

"Busy doing what every business owner loves best," she said. "Catching up the books."

"Then I'm here to rescue you," Jas said. "How about lunch?"

It was close to 1:30. She wondered if he knew she

usually ate lunch late. Knowing Jas, probably.

"Um…okay. Where?"

"Do you know the Vietnamese place a few blocks up Eubank from you? Can you meet me there in half an hour?"

Half an hour. Oh god.

"Sure," she said. "See you."

Amethyst ended the call, set down the phone and put her head in her hands. Well, it wouldn't help her self-assurance to meet him in the sweats she wore now. She pushed to her feet, crossed the hall to her bedroom and opened the closet door. Definitely no silk top this time.

She was dressed in ankle boots, leggings and a tunic sweater in teal when she opened the door to Basil Leaf restaurant. A gold laughing Buddha beside the register greeted diners. A dining room painted in vivid green and glass-topped tables and chairs in dark wood made the place inviting.

She'd seen Jas' green Infiniti parked out front. She spotted him at a table on the right, toward the back. He raised a hand in greeting.

Here goes. She walked to his table and slid into a chair across from him. She had to be radiating awkwardness and discomfort. The other option was fake cheer and friendliness, and that would be even worse.

"I hope you haven't been waiting long," she said.

"Only long enough to order tea and look at the menu."

"Oh. Good."

Amethyst picked up her own menu. It was hard to

keep her mind on the array of Vietnamese dishes. It didn't help that the appetite she should've had by this time of the afternoon had deserted her. She forced herself to concentrate, trying to remember which dishes she'd enjoyed in the past. At least they didn't have to talk while she read the menu.

After the waiter came, poured tea and took their orders, she didn't have that excuse anymore.

There were only a couple of other tables occupied, both on the other side of the restaurant, giving them a degree of privacy. She stared across the table at Jas, hoping she had a pleasant expression on her face.

He gazed back at her a moment, then sipped tea. "How have you been?"

It wasn't the casual question it sounded. Amethyst chose to take it as one. "Good. Melodie and I took Caramela for a walk on the bosque yesterday."

"Ah," he said. "Reviewing the previous day's events, I presume."

"Jas—"

"I can see it bothers you. We can talk about it."

They both knew what 'it' was.

She rubbed her forehead. "Okay. Do you want the honest version, or the don't-want-to-hurt-your-feelings version?"

"I'm encouraged that you don't want to hurt my feelings." He took another sip of tea, leaned back and extended an arm along the seat back. "Let's hear the honest version."

Her mouth was dry. She drank tea, the delicate

jasmine aroma unfurling in her mouth. She set down her cup and put her hands in her lap.

"This isn't going to work, Jas."

He gave a dismissive little wave. "What happened the other night is a speed bump. Nothing more."

"It's more than a *speed bump*."

"I disagree. I frightened you badly when I laid that binding on you. You weren't expecting it, which at the time was entirely the point. I should've guessed I might trigger you. Since it's my doing you reacted the way you did, the least I can do is work to repair the damage."

Her hands were cold. She curled them around her teacup. "Did you ever think you might not be able to?"

"You've gone from considering me your enemy to calling us friends. So no, I don't regard it as impossible."

"This isn't the same. Let's…" She closed her eyes for a moment. "Look, I don't want to negotiate something like this. Let's just stay friends. I'd rather do that than blow up the whole relationship."

"I'm not negotiating. I'm trying to persuade you that this isn't the disaster you think it is. I realize you were embarrassed. I'm sorry for that. That isn't how I wanted to end the day with you."

She picked up her chopsticks and toyed with them. "I know."

"*Did* you enjoy our time together?"

"I wasn't just being polite when I said I did."

"Good. Aside from the stumble at the end, was there anything else you wouldn't want to repeat?"

Stumble, right. "No, but—"

"Then if we'd parted three minutes earlier, we wouldn't be having this conversation."

She squirmed. "I guess not, but—"

"Then let's work on the three minutes of the entire day that *didn't* go well."

She looked at him, exasperated. "It's a pretty significant three minutes, don't you think?"

"Of course it is. That's why it's important to address it."

She shouldn't ask. She really shouldn't. "And exactly how do you propose to do that?"

He leaned forward. "Do you know how phobias are treated?"

She sat back, bracing her hands on the table. "No, Jas. No, no, no."

He rose from his chair, came around to her side and sat next to her. "It's a process of desensitization. You start by presenting the object of the phobia at a safe distance. When the phobic person can tolerate that, you increase the intensity by bringing the person closer to the thing they're afraid of."

She already knew that. *"Here?"*

"We're in a public place," he said. "Nothing can happen."

"Except that you're a wizard. Cast the right spell, and nobody notices anything."

His eyes, dark and intense, held hers. "You're a wizard, too, Amethyst."

She picked up her napkin and scooted away a few inches. "This is ridiculous. I'm not doing this here."

"Then tell me where," he said. "Don't shake your head. I'm serious."

"There *is* no good place, because I'm telling you, it won't work."

He extended his arm across the back of her chair and slid closer. "It will work," he said. "Are you all right with this?" He waved to indicate the distance between them. The *small* distance.

"Come on, Jas—"

"Are you?" he repeated.

"Fine. Yes. Okay?" She concentrated on not leaning back.

He slid closer until his knee touched hers. "Now?"

"I changed my mind," she said. "I'm not okay. This is embarrassing."

"There's no need to be embarrassed. No one is looking. Now raise a ward."

"Seriously?"

"Go ahead. I'll wait."

If she told him to back off, she knew he would. But no, she was going to go along with this. She had no idea why.

She reached for the magic. The ward she shaped guarded against ill-intent, physical force and magical attacks. But she also wove a spell of reflection. Any magic he tried to work on her would be turned back on him. She let the spells settle around her, humming energies of ice-scented blue and shimmering, shifting opalescence that fitted to her like molded armor.

"Good," he said. "Now kiss me."

I can't, she wanted to tell him. But she wasn't going to let him see her quivering like a thirteen-year-old girl.

She wet her lips and leaned forward. He didn't lean closer, but he closed his eyes. That made things easier. Her pulse picked up. Warmth spread from her middle. *Not* fear then. Well.

Tilting her head, she closed the space between them and kissed him.

Jas kissed her back, his lips moving soft and warm on hers. Like the first time—the last time—it was like some rich liqueur spreading through her.

She sat back and opened her eyes. When had she closed them? And when had she put her hand on his arm? She still felt warm, a flush that spread from her middle all the way to her skin.

"There," he said, smiling that smile that brought out the crinkles around his eyes. "Was that so bad?"

Her napkin had slid off her lap. Straightening, she rearranged it, trying not to notice the tingle in her lips, the way she could catch a whiff of his cologne on her skin.

"Don't gloat," she said. "It's much nicer when you're a gentleman."

"That's the second time you've said that. I will certainly be a gentleman, then."

He reached across the table for his cup and utensils and arranged them in front of him. Amethyst was acutely conscious of his nearness, his knee almost touching hers.

"Call a ward whenever you feel the need to," he said. "I won't be offended."

A quiver went through her, though she didn't want to

guess its source. "And what if I always feel the need to?"

He refilled her teacup. "We'll cross that bridge when we come to it."

CHAPTER 4

Do You Wanna Party

J as was up to something.

Amethyst sat at her worktable foiling the glass for an Art Deco stained glass entry door depicting aspens in full golden fall glory. Songs from one of her playlists bopped in the background. Foiling didn't require a lot of mental horsepower, so she had plenty of opportunity to chew over events since The Kiss. Not that she hadn't *already* been chewing them over…and over.

Two weeks, and nothing more than a couple of casual lunches like she and Jas had shared occasionally in the past. He did drop by her office once while Amethyst did her consultant gig at Magus. It wasn't like she kept regular hours, so it meant he was keeping an eye on when she checked in and out of the building.

"So what the hell?" she asked Caramela, who lay at her feet chewing on an Extreme Kong. "First he's all, 'Marry me, marry me,' now he's like, 'Hey, what've you been up to lately? Haven't talked to you in a while.'" She finished running a piece of white glass through the foiling machine and picked up the next one. "He should make up his damned mind."

Skronk skronk went Caramela's Kong in counterpoint to the funk tune playing over the speakers.

Amethyst foiled a few more pieces, tapping her foot half to the music, half in irritation.

"He was probably disappointed in that kiss," she said. "Or maybe he's decided I'm not worth the trouble. Let me down easy, go back to the friendly professional collaboration." She set the glass on the pile with a clink. "That's what I wanted all along, anyway," she muttered. "He could've just let things be. Everything was fine."

I'm hot! boasted the singer in the song that was playing.

"Well, maybe you are," she told him. "Because I'm clearly not."

Caramela got up, shook and went to the door, asking to go out. Amethyst followed her to the back door. Wagging her tail, Caramela waited by the glass door smeared with dog nose prints, then trotted out when Amethyst slid it open. Amethyst went outside too.

It had snowed a little last night. The Sandia Mountains, looming huge over the Griegos' rooftop on the left, were frosted white on the top, like a wedding cake. Even here in Albuquerque, a layer of snow lingered in the shadow of the concrete block wall that surrounded her backyard. She folded her arms against the chill.

Caramela made quick work of her business. Pit bulls weren't designed to be outdoors in cold weather. Besides having short coats, their undercarriage was mostly naked. Amethyst let both of them back inside, then wandered into the kitchen for a snack.

Her phone rang—that techno beat buzzing in her pocket. Something in her middle leapt up. "Shut up," she told it and pulled out her phone.

"Hey, Jas. Whatup?"

"*Whatup?*" he repeated.

Her lips wanted to pull up in a smile. She pursed them to keep them down. "It's the music I've been listening to. Sorry. Can I help you?"

"That's even worse," he said.

"Since we're back on a professional footing, it seemed appropriate."

"We are? I'm sorry to hear that. I was planning on inviting you to a party."

"A party." A burst of happiness bubbled through her. She scowled at it to chase it off, but it kept bouncing around.

"At the home of a business associate," he said. "I suppose you'd call it a cocktail party. Jacket and tie for men, dresses for women."

The bubble popped. "I don't know, Jas. That doesn't sound quite like my kind of thing."

"I understand. I can always get someone else."

"Can I think about it?" her mouth said without her deciding to. She squeezed her eyes shut and caught her tongue between her teeth.

"Not too long," he said. "It's this weekend."

"I'll let you know by tonight. Okay?"

"I'll look forward to hearing from you." She could hear the smile in his voice.

She ended the call before she could say anything else stupid.

Amethyst rested her elbows on the counter, trying to catch her breath. When she was pretty sure her voice would stay even, she picked up her phone again and tapped the icon with Melodie's picture.

"I've got an emergency," she said when Melodie answered. Her voice wasn't steady at all. "I need your help."

"What?" Melodie said, alarmed. "What happened, Wiz?"

"I'm invited to a cocktail party, and I don't have a clue what to wear."

⸎⸎⸎⸎⸎⸎⸎

"What happened to 'he's dialed it way back'?" Melodie said.

They were in Melodie's merlot-red Insight, purring down Menaul. A series of small businesses lined the road on the left; low-slung, 1970s-vintage ranch houses along the frontage road to the right.

Amethyst drummed her fingers on the armrest. "I've been thinking about that. I bet Jas left me hanging for a while on purpose. Then when he dropped this bomb on me, I'd be less likely to say no."

"Huh." Melodie cocked her head as if thinking. "That's pretty baroque, even for Jas."

"You don't know him like I do," Amethyst said darkly.

"If he did plan it, he knows *you* damn well, too."

Amethyst gave a theatrical shudder.

"But I think it's more likely he's been busy," Melodie said. "He *is* CEO of a large company. Or he decided to give you some breathing space."

"Do you hear yourself? You're defending him!"

Melodie snorted. "Hardly. It's Ockham's Razor. The simplest explanation is the most likely."

"Unless you're talking about Jas Harker."

"You could always foil his evil plot and tell him no anyway."

"Not after I already told him yes. I refuse to look like a flake while foiling evil plots."

Melodie slid her a sidelong glance. "Uh-huh. You'd better gird your loins, then. I know how much you love clothes shopping, and this won't be a simple project."

Amethyst slouched down in the seat. "That's what I was afraid of."

The problem with clothes shopping was finding something she liked in her size. Then once she found something she liked, it usually didn't like her.

Amethyst came out of another dressing room with another armful of dresses. Melodie raised her brows in a question. Amethyst shook her head.

"Don't despair, Wiz," Melodie said. "The right one is out there."

"You know what the trouble with dresses is?" Amethyst said. "They're made for people with, you know, *boobs*."

"And the trouble with sweaters, and lingerie. You say

that every time we go shopping."

"Well, it's true. The sizes might get smaller, but they're still designed for a certain shape." Amethyst traced an hourglass with her hands. "You try putting on a frilly babydoll only to discover that the top edge leaves your nipples exposed."

Melodie made a *T* with her hands. "Too much information, Wiz."

"And sweaters. Let's not even talk about sweaters."

"I know, I know." Melodie waved a hand. "They're always lower in the front than in the back."

"Do you have any idea how sloppy that looks?"

"So we'll find something close and take it to a tailor. They'll take up the straps and put a couple of darts in the hips and you'll be fine. Okay?"

"We don't have *time* for a tailor," Amethyst glared at the endless racks of dresses and tops, slacks and sweaters surrounding them. "I know he did this on purpose, damn him. I should just wear that sky-blue thing my cousin forced me into for her wedding."

"I'm pretty sure Jas doesn't want his date looking like an escaped cake decoration."

Amethyst snorted a laugh. That bridesmaid's dress was all frilly petticoats and tulle.

"I did look like that, didn't I?" She thought a moment, an evil grin pulling up one side of her mouth. "You know, now that I think about it, maybe I should wear that dress."

"Remember, Jas isn't the only one who'll be looking at you."

"Thanks a lot, Mel. You had to go and remind me, didn't you?"

Melodie took her arm. "Okay, we're not having any luck at the mall. I know a couple of boutiques we can try."

"Great," Amethyst said. "I already had to drop a couple hundred bucks on one dress I'll never wear again, no matter how long I live. Now I'm supposed to do it again."

"So we'll get you one you do want to wear again. Besides." She jiggled Amethyst's arm. "If all else fails, you can magic one up, right?"

Amethyst gave her a sour look. "Right. And while I'm at it, I'll spin a few plates and balance a bowling pin on my nose. My poor little introverted self is going to have enough trouble navigating a roomful of strangers without also having to keep an illusion running."

At last, the heavens smiled on Amethyst at a little boutique tucked into one of the strip malls along Menaul.

The dress was deepest violet just a few shades short of black. A strap went over one shoulder, leaving the other bare. The material was gathered at the breasts to fall in an asymmetrical skirt, a fluttery triangle of chiffon flowing to her right knee while the hem on the left came mid-thigh.

Amethyst came out of the dressing room, half pleased, half self-conscious.

Melodie's eyes went round. "Holy crap, Wiz."

"I know, huh?" She pulled out the skirt, feeling an unaccustomed girly pleasure.

"No high heels with that," Melodie said, studying her. "The silhouette is already slim enough, even with the full skirt. Maybe a pair of low-heeled sandals. You know what this means, don't you?" She nodded solemnly. "Pedicure."

Actually, the pedicure got bumped to the end. First it was back to the mall for shoes and makeup. Fortunately, Melodie knew better than to try to make her buy a basketful of cosmetics.

"I don't know why Spanish women wear so much makeup, anyway," she said, comparing two cases of eyeshadow. "If I had a complexion like yours, I wouldn't cover it up." She settled on a dusky violet one. "What do you think? Almost the same color as your eyes. They'll look huge when you put it on. Now let's look at lipstick."

"Not too dark," Amethyst warned.

Melodie's lips quirked. Amethyst knew that look. It never boded well.

"So," Melodie said. "Do you want to look at lingerie? For…" One brow rose suggestively. "…*after* the party?"

Amethyst gave her a sweet smile. "You do know I can curse you, don't you? A few words, a little magic, and for the rest of your life, your produce will rot in the crisper and your bananas will turn black after two days."

"O-o-o-kay," Melodie said, holding up her hands. "No lingerie, then." She trailed her fingers along tubes of lipstick and smirked. "You can always just wear stockings. You won't be wearing a bra under that dress, anyway."

"Okay, that's it," Amethyst said. "I'm wearing that puffy bridesmaid's dress."

CHAPTER 5

Charisma

O f course Amethyst wore the violet dress. She might not be girly 99.9% of the time, but that dress brought out the one one-hundredth of a percent.

She didn't try anything fancy with her hair, just caught it back in a pierced silver barrette set with moonstones her grandfather had given her for her birthday one year. Melodie had lent her the white gold ankle bracelet her husband, Marl, had given her. *Don't lose it*, Melodie had said. Amethyst put a spell on it to make sure nothing would happen to it.

Getting ready didn't give her time to be nervous. *After* she was ready was another question entirely.

The doorbell rang.

Amethyst took a long breath, picked up her clutch and coat from the chair by the front door and opened the door.

Jas, waiting outside, took one look at her and literally rocked back. Not much. It was clearly an involuntary reaction, not one for effect.

Amethyst stepped out and closed the door, torn between pleasure and self-consciousness.

He gave a slight bow, turned and offered his arm, not a trace of the smile or teasing lift of the brow she would've expected to accompany such a gesture. She stood, startled.

"I beg your pardon." he said and began to lower his arm.

"No…" She slipped her arm into his, laying her hand on the sleeve of his coat. "Don't apologize."

He bowed his head and walked with her to the car where it waited in her driveway.

She sneaked a glance at him, caught off balance. Where was suave, insouciant Jas Harker? He seemed almost…flustered. He made only the briefest eye contact when he opened the car door and handed her into the seat.

Oh, damn.

Jas circled around to the driver's side and got in. He sat still a moment, then turned and met her gaze at last. His eyes were intense in the dim glow of street and porch lights.

"I'm not often struck speechless," he said. "But I was just now."

It was the kind of thing that would normally have begged for a smart reply. Not this time.

She looked down at the clutch in her lap, suddenly shy. "Thank you, Jas."

They stopped for dinner at a little Italian place in Nob Hill, the funky shopping and dining district just east of UNM. When Jas parked the Infiniti, Amethyst truly understood why the man came around to open the car door and assist the lady out. Climbing out of a low-slung car in a short dress and heels just wasn't the same.

She'd eaten enough meals out with Jas that this part of the evening felt relatively normal. She was used to seeing Jas looking good in a jacket and tie. Only the slide of her hair on her bare shoulders and back, the dress hugging her in unaccustomed places reminded her it was anything but normal. It was when they were back in the car and Jas turned onto Rio Grande Boulevard that things got dicey.

The houses on Rio Grande Boulevard ran the gamut from ancient little adobes hugging the road behind coyote fences to multi-million-dollar estates whose manicured grounds ran all the way back to the river. Amethyst was pretty sure which type Jas' business associate would live in.

As Rio Grande wound north, the house lights grew progressively wider-spaced, more elaborate and farther back from the road. The headlights illuminated winter-brown pastures, old, arching cottonwoods and fences of mortared stone and wrought iron that enclosed acres.

"You've gotten quiet," Jas said.

Amethyst wet her lips. "Have I?"

"Yes, you have. What are you worried about?"

"What am I *worried* about? Are you serious? I'm going to be so far out of my depth I won't even be able to see a glimmer of light from the surface."

"Amethyst, they're people just like any others. Certainly they'll have more money and power than most. But you're a wizard. You have power they can only dream of. If they knew what you are, they'd either fear you or seek your favor."

She threw up a hand. "Sure, and when somebody asks me what I do, I'm supposed to say, 'Oh, I'm the designated wizard at Magus Corporation. I do the magic so my boss can pretend to be a regular person.'"

"No, you tell them you're a stained glass artist. It'll be an excellent opportunity to meet potential clients. Or tell them you're a systems proofing consultant. Or both. That will really impress them."

"Along with my sparkling social skills," she muttered.

He turned to her, his face illuminated by the glow of the dash lights. "I told you a long time ago that wizards have charisma. Do you remember?"

"Yes. And I seem to remember telling you some have it more than others."

He shook his head and turned back to the road. "You have it, too. Your only problem is you don't believe you do. It worked on *me* an hour or two ago. You look good— and at that moment, you knew it." He slid her a sideways glance. "You saw the result."

She gave him a skeptical look. "Thanks for the vote of confidence, but I think you might be a little biased."

He smiled. "That comes dangerously close to accusing me of flattery." He held up a hand when she opened her mouth to argue. "I might—*might* be slightly more susceptible, but I guarantee you, whoever saw you while you were in that state of mind would've felt it. That's the whole trick to it—what you tell yourself. Walk into that room tonight knowing you're a wizard, knowing that no one you see can best you in anything, and you won't have to say a word. People will respond to it."

"I don't know, Jas. It seems…." She thought a moment. "Arrogant. Or something."

"I remember when I met you. You looked like someone had dumped a bucket of water over your head."

She put her head in one hand. "God. Don't remind me."

"What did you think when you first saw me?" he said.

"I thought, 'The best-looking man I've ever seen, and here I am pushing my P-O-S pickup and talking like I have the IQ of a ham sandwich.'"

He laughed.

"Well, what did you think when you saw me?" she said, challenging.

"I thought, 'Good God. She's a wizard, and she's trying to move that P-O-S with sheer brute strength. This will be interesting.'"

She folded her arms. "Liar. You thought I was an idiot."

"Not at all. I was intrigued."

"Huh. And your point is?"

"You reacted to my charisma."

"I reacted to the hot guy who appeared to help me push my truck."

"And with all due modesty, to the truth. I didn't pretend to be anything other than what I am."

"Not much," she muttered. "You pretended you weren't a wizard."

"Fair enough," he said with a dismissive wave of the hand. "Then let's say I didn't pretend to be *more* than I am.

Charisma only comes across as arrogance if you're trying to sell a bill of goods. Are you more honest with yourself by believing you're somehow less than others?"

"Well, no, but—"

"Then don't project that." He shrugged. "It's entirely up to you."

She leaned an elbow on the armrest, drummed her fingers on her leg and thought, *wizard*. In a way, it was a little like working the magic: taking the power within her and reaching out to shape reality.

Jas turned with a startled look then grinned. "Good! Now just turn it down a bit. You don't want to overwhelm the ordinary folk."

"Don't make fun of me. You didn't feel anything."

"Indeed I did." He reached out, laid a hand on her knee. "You'll do fine."

She wasn't sure if the heat that went through her was from his confidence…or where his hand rested.

CHAPTER 6

Magic in the Air

The pep talk was well-timed, Amethyst decided. Jas turned through an open gate onto a long driveway that wound between bare trees. Cars were already parked at the circle driveway at the end: Beemers and Jags, Audis and Mercedes. Jas slid in behind a Porche Cayenne and turned off the engine.

The house was newer, a large Mediterranean with a tile roof and stacked sandstone columns and accents. Tall windows cast golden rectangles onto the landscaping. Low-voltage lighting illuminated flagstone pathways through xeriscaping immaculately tended even in the dead of winter. The scent of pinon smoke spiced the air.

Amethyst's heels clicked on the stone, and the night air traced a chill up her legs even under her coat. The jitters came back.

Wizard, she thought again, not putting as much of a *push* into it this time. *Wizard with a smokin' date looking good in a sweet purple dress.*

It almost made her laugh, but it did make the jitters go away.

Jas smiled at her again and pushed the doorbell.

The woman who answered the door looked more Mexican than Spanish. It took Amethyst an instant to realize she was a maid, and not the hostess. Rich people, she supposed, didn't get their own doors. The maid took their coats and ushered them into the most enormous great room she'd ever seen—not excepting the living room at Jas' house, which was at least at human scale.

This room rose in two stories of glossy plaster walls to an actual groined ceiling. Furniture covered with pillows in russets and golds made artful groupings on the marble tiled floor. A fire of pinon wood blazed in a huge stone fireplace. And throughout the room, groups of people stood or sat, women in black or white or red dresses, men in slacks and coats. The buzz of conversation echoed from the high ceiling, the clink of glasses wove through a background of smooth jazz.

Jas' hand on the small of her back urging her forward made Amethyst realize she'd stopped short. All the nervousness was back.

Think of it as an anthropological expedition, she told herself. *The one percent in their natural habitat.*

The thought helped.

She leaned close to Jas and whispered, "I wonder what the mortgage payment is on three million dollars?"

"Amethyst," he said in a chiding tone, but his lips tucked in a repressed grin.

It occurred to her that he must be relatively confident that she wouldn't embarrass him. It was more confidence than she had in herself.

A man came across the room toward them. "Jas!" he said, shaking Jas' hand. "So glad to see you."

The man loomed over Jas by a good six inches. Jas was a little shorter than average, but he had such presence, Amethyst tended not to notice until he stood with other men.

This one positively dripped money. His brown hair, silvering at the temples, looked barbered just this morning. He wore a platinum and diamond ring that covered most of his first knuckle, a gold watch that looked like it must weigh a pound, and around his neck…was it? Yes, it was. An actual silk cravat.

Standing to one side with a polite smile on her face, she compared him to Jas: slim, not tall, in slacks and coat and one of his usual green ties, this one an awesome black and emerald green paisley. His wore his black hair in a style that looked casually finger-combed, but probably wasn't, and not a speck of jewelry. And damned if Jas, for all his understatement, didn't look classier than the other guy.

Jas put his hand on the small of her back again. "This is Amethyst Rey."

Amethyst jerked herself out of her thoughts and stuck out her hand. "Hi. Pleased to meet you."

She'd missed his name. *Great start, Amethyst.* She gave a firm shake when his hand engulfed hers.

His brows went up and he gave a laugh. "What a grip for such a little lady! You must spend a lot of time at the gym."

"Um…" She resisted the impulse to look to Jas for

help. "I'm a stained glass artist." She mimed holding a glass cutter and cutting a curving line. "My hands are always getting a good workout."

"That explains it, then." He turned to Jas again. "Go ahead and help yourself at the bar. Hors d'oeuvres are there." He nodded across the open-plan room toward a dining area. "Enjoy yourselves."

He gave Jas a manly shoulder pat and wandered off to talk to another guest.

"Was I supposed to give one of those limp lady shakes?" she asked Jas in an undertone.

He took her elbow and steered her toward the bar, where a bartender in a white jacket mixed drinks.

"Don't worry what you're supposed to do. That's one of the advantages of being an artist. You're expected to be eccentric."

"*That's* why you're not worried I'll embarrass you."

"How would you embarrass me?"

She gave an evil smile. "*Dang*, Jas," she drawled. "Didja see that goose egg he was wearing? He'll break somebody's jaw with that thing if he hits 'em."

Jas laughed. "All right. Not *that* eccentric."

At the bar, he ordered her a white zin and himself a Scotch on the rocks.

She sipped her wine and eyed the amber liquid in his glass. Seemed like matters could get difficult if a wizard had too much to drink.

Jas must've noticed her dubious look. "I'm not much of a drinker, but I do enjoy a good single malt once in a while."

She held up her free hand. "No problem. Just thought I'd better know if I'm expected to do damage control."

"*Now* who's worried about being embarrassed?"`

She sniffed. "Nothing you can do can embarrass an *artiste*."

"Not even this?"

He leaned close and slid his hand down her back, perilously close to her butt. And *whoa*, did the heat pour through her at that.

"One more millimeter," she said, "And you get a shock that'll flambé your whisky." She turned her head. "And there I'll be standing," she whispered in his ear, "watching in grave alarm while you yell and jump around, trying to put out your drink."

He laughed softly into her hair and straightened. The look in his eyes, when they met hers, sent fire racing under the violet dress.

"You're a cruel, cruel woman," he said.

She was pretty sure he wasn't talking about her threat.

His hand rested lightly on her waist as they turned back to the room to circulate. It made it hard to pay attention to names and faces. She told the liquid ripple in her middle to settle down and shut up. Damn Jas, anyway.

The party was a Who's-Who of New Mexico movers and shakers. An Intel executive, one of the big land developers, the owners of a couple of companies that contracted for Sandia National Labs.

One of the tech company owners had a trophy wife about half his age. She wore a red dress that looked like it had been spray-painted on, ruby and diamond studs in her ears and her lion-colored hair in a complicated updo. The woman, who had to stand over six feet tall in her heels, looked down on Amethyst and gave her one of those limp lady shakes. Amethyst kept a friendly smile on her face, tried not to feel small and grubby and limited herself to 'pleased to meet you.'

When Jas introduced her to Richard Branson of Virgin Galactic, Amethyst almost bolted for the door. The only thing that kept her from it was the fact that Branson took himself totally un-seriously and seemed to be a genuine and nice guy.

The conversation eventually got around to what she did.

"White-hat hacker," she said.

The term for the person a company hires to test how hack-proof their computers are.

"For the premier computer security firm in the world?" A little corporate-magnate sharpness peeked through Branson's impressed look. "I might have to steal her from you," he told Jas in his cool English accent.

Jas slid her a glance, half teasing, half challenging. "That might be harder than you think."

Especially since 95% of her hacking involved magic.

"You know hackers," Amethyst said with a shrug and a smile she hoped was disarming. "Free agents by nature."

Wizards, too, she thought, reminding herself that no, she wasn't out of her depth here. Really, she wasn't.

To her immense relief, Branson saw the director of the Spaceport Authority not long after and excused himself to go talk to her.

"I'm going to pass out," she told Jas.

"He does have his own charisma, doesn't he?"

"That's not what I'm talking about. Can we please get something to drink? Sparkling water. Anything non-alcoholic."

Jas immediately became serious. "Of course."

He conjured a spell of avoidance, just enough to discourage anyone from engaging them. Better than studiously avoiding people's eyes.

"Thanks," she breathed. "I am *so* not wired for talking to Important People."

"You talk to me."

"Trust me, I was totally intimidated when I first found out who you are."

"You did seem that way, yes," he said. "For a smart, capable woman, you intimidate easily."

"Put me in front of a computer or a sketch pad and I'm fine. With people?" She waggled her hand back and forth. "Not so much."

They reached the bar, where she asked for a limeade.

Jas touched her arm. "Let's get something to eat and find a quiet place to sit down for a few minutes."

She held her limeade in both hands, resisting the temptation to press the cool glass to her face. "That sounds good."

It was strange, confiding in Jas like this. She didn't quite know how that had happened.

They made a pass over the hors d'oeuvre selection. No jalapeño tortilla wraps or barbecued cocktail weenies here. No, there were crostini and mini seafood salads on scallop shells; endive leaves stuffed with marinated veggies and squares of cheese; little puff pastries that tasted of lemon and basil that almost evaporated when she bit down on them. Jas found a spot at the end of the banco that flanked the fireplace and sat down with her.

Amethyst sipped her limeade and ate nibbles off a Mexican glass plate, catching her breath.

Jas sat quietly beside her for a few minutes. "We can go, if you'd like."

"No, I'll be fine. Just… If the governor's here, please don't introduce me yet. Okay?"

"I think I heard someone say she is."

Amethyst looked around, alarmed, then stopped. "You're messing with me, aren't you?"

He put a hand over his heart. "On my honor, it's the truth."

She watched the people with their fancy clothes and expensive jewelry. A bad feeling uncoiled in her gut, like midnight was striking and the real world was about to intrude.

"Politicians tend to be more accessible than corporate types," Jas said into her silence. "I don't think you'll have trouble with her."

He was being kind. She appreciated it, but it didn't change the fact that they lived two very different kinds of lives, even if they were both wizards.

She set her plate aside. "I think I need to splash some water on my face. Do you mind?"

He was instantly on his feet, offering his hand. "Of

course not. Take your time."

It was his usual smooth charm, but she saw a flicker of concern in his eyes. She let him raise her to her feet. Sudden gloom pressed down on her.

Damn, she thought. *When did this get to be so hard?*

She squeezed his hand, then went to find the bathroom.

It was occupied. She'd just turned to find a strategic spot to wait when the door opened and Trophy Wife came out, a little unsteady on her feet. For a moment, Amethyst thought she was drunk. Then she saw how pale the other woman looked, how tight her face was.

"Are you okay?" Amethyst said.

Trophy Wife started, then she averted her gaze again. "I'm fine, thank you for asking."

She made to go past, but Amethyst touched her arm. "Are you sure? You look like you need to sit down or something."

Amethyst didn't know why she pressed, except the woman seemed so *not* fine. Trophy Wife hesitated, looking down the hall with something like dread.

"I'm Amethyst. We met a little earlier. I'm sorry, but I've forgotten your name. I'm terrible about stuff like that."

"Jessica," Trophy Wife said, really looking at her for the first time. "You are? I thought it was only me."

"Well, I feel better now," Amethyst said. "Because here I was thinking it was only *me*."

"I'm not sure if I can go back in there," Jessica said in a low voice.

Amethyst would've laughed if it hadn't been so depressing.

"I know," Amethyst said. "But I don't think we'll be able to hide in the bathroom all night. If they don't come looking for us, we'll have people pounding on the door, wanting in."

Jessica did laugh. "That's true."

"If you'll excuse me while I have my own panic attack," Amethyst said, "maybe we can go back in together."

Jessica gave her a very nice, very white grin. "I'll wait."

She did wait, which told Amethyst how uncomfortable the woman must be. When Amethyst came out, they stood awkwardly for a minute.

"See, this is the problem," Jessica burst out. "If I have to make one more minute of small talk, I think I'll throw up. Again." She paused. "I mean, everybody is so smart and so talented. They have all these degrees, and they run charities and own boutiques and they're on this or that non-profit board. And me? I shop. I party. Like, how much good is *that* supposed to do anyone?"

If she realized that, she was way ahead of a lot of people.

Amethyst started back down the hall toward the noise and motion of the party, more or less forcing Jessica to follow. Fused glass wall sconces in amber and citrine and cream cast cones of light on the faux-painted plaster.

"And I'll bet they're all at least ten years older than you are," Amethyst said. "If you could get them to tell you the honest truth, they were probably doing the same thing at your age."

Jessica stalked along beside her in her four-inch heels. "I'm afraid my husband'll get bored of me. I'll make him ashamed," she said, almost too low to hear.

The words rang in Amethyst like a bell of truth. No. That *couldn't* be what had been gnawing at her all night.

They'd made it back to the great room, opposite the bar and kitchen. Here, in a corner between a window and shelves displaying a collection of Pueblo pottery and carved kachina figures, it was quieter. Most of the guests were gathered nearer the refreshments.

Amethyst was absolutely the last person in the world who should be giving relationship advice. But an observation was probably safe.

"I thought your husband looked pretty proud of you," she said.

"Really?" Jessica looked torn between hopeful and doubtful. "I know some people say I married him just because..." She shrugged one elegant bare shoulder. "You know. His money and all. But that's not true. I love him. He makes me feel special."

If ever the universe was trying to tell her something, it was right now. Amethyst had a sudden, intense desire to escape the conversation.

"Then what're you doing hiding here with me?" she said with a smile.

Jessica blinked. "I guess you're right." She looked around. "There he is. Thanks, Amethyst." She stalked off across the room, vivid and graceful as a flamingo.

Amethyst turned back to the window. The reflection of the party going on behind her moved like ghosts across the glass. The warmth of the room, the clink of glasses, the occasional laugh that bubbled up out of the ebb and flow of conversation contrasted with the stillness of the moonlit garden outside.

One shape detached itself from the kaleidoscope images, growing clearer as at neared: Jas. She held in a sigh and turned.

He held out her glass of limeade. She took it and sipped, conscious of his gaze on her.

"You have that 'this isn't going to work' look on your face again," he said.

She put on a smile she hoped looked sincere. "I'm fine."

Jas studied her. "I saw you talking to Trevor Bayford's wife. Did she say something to upset you?"

"Why would she do something like that?"

"Obviously something happened."

"Nothing happened, Jas. We talked a little. She's a nice young woman who loves her husband and feels overwhelmed and inadequate. That's all."

"Ah." Sudden comprehension showed on his face. "I hope you told her that her husband wouldn't bring her to meet his business associates if he felt she was in any way inadequate."

"Something like that," she said.

"Good. I suppose this…" He gestured around him. "…is all new to her. Once it's no longer quite so new, I doubt she'll find it as daunting."

"Maybe not," she said. "I guess it depends—"

The magic suddenly lurched like someone had sent a jolt of electricity through it. The same instant, there came an odd *foomp* and rush of heat. A couple of women uttered startled screams and someone cursed aloud. Amethyst spun.

The fire was... She blinked, trying to make sense of what she saw. It was *clawing* out of the fireplace, a shifting, shimmering shape more alive than any flame had a right to be.

"What the *hell*," Amethyst said.

People scrambled backwards. The bartender grabbed a bucket of ice and shouted, "Where's the fire extinguisher?"

The thing crawling out of the fireplace expanded, ballooning outward, licking upward, its red and orange and yellow light flickering across the shocked faces of the people in the room.

Jas' eyes were narrowed, scanning the room. "It's a summoning. What the bloody hell does he think he's doing?"

Amethyst scrambled for a spell that would get rid of the thing, but blank shock was the only thing in her head at that moment. Desperate, watching the fire fill more and more of the room, she started pulling energy out of it.

It was big medicine. It wasn't a proper counterspell, magic directed to a specific purpose, but rather using her power to force the magic out of the spell and back into the ether. Something like trying to use a high-powered fan to blow smoke back into a bottle. Her power thrummed and shivered with the strain. The fire spirit, demon, elemental, whatever-it-was shrank back, dimming and thinning. It gave an angry hiss, like a doused campfire, but didn't show any signs of returning to a normal fire.

Jas whipped around. "What are you doing?"

She panted, sweat prickling along her hairline and nape. "The only thing I can think of!"

"No. Banish it." He grabbed her wrist and the outline of a spell formed in her mind. "Like this."

She and Jas were linked—she'd done it herself a year ago. It had been unintended, but the end result was the same: she could use Jas' power, and he could use hers, effectively doubling the power of each.

It was hard, shifting her power into the new spell, like grinding gears. Jas used the link to give her a little push and the spell took form. She immediately saw how it worked—it snipped off the root to whatever dimension the spirit had been summoned from, leaving it to wither or forcing it to return.

Amethyst didn't know which the fire spirit had chosen—or if it was even capable of choice. But it evaporated like burning tissue paper and fizzled out.

People clustered in muttering, exclaiming groups as far from the fireplace as they could manage. A few of the women clung to their men. The bartender had reached the fireplace and chucked the bucket of ice and water on the fire. It hissed much like the fire spirit had and spluttered out in a gout of pinon-scented smoke and a spattering of wet ash.

Amethyst slumped, drained from the expenditure of

power. Jas slid a supporting arm around her, but still scanned the room with that narrow look.

"Someone," he said, "is in a great deal of trouble."

"That was a stunning example," said a man's voice with a Scottish accent, "Of the work of Gramarye FX."

People gasped and looked around. The voice seemed to be coming from a spot a yard or so in front of the fireplace. A spot now glaringly empty.

"Come on," Jas said under his breath.

The magic swirled again in answer to a wizard's power. A fold in the air seemed to form, opening to produce a man.

He was big and tall and looked to be in his forties (which didn't mean much when estimating a wizard's age). He had the most amazing henna-colored hair, a dark, dark brown with a distinct reddish tinge that wore long and loose with... Amethyst's gaze traveled down from his coat. A kilt. An actual kilt, with knee-high stockings and garters under it.

A few more startled squeals and excited exclamations greeted his appearance.

The man made a stagey bow. "Dougal Balgaire, owner and founder Gramarye FX. I hope you enjoyed the demonstration of the effects my little startup can produce."

He turned and, meeting Amethyst's eye across the room, raised the glass he held to her.

She swallowed hard. She'd just blown her cover. Not to the civilians in the room, of course—it wasn't like any of them could see the magic she'd just worked. But certainly to this wizard.

Jas looked ready to start a wizard's war right there in the middle of the cocktail party.

Mr. Gold Watch, the host of the party whose name Amethyst hadn't yet managed to get, stepped forward and slapped Balgaire on the back.

"I didn't believe you when you said you could do that kind of thing in an ordinary setting," Mr. Gold Watch said. "I'm impressed. Extremely impressed."

Uncertain applause peppered the room. A few people laughed nervously and someone gave an approving whistle.

Amethyst watched in disbelief. "Yeah, but if we hadn't stopped that…"

"I suspect," Jas said quietly, "that was exactly the point. To find out if he would be stopped."

"Shit," she said under her breath. "It was a setup. And I walked right into it, didn't I?"

Jas, his arm still around her, gave her hip a reassuring pat. "Under the circumstances, I doubt you gave away anything he didn't already know."

She looked a question at him, worried: *Does he know you're a wizard?*

He shook his head. "As long as you're here, I'm fine."

Knowing the keenness of wizards' senses, he was talking in code: as long as Amethyst was there, any wizard present would assume the magic worked was her doing. And Jas was very, very careful to keep the spells he wove subtle and untraceable so no other wizard would realize he was one, too. It gave him an edge he wasn't willing to lose.

A fan club of sorts had gathered around Balgaire. He laughed and nodded and seemed to be enjoying himself immensely. Once he clapped and pointed across the room. Heads turned, necks craning. Liquid leaped out of someone's abandoned glass on a table, did a dolphin twist in midair and splashed back into the glass. This time, the applause was certain and enthusiastic.

"I'll have to let you take the lead, Amethyst," Jas said.

"Thanks a lot," she muttered.

She'd had her fill of confronting other wizards, which is what seemed to happen every time she met a new one. It was comforting to know that Jas was her ace in the hole— a strange thought, considering he was the very first wizard she'd ever confronted.

She was still trying to decide the best way to confront *this* particular wizard when she realized he was gradually making his way in their direction. Amethyst thought she ought to be getting nervous about now. Instead she folded her arms and waited, half curious to see what he'd do, half disgusted that they'd probably end up circling each other like two strange dogs.

Balgaire paused at the bar to refresh his drink, and to shake the bartender's hand. "Good work, man," he said, then resumed wandering in their direction, chatting and laughing with this person and that.

Amethyst had long since finished her limeade and now sipped melted ice, growing increasingly impatient.

"Take your time, why don't you?" she muttered.

Jas chuckled.

She wondered if Balgaire had a history on the stage.

He certainly knew how to draw out the suspense. Eventually, he stopped in front of them.

"Dougal Balgaire," he said, offering his hand.

Jas shook it and introduced himself and Amethyst. She folded her hands, ignoring his outstretched one.

Balgaire lowered his hand and hooked it in his belt. "I'm afraid my poor display's left you unimpressed," he said in his brogue.

"Flashy and self-indulgent," Amethyst said. "And if you'll excuse me for saying so, really, really stupid. How much damage control were you prepared to do?"

He grinned. "Why, lass, you did it all for me." He took her hand and bowed over it. "And for that, I thank you. I did hear you're no one to fook with."

"Watch your language around a lady," Jas snapped.

"Och, now. Ladies aren't so delicate where I come from."

Amethyst retrieved her hand and laid it on Jas' arm. "That's okay, Jas. Old Oscar Griego from next door could see his 'fook' and raise it a 'mutha'...um, something else."

Jas' lips twitched, but his black stare didn't waver from Balgaire. "Then let's call it respect. And I think this..." Jas gestured at the other wizard and let the pause draw out long enough to be an insult on its own. "...*fellow* owes you that, under the circumstances."

Balgaire laid a hand over his heart. "On my word, I never meant a bit of disrespect."

Definitely a stage background, Amethyst thought.

"So," she said. "Your point in all this?" She waved a hand in the direction of the fireplace.

"Why, for business connections." Balgaire grinned. "And venture capital."

"Really," Jas said. "Speaking for myself, I've backed startups before. Confidence is certainly an element of success. "Unfortunately, *over*confidence isn't a good selling point. It causes people to make…" He glanced at Amethyst. "…stupid mistakes."

"Ah, I see you trust the lady's opinion of my work."

"That I do," Jas said.

"A powerful man like you." Balgaire switched his attention to Amethyst. "How is it, knowin' you've got more power than any man? Ah, I should say, *almost* any man."

She couldn't decide if the remark was funny or irritating.

"Be careful, Dougal," she said. "You'll date yourself with comments like that. Women these days don't have to wring their hands on the sidelines while the men do all the heavy lifting."

"Oh, aye, that's why they hang all over me, then."

Privately, she thought it had more to do with the kilt and the accent than anything else. She gave Jas a 'spare me' look.

"Lucky man," he said dryly.

Amethyst was pretty sure Jas didn't have any trouble attracting women, himself.

"It's got to be hard for the both of you," Balgaire said, "goin' against the natural order of things."

Amethyst turned to Jas. "Help me out here. Is he insulting us? Or is he coming on to me?"

Jas tilted his head as if thinking. "I'd say he's questioning my masculinity while trying to drive a wedge between us."

Balgaire rocked thoughtfully on his heels. "The truth of it is, I'm wondering about the man who owns a company called *Magus* Corporation."

Her palms went sweaty. "Damn," she said and thought, *Damn, damn. He knows.* "I was getting ready to be all flattered."

Jas shot her a look, opened his mouth to say something, then barked a surprised laugh and turned back to Balgaire. "Are you saying *I'm* a wizard?"

Right then, Amethyst knew exactly what to do.

She called back the moment a couple of years ago when she'd realized what Jas was, that he'd wooed her for weeks to draw her in, to lull her. All the hurt and betrayal flooded in as if it had only been waiting.

She took a step back. "Are you, Jas? Does he have it right? So help me God, if you've been lying to me all this time, setting me up as your front man, your *fall* guy—"

"Don't be ridiculous," he snapped. "Would I have hired you if I were capable of doing what you are?"

"If you thought you had something to gain by it, damn right you would. You think I don't know that?"

Damn, the anger was still there. She thought she'd gotten past all that.

His nostrils flared. "If you feel that way," he said with chilling calm, "why are you here?"

The bottom dropped out of her middle, like a misjudged step in the dark.

"Dear me," Balgaire said. "I've gone and started a lover's quarrel. I'd best be going."

Amethyst rounded on him. "Ya think? Hey, by the way, thanks for a *lovely* evening. I'll be sure to look you up sometime and return the favor."

He held up his hands. "Now, now, no need for that. I meant no harm."

She narrowed her eyes. "Well, I guess it's too bad, then, since the harm's been done. Better look for work in LA, Dougal. I have a bad feeling none of the film studios in New Mexico will want to hire you."

Balgaire looked like he very much wanted to say something, but had the good sense to beat a hasty retreat. Amethyst watched while he made his excuses to the host and hurried—without seeming to hurry—out the door.

She let out a breath and closed her eyes. "Don't be mad at me, Jas."

He didn't say anything for a long, painful moment. "That sounded serious, Amethyst," he finally said.

Her mouth was so dry she couldn't swallow. "So did you."

"What you said...caught me by surprise. I didn't think you still felt that way."

She looked down into her empty glass. "I don't, mostly."

"Mostly."

She plunked the glass down on a table. "Look, I'm sorry, okay? I'm sorry I don't get over things easily. I know it has to be frustrating. It's frustrating for me sometimes, too. If it makes you feel any better, it caught me by surprise, too."

Turning away, she folded her arms, concentrating on not hugging herself. "Well, what do you want to do?" That was a much bigger question than she wanted the answer to. She immediately backtracked. "It's not like I can leave. I wouldn't embarrass you that way."

"Amethyst..." He touched her arm, turned her to face him. "It was a difficult situation. I won't fault you for how you handled it." He took her hands. "Thank you."

She leaned back. "What?"

"Thank you," he said again. "For coming with me tonight. For so artfully turning aside suspicion. For being willing to use..." He gave a regretful shrug. "...what happened between us to shield me."

"I— What I said. About you having something to gain by it," she began, stumbling. "I didn't mean to hurt you."

His crinkly smile came. "That's twice now you haven't wanted to hurt my feelings. A year or two ago, you would've happily eviscerated me. I'm making excellent progress."

"Not eviscerated you," she said, scowling to hide a smile. "Only ripped you a new...um, orifice."

His hands tightened on hers. "Would you like a change of scenery? I've filled my quotient of networking for the evening."

Amethyst closed her eyes in pure bliss and sighed. "I thought you'd never ask."

He made a show of running his finger under his necktie. "There you go with that voice again." He cleared his throat. "Do you like to dance?"

"I love to dance." She paused and considered. "As long as it's not Regency or something. The way you offered your arm at my front door has me worried."

"No, in the Colonies it was more jigs and country dances."

She laughed, then stopped. "Are you saying you—" She shook her head and held up her hands. "No, don't tell me. I don't want to know. It would be too weird if you're that old."

"All right. I won't tell you." He held out his arm once more.

Amethyst slipped her arm into his. "Although it might be interesting to see you in a waistcoat and cravat."

"We'll see," he said, sliding her a teasing smile.

❖ ❖ ❖ ❖ ❖ ❖

Dancing with Jas at the Route 66 Casino nightclub was much more enjoyable than talking to Important People at someone's three-million-dollar estate on the bosque. Jas might still be a wily schemer, but he made one helluva dancer.

It would be so, so easy to fall under his spell again. More than once she opened wizard's senses to see if he was doing anything with the magic. But it seemed the only magic was the ordinary kind—the gentlemanly attention he paid her, the way he smiled at her, the pressure of his hand on her waist, light in his dark eyes when he looked at her.

And if she lowered her guard, what then? She liked to

think he wouldn't try another binding. She trusted him that much, anyway. But if it turned out he had some other ulterior motive...

She didn't want to think about it. Not now.

He pulled into the driveway at her house and turned off the ignition. Silence expanded into the car, thick and heavy. In the dim light, he turned to her, a question on his face. Something in Amethyst's middle fluttered. Whether it was excitement or nervousness, she couldn't begin to guess.

She drew a steadying breath. "I'd like to invite you in, but you have to promise not to take advantage of me. I'm not a cheap date."

"I assure you," he said. "I most certainly do not consider you a cheap date."

"Okay, then. Would you like to come in for a cup of coffee before you head home?"

"I'd love to."

Something about the way he said it made goosebumps prickle up her arms.

She waited for him to come around and help her out of the car, then concentrated on her hand in his, avoiding his eye.

Caramela's happy greeting at the door pulled the plug on the tension. This time she gave Jas a cursory sniff as if to say, *Oh, it's* you *again*. He bent and scratched under her chin. Caramela gave a mollified wag then went and flumped down on her bed. It was *way* past her bedtime.

Amethyst reached to take off her coat. Jas stepped forward to help her, then laid the coat over the arm of the sofa. He glided his fingertips down her arm, took her hand and stood still, waiting.

Her heartbeat immediately ramped up, not entirely unpleasantly. In fact, not at all unpleasantly.

She wet her lips. "I'm going to try this without a net." In other words, no wards. "But if you—" she began, threatening.

He put his fingers to her lips, stopping her. "If you don't feel comfortable, don't do it. I can wait."

She gave him a skeptical look. "Jas, no man is that patient."

"Men have lost the art of patience. If they'd bother to try it, they'd find it yields its own rewards."

She wasn't sure why that statement made her insides do funny things.

Very gently, he cupped her face in both hands then paused, watching her. She put her hands on his arms and waited for the panic to flare again, but nothing happened. Well, not quite *nothing*. Her breath quickened and her pulse fluttered in her lips. She tilted her face to his.

He bent his head and kissed her. She closed her eyes and leaned into him.

Still holding her face, he drew back enough to meet her eyes. His thumbs traced gentle arcs on her cheekbones. "All right?"

Her heartbeat was definitely racing, but the sensations thrumming through her didn't have anything to do with fear.

"Good," she said, not entirely steadily.

"Only 'good'? I'll have to work on that."

He slid his hand behind her neck, encircled her with his other arm, still very gently, giving her the chance to pull away if she wanted to. Heaven save her, she didn't want to.

He brushed his lips lightly against hers, his breath a warm caress on her cheek. He kissed the corner of her mouth, then took her lips again.

His scent surrounded her like a nighttime thunderstorm, the tang of warm rain on desert plants and musky earth. The sensation of his lips moving on hers, the flex of his fingers in her hair raced across her skin like lightning. Her heart beat like thunder.

Her hands moved without her deciding to, around his neck, his chest. He pulled her closer, pressing her against the lean firmness beneath his shirt. She melted into him, tipping back her head to invite a deeper kiss. His tongue traced the rim of her lips then slipped between.

A little sigh escaped her as she opened her mouth to meet him. His hand slid down her back to her bottom, pressing her even closer. Liquid fire rippled its way through her. She shifted her leg, his thigh inside hers, close enough to feel how *he* was reacting.

Breaking free of her lips, he kissed his way along her jawline to the sensitive place below her earlobe.

"Amethyst," he breathed, then traced the rim of her ear with his lips.

She shivered and tipped her head to the side, kissing the delicious-smelling hollow of his throat. His breath shook against her skin. His hand cupped her bottom and his fingers tightened in her hair. His mouth moved lower, tracing the line of her neck to her shoulder.

"Amethyst." His voice was husky. "If you want to escape with your virtue intact, you'd better send me home."

His lips and hands said just the opposite. So did hers, moving over the muscles of his back. She felt dizzy, drunk, her head spinning and heat throbbing through her.

Somewhere, a little sense flickered. *Wait*, it said. She wanted to ignore it, but it shouldered its way past all the spinning and throbbing, growing larger and more insistent.

Wait. Wait.

Amethyst made herself let him go, put her hands on his chest. He shifted his grip, too, resting his hands on her waist. His eyes were closed, his chest rising and falling under her touch.

She was suddenly, horribly embarrassed. Here she was supposed to be resisting his spell, and it had been Jas himself who'd had to remind her of it. The heat that had been running so high in other parts rose to her face.

She extricated herself as gracefully as she could. "Sorry," she muttered.

Jas' eyes popped open. "*Sorry?* What in God's name for?"

"I, um, well…" *For being ready to ravish you? For being a tease?* No. "I forgot all about the coffee."

He just stared at her in either bewilderment or disbelief, then bent over laughing. Finally, he straightened. "I think I'll have to take a rain check on the coffee."

"Oh. Okay," she said, not sure if she was relieved— or disappointed.

"Thank you for coming with me tonight. It was…"

He touched her cheek. "…perfect."

Maybe not perfect, but pretty damned close. She should probably tell him so, but couldn't quite manage to do it. Why not?

He gathered his coat and crossed to the door. Amethyst trailed after, trying to think of something to say that wouldn't sound lame or too formal. Or worse still, too flippant.

He stopped outside the door. "Sleep well, Amethyst."

She grinned. "Oh, yeah, sure. You too."

He returned the grin. The look in his eyes challenged her to change her mind.

Not yet, that little voice in the back of her head whispered. It was right. If things had kept on going, the morning-after regret would've been absolutely classic. And Jas must've realized it before she did. Now *that* was a strange thought.

She shut the door, leaned against it and blew out a breath.

Neither of them would be sleeping well at all tonight.

CHAPTER 7

Fear of Falling

methyst woke feeling like she'd been sick with a fever—dizzy, a little fuzzy, physically lighter than she should. She opened her eyes, pulled her arms out of the warm cocoon of bedding and stretched.

Happiness flooded through her. She lay for a moment looking out over the familiar landscape of her bedroom, the rumpled sheets, the dresser mirror reflecting way more light peeking through the blinds than usual when she got up.

Caramela's tail whapped a good-morning greeting on the comforter and she, too, stretched, front feet paddling the air. Amethyst reached over and grabbed one. That led to a game of keep-away feet, Amethyst grabbing Caramela's toes, and Caramela opening her wide, pink mouth in play bites and snatching her feet away. Getting rowdy, the dog launched herself off the bed and ran off down the hall.

Amethyst laughed, rolled out of bed and padded to the closet to get dressed. Seeing the violet dress hanging inside, she suddenly realized why she felt happy. Just as suddenly, the happiness spluttered out as if doused with a fire hose.

She scuffed on slippers and slouched down the hall to let Caramela outside. Late morning sunlight shining through the stained glass panel hanging in the kitchen window scattered color across the countertop. She picked up her phone where it rested in a pool of garnet light.

Melodie had texted her around 9:30: **call me.**

Again at 10:15: **U up? call me!**

Then again a little after 11:00: **Get up. I'm coming over.**

Amethyst squinted at the clock on her phone: 11:14. She dropped the phone and hurried back to the bathroom to get ready.

The doorbell rang. She spat out a mouthful of toothpaste, wiped her face and hurried to the door.

A young woman with hot pink hair and wearing a green polo shirt embroidered with *Bella's Blooms* stood outside holding a vase of flowers. Amethyst, trying not to wince at the color scheme, thanked her, took the flowers and carried them into the kitchen.

Purple roses and green hydrangeas tied with green and purple ribbons sprouted from a tourmaline vase, green glass streaked with purplish pink. The vase looked like it might have been hand-blown. Not the sort of thing found stock in a flower shop.

The symbolism was obvious: Jas' green and her purple. Something tugged under her heart as she pulled the little card out of its envelope.

It bore only one word: *Magic.*

Amethyst leaned on the kitchen counter and sank her head into one hand. The doorbell rang again.

Caramela's gruff barks turned into a welcoming wag and a pit bull grin when Amethyst opened the door to Melodie.

"Well?" Melodie said by way of greeting.

"Oh, Mel," Amethyst said and led the way to the kitchen.

Melodie headed straight for the flowers on the breakfast bar. She picked up the card, which Amethyst had left on the counter.

Her brows went up and she cocked her head in a question. "Here are flowers in a very nice vase. Here's this card." She waved it, then pointed it at Amethyst. "Then there's the look on your face. What happened?"

Amethyst filled a kettle and got mugs and a couple of tins of loose-leaf tea out of cupboards. "About what you'd expect. Party, dancing afterwards."

"Yeah, yeah. And after that?"

"We came back here."

Melodie tapped the little card on the countertop.

Amethyst got out bread and peppered turkey breast for sandwiches. "Well," she said to the inside of the fridge as she took out lettuce and mayo. "We kissed."

The sound of the card tapping on the countertop abruptly ceased.

"If he did anything like he did when he kissed you a couple of years ago," Melodie said, "I will personally go kick his ass—wizard or not."

Amethyst would've laughed at the picture that made,

but couldn't quite manage it. "No. Nothing like that."

She pulled out the cutting board and started slicing a cucumber. Melodie moved around the kitchen, taking out plates and a knife and applying mayonnaise to bread.

"It was..." Amethyst closed her eyes. "Awesome." She turned a bleak look on Melodie. "If he hadn't stopped, I have a feeling we would've ended up doing it right there in the living room."

Melodie opened her mouth to say something, closed it again and frowned. "*He* stopped. So...is that the problem? You're feeling embarrassed and rejected?"

Amethyst felt absurdly close to tears. "I don't know what I was thinking, agreeing to see him like this. Romantically." She cleared her throat. "I'm going to have to break it off."

Melodie looked at the flowers, then back at Amethyst. "Wiz, I hope you know he'll be blindsided. And somehow I suspect Jas Harker isn't the kind of man who takes blindsiding well. If you break it off, you'd better be ready to have *no* relationship."

Amethyst splayed her hands on either side of the cutting board and closed her eyes again. "I know. It's unfair. It's despicable. But I can't start falling for him again."

Melodie wet her lips. "Far be it from me to try to talk you out of this, but why not?"

"I like...being...with him. This morning..." God, it was so hard to get the words out. "When I woke up, I was *happy*. But Mel, what if he hurts me again?"

Melodie was silent a moment, folding turkey and

cheese slices onto the sandwiches. "The problem is about more than that binding, isn't it?"

Amethyst nodded, not trusting her voice.

Melodie put the sandwiches on plates and set them on the breakfast bar. Amethyst hitched onto a stool beside her and bit into her sandwich. She had to chew a long time before she could convince her throat to swallow. Beside her, Melodie worked on her own sandwich.

"If you're worried he's only after a casual fling," Melodie said, "I think the multiple marriage proposals might put a dent in that theory."

"Yeah. But what *else* does he want?"

Melodie's eyes went round. "Oh." She put down her sandwich, wiped her fingers on a napkin and put her hand on Amethyst's. "Wiz, what do you want me to say? Because ordinarily I'd say the problem is you *are* starting to fall for him, and it scares you. If we were talking about anyone besides Jas, I'd say you'd better take a deep breath and wait before you do anything as drastic as breaking it off."

"But we aren't talking about anyone else. I'm heading down exactly the same path I did two years ago."

"Is it really the same path?"

Amethyst curled her hands around her mug, letting the warmth seep into her cold fingers. "Not really. I know him better now. He's not just some amazing fairytale prince who popped into my life to sweep me off my feet. Mel, he's been trying hard for a long time, I have to give him that. But if I still feel this way now, after everything he's done to show me he made a mistake, is it going to be any better a month from now, or two months, or six?"

"You've also been keeping him at arm's length for a long time. If you let yourself get closer…" Melodie trailed off, looking troubled.

"Would you?"

Melodie gave a short, humorless laugh. "I think you already know the answer to that."

Amethyst lifted her mug to drink, then put it down again, staring into it. "See? We both keep coming to the same conclusion."

"I know," Melodie said. "So why are we both so miserable about it?"

❖❖❖❖❖❖❖

Amethyst sat staring down at her phone. Some fifteen minutes ago, Melodie had hugged her and left her to her fate. She'd been sitting exactly like this since, the sandwich with a single bite out of it by her elbow, her tea gone cold and the flowers on the counter accusing her.

She could take the coward's way out and send Jas a text. Plenty of people did just that. But he deserved better. She put her head in one hand and closed her eyes. He deserved to be blindsided in person.

Well, one thing for sure, she didn't trust her voice. She picked up her phone and tapped in a text:

I owe you a coffee. My house 2PM?

A text came right back: **I'll be there.**

CHAPTER 8

Damned If You Do

It was a grueling couple of hours, waiting for Jas. Amethyst touched a heat spell to her tea and made herself eat the sandwich. She tidied up (even though she'd already tidied up yesterday). She went out into the backyard for poop patrol. The warm, high-altitude winter sun didn't do anything for the cold spot in her belly.

All the while, she rehearsed in her mind what she'd say to Jas. Something like, *It's my problem, not yours. I know you've done your best, but I just can't get past what happened...*

She made her way back to her bedroom about 1:30 to change into cords and a soft cowl neck sweater. She started a pot of coffee and put fresh water in the kettle for tea. She cut up veggies for dipping and arranged crackers on a fused glass plate with sandstone-red shapes against a turquoise background.

She checked the clock on the stove: 1:56. He'd be here any minute.

Her mouth was dry. Her stomach was upset. She put placemats and napkins on the table, then went into the bathroom to check how she looked one more time. The clock on her nightstand read 2:07.

Jas was usually pretty punctual. If anything, she'd expect him to be early, not late. Unless he'd somehow gotten wind of what she had planned—

No, that was stupid. Of course wizards had ways of eavesdropping, but not on another wizard whose house was warded up every which way to Tuesday. Not unless he knew some kind of snooping spell she didn't—

Knowing Jas, he just might.

Stop it, Amethyst. There'll be plenty of time for a guilty conscience later.

She drifted into her workroom. She was in the process of pinning the pieces of the fall aspens window over the pattern in preparation for soldering. She sat down at her worktable and pinned a few more pieces. Her eyes kept drifting to the wall clock. When it finally read 2:13, she pushed away from the worktable and went to the window. If she looked through it from the far end, she could see most of her driveway.

Jas' green Infiniti was parked there. Her heart abruptly crowded into her throat. She took three deep breaths and made herself walk slowly into the living room. The stained glass panel she'd conjured in her very first effort in handling the magic glowed gently with its own ethereal light.

No doorbell. No knock at the door. She made a not-very-successful attempt to wet her lips.

What the hell? If he was sitting in his car on the phone, she was going to open the door, rip the damn phone out of his hand and stomp on it.

She waited a minute more, chewing on the inside of her lip, then strode for the front door.

The sound of voices nearby greeted her when she opened it, a woman's laugh and a man's voice. *Jas'* voice. Amethyst took a few steps down her front walk, past the jut of the garage, looking to see *what* the *hell* was going on.

Heather Purdy, her next door neighbor, stood on the far side of the driveway talking to Jas.

Heather had hair the color of fine whisky, blue-topaz eyes and a figure that filled out anything she put on. Today it was faded skinny jeans with an artful hole high over the thigh and a turtleneck sweater a few shades lighter than the flower delivery girl's hair had been.

She laughed at something Jas said and gave him a playful shove. Cold fire shot through Amethyst, rooting her to the cracked concrete of the front walk. Heather looked up and caught sight of her.

"Amethyst, honey," Heather called. "I was just making the acquaintance of your friend Jas. I've been seeing his car here and have been just *itching* with curiosity."

"And you finally found your chance," Amethyst said with a grin that probably showed too many teeth.

Right at that moment, it was all she could do to keep from cursing Heather with split ends, chapped lips, pimples, toenail fungus and drooping boobs.

The reaction took her aback. Heather had been a godawful flirt from the day she moved into old Mr. Meadows' house, but as far as Amethyst had ever seen, it was men's attention she was after, not necessarily the men themselves. Although if a man proved interested, she was pretty sure Heather wouldn't turn him down.

Jas circled the front of his car to slip his arm around Amethyst's waist and give her a kiss. "How are you today?"

It was a very nice, very sweet kiss, enough to filter through her unexpected anger at Heather. She backed off to find him smiling at her, as if there was no such thing as boobilicous Heather standing eight feet away.

"Just great," she answered him, trying to regain her footing.

Not that she had much footing to regain to start with.

Keeping an arm around Amethyst, Jas turned. "It was a pleasure to meet you, Heather."

"Oh, definitely," she said, dimpling. "I hope I can get you…and Amethyst," she said after a pause so brief Amethyst wasn't sure it was a pause, "to come over for coffee and cookies one day. I just love showing off my new house to people."

An arsonist had burned down Heather's house a year or so ago. Amethyst had always had a bad feeling that it was *her* house that was supposed to have burned, but her wards shunted the arsonist's attentions to the nearest substitute. Fortunately, Heather seemed pretty happy with the cute, new northern New Mexico-style one built to replace the old house. Amethyst had taken the precaution of putting wards on that one.

"Thanks, Heather," Amethyst said, trying hard to keep both guilt and a certain lingering nastiness out of her voice. "That's nice. We'll keep it in mind. Right now, I already told Jas I owed him a coffee."

She linked her arm in his, turned and marched with him back up the front walk.

Jas heaved a sigh when she shut the door. "Thank you for the rescue."

Amethyst shot him a look. "Somehow, I suspect you're perfectly capable of rescuing yourself."

"True," he said. "But she's your neighbor. I'd hate to cause problems."

Amethyst grunted. If she was going to cut him loose, she supposed she didn't have any business being irritated about Heather's attentions. *Or* giving him a hard time.

Her conscience started pricking her like a cactus spine in her sock. *Shut up*, she told it. It shut up, but her stomach took up the chorus.

"You'll have to tell me if the coffee is okay," she said. "If it's not, I can make another pot."

"I'm sure it will be fine."

She made herself busy in the kitchen, getting mugs, milk, sugar, putting tea in a strainer for herself. It was chamomile and mint this time. She really, really needed that chamomile. Now besides her stomach doing unhappy things, her heart made strange, painful squeezes, like someone wringing out a sponge.

"I see you got the flowers," Jas said behind her.

"Oh!" She spun. "Oh, yes. I'm sorry, I totally forgot. They're beautiful. Thank you. Thank you so much."

"It was my pleasure," he said, studying her. "Amethyst, is everything all right?"

Oh, damn. Oh, hell. Oh, shit. Now's your chance. Tell him.

She turned back to fussing in the kitchen. "Heather just kind of…set me off. Sorry. Her cousin Emily's boyfriend used to live next door. In fact, he'd lived next door with Mommy and Daddy ever since I've lived here." She was blathering, but it was better than facing Jas. "Emily finally pried him out and got him to move in with her in a place near Old Town. Said it was so Gary could be closer to UNM for classes, but I think it was because of Heather. Emily has a pretty short fuse when it comes to Heather's flirting. I guess I would too if I'd lived with it all my life."

Sweet Mary in Heaven, what was she thinking? Telling him that Heather's flirting bothered her. Talking about *boyfriends!*

She gritted her teeth, put what she hoped was a pleasant expression on her face and turned to hand Jas his mug of coffee.

He gave her another of those smiles like he had a few minutes ago, not his usual charming one, but one that seemed specially crafted for her.

"Well, when you move from this house," he said, "I hope it will be for reasons other than Heather's flirting."

That sounded an awful lot like another roundabout marriage proposal.

"Jas—"

Say it, Amethyst. Just say it, dammit. Get it over with.

"What?" he said, teasing, but like his smile, in a different way. But different how?

"Never mind," she muttered.

She sat down at the dining room table. Jas doctored

his coffee and put veggies and crackers on his plate. Amethyst did the same, slowly, wondering what excuse she'd give for leaving them uneaten.

She watched him. Why couldn't she just *tell* him? It wasn't going to work. It would never work. They might as well admit it and end the torment. She swallowed on a dry throat and took a breath, ready to force out the words.

Then it struck her what was different about him today.

He was *happy*. He was happy to be here, sitting drinking coffee with her. No offhand charm, no sly suggestions, no knowing smiles. Just happy.

Happy…like she'd been this morning, before all her defenses had slammed back into place.

The realization rolled over her, powerful enough to make her dizzy. She looked at the flowers where she'd placed them as a centerpiece on the table, thinking of the card that had come with them: *Magic.*

He'd meant it. The flowers hadn't been part of some calculation to soften or beguile her. He'd truly enjoyed their evening together, and wanted to let her know it.

The tension that had wound her so tight evaporated. This wasn't a wreck hurtling toward her, impossible to avoid. It was… She didn't know what it was. Maybe, just possibly, it was something honest.

She picked up a carrot stick and crunched it, the choking tightness in her throat gone.

"I've been thinking," Jas said, "about what we should do next weekend."

That 'we' caught her off guard, then realization hit

her. *She'd invited him over today.* Since she hadn't told him what she'd intended to, how else could he take the invitation but acknowledgment that they *were* a 'we'? How—and more to the point, *why*—had she managed to do exactly the opposite of what she'd intended?

Caught, she fumbled for a reply. "It's still *this* weekend, Jas."

"So it is. What do you want to do?"

"Now?" She definitely wasn't going to get a chance to fall back and regroup.

"A few hours of a very nice day remain."

"I, um, was going to take Caramela to the dog park."

"Why don't we go after we finish our coffee?"

"You want to go to the dog park and throw a ball for Caramela?"

"Why not?"

"You never struck me as a ball-throwing kind of guy."

"I'd like to turn that into a suggestive comment, but I can't quite figure out how."

She rolled her eyes.

"You don't seem the type to own a pit bull," he said.

She twirled a broccoli floret in the dip. "There were some renters a couple of houses down from Heather. Caramela was basically a four-legged burglar alarm living in the backyard with their junk. When they moved, they left her behind along with the other junk they didn't want." Amethyst bit off the head of the broccoli. "So she came to live with me."

"You see," Jas said quietly after a moment, "Today

I've learned something else about you. You have a kind heart."

If he'd deliberately set out to prick her, he couldn't have done a better job. *If only you knew the bullet you just dodged*, she thought.

Caramela had heard the words 'ball' and 'dog park' and was dancing around, nudging Amethyst with her nose.

"Okay, okay, I'll ask Jas if we can go soon," Amethyst told her.

He took a last sip of coffee and stood. "I'll get our coats."

Strange how intimate that felt, Jas going to her hall closet for her coat. Amethyst went into the laundry room for Caramela's leash and ball, Caramela dancing around her the whole way. She danced while Jas helped Amethyst into her coat, but settled down when Amethyst bent and put her hands on her shoulders.

"Let's get ready to go out," Amethyst told her and called the magic.

Amethyst clipped on the leash and straightened. Jas gave her a questioning look.

"It's a little ward against ill-will," she explained. "A lot of people don't like pit bulls."

She didn't mention that she'd also worked a spell of distraction. Something to occupy Heather as they walked past her house. Maybe a smoke alarm going off or an insistently beeping microwave. Electronics were *so* susceptible to magic.

Amethyst felt…odd, walking with Jas. Although why walking along Eubank toward Los Altos Park should be any different than walking in Santa Fe, she didn't know. Maybe because, like her coat closet, it was part of her home space, places she'd rarely let Jas enter.

The happiness of the dog and the happiness of the man beside her, stylishly casual in his distressed leather jacket and designer jeans, gradually wore away her awkwardness. There was only the brilliant afternoon, the cold air and sunshine, intense even in winter.

Eubank was a busy street, and the noise of the passing traffic made much talking impractical. It wasn't far to the park, though, maybe only half a mile or so.

The park was brown with winter, the trees casting only a tracery of shade. As usual, dogs bounced around the fenced-in area, running, playing, barking, their people looking on, hands tucked in pockets for warmth. With the spell on Caramela, no one gave the dog evil or wary looks.

Inside the fence of the big-dog park, Amethyst unhooked Caramela's leash. Caramela focused on her the way only a pit bull can as Amethyst took the Chuckit ball-thrower out of her back pocket and the ball out of her jacket pocket. She popped the ball into the Chuckit and let fly. Caramela flew as well, running just as fast to return the ball as she had to chase it, pure, thoughtless joy.

Jas, true to his word, took his turn with the Chuckit. Amethyst hadn't thought he really would. But yes, there he was, Jas Harker, wizard and CEO of Magus Corporation, urging Caramela to go deep before he threw the ball. There was the same happiness she'd seen earlier, his enjoyment of something as simple as playing with a dog.

A warm little bloom unfurled under her heart. She

didn't want to examine it too closely.

The ball arced high through the air, whistling, and Caramela raced after it, although not quite as fast as before. Pretty soon, Caramela's tongue lolled dripping from her wide, pink mouth.

Amethyst took the slobbery ball and clipped Caramela's leash back on. "Time to take a break, crazy dog."

They left the fenced-in area and found a bench to sit on. She took a water bottle from her other pocket and filled a collapsible bowl. Caramela lapped noisily.

"Did you ever have dogs?" Amethyst asked.

"I had a few hunting dogs I was fond of," Jas said.

Hunting dogs. She pictured men on horses coming home with their winded dogs to a lantern-lit house. No, still better not ask how long ago it had been.

"We always had a dog or two when I was growing up," she said. "I'd forgotten how much I missed them until I got Caramela."

The sun was descending to an early sunset, not much more than an hour away, and the air was decidedly cooler. Even so, Caramela lay at Amethyst's feet, panting. Jas sat beside her, his arm extended along the bench behind her. And damned if it didn't feel comfortable. After all this morning's agony, had she given up that easily?

"So, next weekend," Jas said. "I thought this time we might do something that includes your friends."

That idea made her shiver. She bent and smoothed a hand along the soft, short fur of Caramela's head and neck. "I don't know if that's a good idea." Sighing, she straightened. "Melodie is, and I quote, not a big fan of Jas Harker."

"Ah," he said. "I wondered why I've encountered her only once or twice. I'd hoped I'd mended her opinion of me. I suppose I'll have to convince her that I'm not the devil incarnate."

Amethyst closed her eyes. "Please, Jas. No convincing. If you start convincing, she'll be *sure* you're the devil incarnate."

A teasing glint came into his eyes. "I hope you realize I can easily take that as a compliment."

She gave him a disgusted look. "You would."

✥✥✥✥✥✥✥

"All that anguish, wasted," Melodie said.

Amethyst had called to tell her about the interview with Jas. Now, Bluetooth headset clipped over her ear, Amethyst stood at the sink peeling the charred skin off some roasted green chile.

"Well," she said, "I'm sure not going to go through with something like that just for the principle of the thing. Besides, it hardly seemed fair to hurt someone so that I won't get hurt."

Melodie's snort came clear over the headset. "That's what I was trying to tell you this morning, but you didn't want to hear me."

"I heard you, I just didn't want to listen."

"I'm going to regret being the voice of reason, aren't I?" Melodie said on a sigh.

Amethyst laughed. She was glad Melodie wasn't here in person. She wasn't sure how much she wanted to see her reaction to what was coming next.

"Jas and I are going snowboarding next weekend. You and Marl are invited." Marl was Melodie's husband.

Dead silence on the other end of the line. Amethyst bit her lip and waited.

Then finally, "You don't know how to snowboard. *I* don't know how to snowboard. If Marl ever went snowboarding, he never said anything."

"That was pretty much my argument, too. Jas said it'll be fun, all of us learning together." Amethyst dropped the green chile into the food processor and started peeling tomatillos. "I'm a little ashamed to admit, it *does* sound like fun."

She'd wanted to learn to snowboard for a long time, but it just never seemed to happen.

More silence. "If I say we're busy, this will just come up again later, won't it?"

Itchy prickles ran under Amethyst's sweatshirt. "Well…I guess it's a possibility at this point. You could always wait it out and see. You won't hurt my feelings."

Melodie sighed again. "I've already spent a year hoping I wouldn't encounter Jas." This time the silence was a thinking one. "I think I can promise to be civil."

"Thanks, Mel," Amethyst said on an outrush of breath. "I won't ask for more. I can't promise you'll have fun, but it should be…interesting."

"I can't wait," Melodie said without enthusiasm.

CHAPTER 9

Unexpected Visitor

That invitation to coffee had been a severe tactical error. After the evening they'd had at (not to mention *after*) the cocktail party, how else could Jas take their situation but *damn the torpedoes, full speed ahead?*

So here she was at Flying Star, sitting in a booth next to Jas scarcely 24 hours after the last time she'd seen him.

Amethyst thought she should be feeling trapped, desperate, panicky. At least awkward or weird. But no. She only felt weird because she was... Well, she was enjoying the time with him. What she *should* be doing was trying to figure out a way to slow...things...down.

"I don't think that cake has any evil designs on you," Jas said. "If that's what you're worried about."

She found herself frowning at the slice of chocolate-orange mousse cake in front of her, her fork hovering over it. She cut a bite, not turning to look at him where he sat so close. The rich, fluffy chocolate with its orange aroma chased away much of her discomfort.

The night pressing against the restaurant's big windows, the tiny flecks of snow drifting past the parking lot lights outside, made the restaurant with its sunken central dining area and tile-mosaic columns feel that much cozier.

"Um, no," she said.

"Neither do I have any evil designs on you."

"I kinda got that after you passed up multiple opportunities for villainy."

He gave a ghost of a laugh and took a bite of his own dessert, a mixed fruit tart. "Then what? That I'll be encouraged to ask you to marry me again?"

"Something like that," she muttered to her cake, making designs in the mousse with her fork.

"Perhaps you're more worried about your answer."

That did get her to turn. "Try me."

He leaned close and brushed his lips against her temple. "I'd love to."

She ignored the tingle that went through her. "You really want to be wearing that fruit tart, don't you?"

"I find it interesting that comestibles seem to be your weapon of choice. Last time you threatened to set my whisky on fire."

"Minimum effort, maximum effect," she said…

…And abruptly realized that he'd teased her right out of the fidgets.

How did that work? And dammitall, now she was feeling all warm and happy again. He couldn't be calculating this. Jas might be shifty and cunning, but he couldn't possibly know her that well.

"Am I allowed to ask what you're looking for in a husband?" he said.

"You're full of hypothetical questions tonight. So hypothetically, I'd refuse to answer."

He tsked. "I'd never have expected you to be so missish."

"*Missish?*" she said on a half-choked laugh. "If you're going to use a *Pride and Prejudice* reference to insult me and hope I don't get it, you'll be sadly disappointed." She sniffed and turned back to her cake. "Besides, that's not missish. It's just smart strategy to withhold key information when dealing with psychics, con artists and…" She raised a brow. "…*charmers.*"

He bowed his head. "Thank you."

"Any time." She took a bite. "Anyway, I'd think by now you'd know what makes good husband material."

"Hmm," he said. "Constancy? Dependability?"

He'd certainly displayed those in abundance since they'd become reacquainted, she had to give him that. "Unless I'm into bad boys. Then it's just boring."

"If you preferred bad boys, you wouldn't still be angry with me about that binding."

"Hmph."

"Gentleness and tenderness?"

"Well, duh. *Despite* what you might have read in a certain book about another billionaire."

"There were three of them."

She made a shooing motion in reply. "Persistence."

"Now you're trying to trick me," he said.

"Me? Never."

"The ability to provide for a wife."

"Nice, but anachronistic."

"Even when it includes fast cars and wind sculptures?"

"Remember." She poked her fork in his direction. "You promised no expensive gifts."

"Yet." He touched his cup and steam suddenly rose from the coffee. "How about protection?"

She had to think about that one for a minute. Her experiences with other wizards really had been uniformly unpleasant. "Maybe. But that's a pretty...I don't know...cold-blooded reason to marry someone."

His eyes danced. "I'm glad you think so."

"Okay, fine. I'll give you a hint." She leaned an elbow on the table, angling to face him. "Respect. Compatibility. I'm sure there's a way to fake those." She gave a smug smile. "But not over time."

Sudden understanding washed across his face. "Ah."

She would *not* ask what the big revelation was.

His hand came to rest on her knee, not suggestively, but with a squeeze of reassurance. "We can take all the time we need, Amethyst."

Her heart turned over. She sipped water, swallowing the unaccountable thick feeling in her throat.

"Okay." She closed her fingers around his.

❖❖❖❖❖❖

Thank god the weekend is over.

Amethyst enjoyed roller coasters, but it was always nice when they stopped and you stepped off onto solid ground again. When you had the chance to catch your breath.

And God knew, she really needed to catch her breath.

She sat at her desk sketching out a design for a new window, this one a geometric cholla cactus in bloom, all jointed angles in diamonds of brown and olive glass with brilliant magenta petals. She still had the fall aspens to finish pinning for soldering, but designing took up more mental real estate. And she really didn't want the opportunity for a lot of thinking right now. It only made her more confused.

The doorbell rang. As usual, Caramela leapt up from her place at Amethyst's feet, her barks marking her progress down the hall and to the front door. Amethyst sighed, got up and followed.

Caramela stood at the door, her tail whipping in a stiff wag and her front end hopping with each bark. Amethyst hooked her fingers in the dog's collar and opened the door.

A big man wearing a kilt and long, henna-colored hair stood outside.

"Good morrow, Miss Rey," the wizard Balgaire said.

The last time a wizard had shown up at her house uninvited, he'd attacked her. Her only advantages then were that his powers were only newly restored, and she was better able handle modern magic—which, as she understood it, was wilder and more potent than it had been in past centuries.

So Amethyst instantly snapped up the strongest shield spell she could conjure. Caramela, no doubt feeling the surge of magic, not to mention Amethyst's sudden tension, bristled from skull to halfway down her tail. Threatening snarls mixed with her barks.

"Back up," Amethyst told Balgaire, stabbing a forefinger over his shoulder. "Off the porch."

He spread his hands in a theatrical gesture. "Now, lass, no need for that—"

"Back," she said again. "Now. Onto the driveway."

If he was going to try anything, she wanted it in full view of the world.

His gaze flicked to Caramela. The dog's ears were back, her lips wrinkled up off her teeth. Serious threat, no longer only alarm barking.

"Aye, aye, very well."

Balgaire did indeed *back* up. It was not a good idea to turn one's back on a dog as serious as Caramela was right now. Amethyst followed as far as the front walk, laid a hand on Caramela's head and shushed her. A brush of magic got through to the dog where mere words wouldn't have. She settled, still grumbling and hackles still bristling.

A sunset red Cadillac SUV of some kind was parked at the curb in front of her house. She'd never seen one like it before, but it looked exactly like the kind of thing Balgaire would drive, fancy and flashy.

Amethyst folded her arms, nevertheless yet touching the magic, ready to use it if she had to. Through it she felt Balgaire's alarm, a prickly roil of surprise underlain by the bitter tang of adrenaline. Good. At least he took her and Caramela seriously.

"*What*," she said, "are you doing here?"

"I came to apologize." He stopped, wet his lips.

Amethyst wondered how they must look, bristling woman and bristling pit bull. Then she laughed.

"What do you really want, Dougal?"

"Truly," he said. "It was an ill thing, what happened at the party. I want to make amends. Let me take you to dine."

A little alarm bell started going off in her head. This was beginning to feel too much like stalking. Worse still, she wasn't sure if she was the one being stalked.

"Uh-huh. And why should you bother?"

He glanced again at Caramela, then took a step nearer. "You defeated the drake laird. I know what I owe you, lass. My life. My power."

That again. The dragon lord. The *first* wizard she'd had to fight for her life. The uncomfortable side effect of destroying him was that the power of the wizards he'd drained had been returned to them. Thus the sudden reappearance of wizards in the modern world.

"Thanks duly noted and accepted," she said. "Next time, send a card."

"Morning, Amethyst," a familiar voice chirped.

Amethyst looked past Balgaire to see Heather sashaying down her driveway, ostensibly toward the mailbox cluster at the curb. Today she wore moccasins, an off-the-shoulder chenille sweater and cords that mapped the topography of every curve.

Balgaire turned as well, first only his head, then the rest of him.

Heather was abruptly far more welcome than she'd been Saturday afternoon, when she'd had her sights locked on Jas.

"Hi, Heather," Amethyst said.

Heather's usual pert smile wavered when her gaze fell on Balgaire. Inveterate flirt and man-chaser that she was, she nevertheless stopped in her tracks. She looked, to use Jas' words, like somebody had dumped a bucket of water over her.

Heather's eyes went from Balgaire's face to his booted feet and back up again, lingering somewhere in the vicinity of his kilt. Her chest rose, which did even more amazing things to her already amazing bosom.

Balgaire gave a stagey bow. "Miss Rey, will ya not introduce me to the young lady?"

It was all Amethyst could do to keep from shouting and pumping her fist.

"Dougal, meet my neighbor, Heather Purdy. Heather, this is Dougal Balgaire."

Heather came up the driveway as if reeled in and held out a hand to shake. Balgaire took it and kissed the knuckles. Heather blushed, actually *blushed*, giggling.

"My goodness! Where do you *find* these men, Amethyst?"

"Seems they always manage to find me, somehow," Amethyst said. An idea was beginning to take shape. "Dougal owns a special effects company. I met him when he gave a demonstration at a party Jas and I went to Friday night. It was…" She searched for something besides 'incredibly stupid' and 'disgustingly arrogant.' She finally settled on, "Amazing."

"Really!" Heather said.

"He was just asking me to lunch," Amethyst went on, "but I have a commission to finish. Maybe you could take my place?" She turned to Balgaire. "Heather is a publicist. She could help you get some traction for your new company."

Balgaire's eyes didn't leave Heather, making the same trip up and down that hers had. He smiled. It was an enchanting smile, an utterly satisfied smile.

"Indeed! That sounds promising. *Most* promising."

Heather blushed again, not missing the subtext in the least. "I'd be happy to do *anything* I can."

Amethyst struggled not to roll her eyes.

"Well, Amethyst," Heather said, "if you're sure you're too busy…"

"Absolutely buried," Amethyst said with a helpless gesture.

Heather turned to Balgaire. "Then come on in while I get my coat and purse."

"I'd be delighted, Miss Purdy."

Heather laid a manicured hand on his forearm. "Please, call me Heather."

Balgaire turned back to Amethyst, first putting his big hand briefly on Heather's. "Good day to you, then, Miss Rey. It was a pleasure to see you again."

He reached out as if to take her hand and kiss it (bastard!), but Amethyst bent and patted Caramela on her muscular side.

"Come on, Caramela. Back to work." She headed for the front door.

"Are you new to town?" Heather said behind her. "I

could take you around, show you the sights after lunch."

"Aye," Balgaire replied, a caress in his voice. "I haven't yet seen the half of what I'd like to here."

Amethyst closed the door on Heather's giggle. Damn. What if they jumped each other's bones as soon as they went inside? No, Heather might be a flirt, but Amethyst didn't think she was a ho. Or if she was, she was pretty sure Heather wouldn't advertise it to the neighborhood.

Amethyst knelt in front of Caramela and gave her a kiss on her bulging cheek. "Did I ever tell you what a good dog you are?"

Caramela gave her a kiss on the cheek back, wagging and panting.

Amethyst stood and patted her thigh. "Come on. Let's get some hot chocolate. I need it after that."

She made her hot chocolate and heated up some leftover chile verde, giving Heather and Balgaire enough time, she hoped, to leave. When she peeked out the front blinds again, sure enough, Balgaire's Cadillac was gone. Good. Except he'd have to come back to drop Heather off home. Unless they ended up having a wild night at his place.

Shuddering at the image, she returned to the kitchen to clean up after lunch and think what to do next. She kept coming to the same conclusion.

She put her bowl and spoon in the dishwasher, leaned on the counter and sighed.

"Well, Caramela. Looks like we're going to have to make ourselves scarce for a while."

CHAPTER 10

Divide and Conquer

Amethyst had brought Caramela with her to the Magus Building once or twice. She didn't shed much, she was well-behaved, and she loved people. Well, except for stalker-y wizards, maybe. With stalker-y wizards in mind, she brought the dog with her this time.

She pushed open the tall doors of Coke-bottle-green glass and stepped into a lobby like a fairy cave. Her own stained glass flanked the door, a design of koi and lily pads in swirls of green water. The floor of water-smoothed pebbles in green and pink and beige embedded in urethane stretched away to a bank of elevators and the security desk. Dotting the space between were sculptures: a dragon made of junkyard parts, a fused glass frit panel depicting a tree-lined series of small waterfalls, a lump of polished, greenish marble carved to suggest a wolf lying with its tail curled around its paws.

The most striking of all was a fountain, a glossy black boulder ten feet tall and shot through with chips of brilliant color. Water cascaded down its face and disappeared into the pebbles surrounding its base. The murmur of water echoed through the lobby, weaving in and out of the voices of the people there. Caramela beside her, Amethyst walked toward it.

Amethyst had spent a lot of time by that fountain over the last year. Jas had obviously noticed, because sometime last winter during one of her visits, she'd found a bench made of a slab of redwood inlaid with turquoise had been installed beside it. Jas had never said a word about it, and neither did she, but gratitude for his kindness washed over her each time she sat on the bench.

As always when she entered the building, she called a little spell. People crossing the lobby, the guards at the security desk would be aware of her presence by the fountain, but have no interest in what she did there. If not for the spell, they'd think her stranger than most of the programmers.

Because as always, she stepped close to the fountain, trailed her fingers in the water purling over the stone and said, "Hi, Talys."

Amethyst, a liquid voice replied, flowing through her mind. Silver reflected in the ripples around her fingers. *You're troubled. Why?*

She sat on the bench. Caramela, putting her ears back and wagging at the fountain as if greeting a familiar friend, lay down at her feet.

Amethyst sighed. "I wish you were still my familiar. Everything would be so much easier."

She'd first met him as the spirit inhabiting a '69 Mustang Mach I. Then he'd taken the form of a man.

Who then would guard the magic? he said.

"I know, I know. And at least I have you…" She shrugged. "…here."

Better than nowhere at all, she didn't say. Although sometimes she wondered, *was* it really better? Each time she spoke to him now, as the guardian, it reminded her all over again: Talys, her trusted partner in magic, her friend, her *lover*, was gone. Forever.

She sat silent, listening to the water's soothing voice. Talys only waited. She supposed time meant nothing to him now, being of pure magic that he was. Time, or the small distresses of one young wizard.

"If you were still with me," she finally said, "I wouldn't have to worry about why wizards are sniffing around."

Certainly you have power enough to discourage them.

"Oh, sure I do. The problem is these…these stupid *men*, who look at me and say, 'Pfft. Nothing to worry about there.' And then things get ugly. People slap spellbindings on me. They hold my friends hostage and try to drain my power. Kidnap me to sell me to the government to experiment on." She put elbows on knees and chin in hands. "Damn wizards have more respect for my dog than they do for me."

The old Talys, *her* Talys, would've said something droll and British and made her laugh.

They will learn, he only said. *You will learn.*

He was like water now, reflective, impossible to grasp; like the magic itself, aware of all, a part of all.

The magic thrummed around and through her like an

electric charge. This was what Talys guarded: this place, the wellspring, the source, the heart of the magic. It was soothing and vitalizing at once, driving out weariness and worry, recharging the power drained in the meeting with Balgaire. She always felt better here—sharper, stronger, more competent.

So watching the silver-gilt water pour down the black, light-flecked face of the boulder, thoughts occurred that hadn't earlier.

"The whole problem," she said, "is that I can't figure out what this guy Balgaire is up to. Is he after me? Jas? Is he after—" She straightened, flattening her hands on either side of her. "Talys, has he come *here*? Does he know what you're guarding?"

The magic is for all.

"I know that. But would you know if he came? Would you be able to tell he's a wizard?"

I know the ocean of existence around me. I know the pulse and flow of magic.

She tapped her fingers on the bench, trying to decipher that. "In other words, you know when a wizard uses magic, and where the magic is used, but as long as they're not doing anything too egregious it's barely a blip on the radar."

Talking with Talys was often like that now. She ended up following a spiral that would bring her, if she let it, exactly where she needed to be.

She sighed and got to her feet. "Thanks, Talys. I guess I'd better go see if I can find Jas."

❖❖❖❖❖❖

Jas was, naturally, in meetings all afternoon. Amethyst left a message with Sylvia, his assistant, then logged on to her über-secure account to get some work done.

She was just setting a spell into a module of code when Caramela raised her head and said, "Woof."

Jas stood in the doorway decked out in full CEO regalia—custom-tailored suit, expensive shoes and one of his usual green silk ties. This one was a conservative stripe in black and warm green, like a pond banded with shadows. The one outfit probably cost as much as her whole wardrobe. And wow, could he ever wear it. 'Woof' indeed.

He bent and kissed her. "There," he said. "You can't go a day without seeing me."

"Of course I can't."

Damn. Where had *that* come from?

For about a nanosecond, Jas looked surprised, then for another fraction of a second, pleased. He turned to pull out a chair from the credenza in front of her office window. She suspected he wore a grin he didn't want her to see.

When he turned around, the expression on his face was perfectly pleasant. He settled into the chair and nodded at the lines of code on her computer screen. "What are you working on?"

"I set an aggressive reflective spell in a remora. The remora will track an attacker and the spell will return an attack that much worse."

Jas whistled softly. "I'm glad you're working for me. You'd be a terror as a freelancer."

"Thank you."

She hit a key to save her work and logged out. The light outside her window was fast deepening to dusk. Behind the lighted squares of the neighboring building's top-floor windows, the Sandia Mountains loomed dark against deepest indigo. A reflection of herself, Jas and the office floated over the view.

"I had an unexpected visitor this morning," she said. "Remember our friend Dougal Balgaire, from the party Friday?"

Jas' pleasant expression vanished. "*What?*"

Amethyst sat back in her chair. "Don't worry. I deployed my secret weapon—Heather."

"Don't *worry?*" he said. "Balgaire will be guaranteed to return now. Did you think of that?"

She tensed. "Yes, Jas. As matter of fact, I did." The bitter taste of fury ran over her tongue. "Is this jealousy? Because if it is, I'll tell you right now, it's a deal breaker. I don't do that crap."

"Like you didn't when Heather and I were talking?" he shot back.

She shoved to her feet, so mad she could feel the thick, fast thud of her heartbeat. She snatched up her purse and Caramela's leash from under her desk. Caramela watched her with round eyes and drooping ears, not at all happy with the sudden change in atmosphere

"You know what, Jas? I don't need this."

She snapped on Caramela's leash and headed for the

door.

Jas stood too, imposing in the power suit. "What don't you need? Someone to point out that you have no business getting angry over behavior you engaged in yourself?"

"Oh, hey, knock yourself out if it makes you feel better." She fisted her hand on her purse strap. "But don't *ever* imply I'm stupid."

"It's difficult not to when you leave yourself wide open for further trouble."

"What did you want me to do? Blast him in the middle of the driveway?"

"Think. Use your wits."

"I did. I'm not *clever.* I'm not cunning. That's your thing. I do the best I can with the tools I've got. Sorry they're not up to your standards."

She turned her back on him, jerked open the door—

And stopped. As if it had only been waiting for her to stop arguing, shut up and listen, a bad thought dropped on her. The anger abruptly drained away.

She turned. Jas stood in front of the window, radiating power and anger. He might've been intimidating, but it was like she observed him from a distance.

"Is *this* what he's up to?" she asked.

Jas looked at her like she'd fallen on the floor frothing at the mouth. "What are you talking about?"

Her thoughts skipped ahead. "I keep wondering what Balgaire is trying to do. Have you noticed every time he shows up we end up fighting? Maybe that's it. Maybe he's trying to split us apart for some reason."

And she didn't like the reasons that occurred to her, the least noxious of which was that he intended to be ready with a shoulder to cry on.

The anger faded from Jas' face and his brows crooked in a thinking frown. "You're possibly right."

She crossed her arms. "Of course I am. The woman is always right. You should know that."

He slanted her a glance at her as if trying to decide whether or not she was serious. She wasn't, mostly. But she was still smarting from that argument.

"For someone who wants to take things slowly, you're presumptuous about the relationship."

"I learned from the best."

A smile hinted at the corners of his mouth. "I'll have to be more careful what I teach you."

He stepped past her and shut the door. He lifted her purse off her shoulder, set it on the desk and took her hand.

"I'm not jealous, Amethyst, and I certainly don't believe you're stupid. The last thing I want is to get at cross purposes with you. I've had enough of that."

She nodded once, took a breath, pushed it out again, trying to push out the anger at the same time.

"Me too," she admitted. "I don't even know how it got started."

"It started because I was—am—alarmed and concerned. It's clear Balgaire intended to flush you out at the party. I, too, have been wondering why. Now he appears on your doorstep." His grip on her hand tightened. "I don't like what occurs to me, and frankly, I have no intention of waiting to find out what he plans. I don't care if he discovers I'm a wizard. I *will* put a stop to it."

Amethyst pulled her hand away. "No, you won't. Yeah, yeah, go ahead and give me a look. If Balgaire knows you're a wizard, so will everybody else. If everybody knows you're a wizard, you might as well just die in a plane crash or something and will your assets to your new self, because you won't have a hope in hell of functioning the way you have for the last however-many years."

Jas folded his arms and perched on the edge of the credenza. "Haven't you become brash."

"Gosh, so sorry. We all know women should never question a man's superior wisdom. In the future, I'll make sure I only talk about fluffy little kittens." She picked up her stuff again.

"Amethyst—" Jas put a hand over his face.

"What?"

He didn't answer. After a minute, she realized he was laughing silently.

She propped fist on hip. "What?"

He lowered his hand, still grinning. "I'm trying to imagine you talking about fluffy kittens."

"Just because I write code and like cars doesn't mean I can't mush on puppies and kittens as well as the next girl."

"Then I suppose you won't mind me being male about this situation."

"Depends on how you go about it."

"What about this," he said. "I'm perfectly capable of

making his life unpleasant without magic. I might just do that. If I'm feeling generous, I might tell him what can happen before I do it."

Truth be known, she'd be perfectly happy if Jas would make Balgaire go away. "That's up to you," she said.

He studied her for a long moment. "Are we all right now? Because I'd like to make a suggestion, and I don't want you to take it the wrong way."

She reached down and stroked Caramela, who sat panting anxiously.

"Okay," Amethyst said. "Let's hear it."

"Why don't you borrow my guest bedroom for a while. I don't like the idea of your being alone. Not that you're unable to take care of yourself, but why put yourself in a position where you have to?"

Amethyst raked a hand through her hair. "To be perfectly honest, *I* don't like the idea of being alone, either. But—"

"Bring Caramela, of course."

She bit her lip, thinking. If it weren't for the argument, she might've thought this was all part of a plot to get her to move in with him. She knew from experience how wily Jas could be. But now—

"Don't worry about problems," he said, obviously misinterpreting her hesitation. "We'll handle them."

"I don't know, Jas. Maybe I'm overreacting. For all I know, Balgaire really only came to apologize. It was probably stupid to come scampering down here to tattle on him."

Jas had started shaking his head at the word

'overreacting.' "No. Listen to your instincts. What was your reaction when you found him outside your door?"

"Alarm. Caramela was barking the house down, too. We backed him off the porch."

"Exactly. You might have overreacted. I might have overreacted. Not both of us."

She gusted a sigh. "Great."

He tapped his lips thoughtfully. "I have another idea," he said. "Let's trade houses. You stay at my house for a week or two, I'll stay at yours."

Amethyst just stood stunned for a moment. *My god. He's serious. He's really concerned about me.* That's *why he was so mad.*

She stammered before she could get out a reply. "You can't do that! You can't…can't turn your life upside down because I got spooked by a guy in a skirt!"

"It'll solve several problems." He ticked off points on his fingers. "It will serve to discourage him. If he is trying to divide us, it will prove that he hasn't succeeded. It might possibly enlighten us as to his motives. And finally…" He gave a thin smile. "I might get the chance to discuss a few things with him."

"Yeah, and we still have the same problem. What if he tries to throw down on you? Even with the protective spells on my house, even with protective spells on your person, you might end up forced to use wizardry. For all we know, that's exactly what he's angling for. And besides, hiding out at your house makes me look like a gutless weenie."

He folded his arms and frowned. "Amethyst."

"Hey, you were the one who told me I shouldn't show weakness." She shrugged. "If it makes you feel better, I have exactly zero interest in going toe-to-toe with Mr. Balgaire. So here's another idea. Why don't you stay in *my* guest bedroom? It has all the advantages you just mentioned without leaving you exposed and me tucking tail."

A slow smile spread across his face. One black brow inched up.

She leveled a finger on him. "Do not smile like that. You're the one who said not to take it wrong. And just so you know, Caramela sleeps with me."

The dog, hearing her name, licked Amethyst's hand and wagged her tail.

He held up his hands in surrender. "I'm sorry. You caught me off guard. Yes, that's an excellent idea. Also…" The smile and the quirk of the brow came back.

She narrowed her eyes. "Also…what?"

"What do you think? I was only going to say that I'll learn if you truly squeeze the toothpaste tube in the middle and put the toilet paper roll on the wrong way."

CHAPTER 11

Stay the Night

I t was going to be weird. Amethyst hadn't thought about that part when she suggested that Jas stay with her. But she thought about it now, remembering how strange it had felt when he'd opened her coat closet for her coat.

He'd gone home to change and pack a few things. She'd gone to Scarpa's for dinner, where she picked up a primavera pizza, spinach salad and an apple tart for dessert.

Amethyst pulled up Flint. The modest little houses looked cozy, windows glowing with warm light, winter-bare landscaping sketched in charcoal lines in the light of streetlights. One house still stubbornly sported Christmas lights. She crested the little hill where she could see her house ahead on the right.

Jas' Range Rover Evoque was already parked in the driveway. Her stomach did a funny little flip, not sure whether to be relieved or nervous. Although the nervousness might be from wondering where Balgaire could be.

She sent a flick of magic ahead to open the garage door and disarm her wards. The Range Rover's lights came on and it pulled into her garage, a tight fit in the single-car space. Amethyst pulled her Outback onto the driveway behind it, gathered up the pizza box and the bags containing the rest of the food and opened the rear door with another magical nudge. Caramela bounded out and trotted into the garage.

Jas was pulling an oversized duffle from the backseat. This time Caramela gave him a sniff and a cautious wag. Jas patted her, slung the bag over his shoulder and slammed the door.

He raised a brow. "I assume you knew it was me."

"It's your—" She stopped. "Oh. The car might've been under illusion." She turned to close the garage door to cover her embarrassment. It went down with considerably less rattling than her old one had. "Well, I'd sense an illusion, anyway," she grumbled.

"If you're looking for one, yes."

This time he raised both brows, maybe waiting for her to tell him she had been looking. She only met his gaze, daring him to ask. He didn't.

"If you don't already have a ward in place against illusion, I'd recommend you add one." He took the pizza box from her. "I certainly have."

She grinned. "I bet. How far down the street does it extend?"

"That," he said, "is privileged information."

To torment him, she'd created the illusion of a loud party at his house a couple of months ago. The neighbors had called the Party Patrol and everything. His retaliation was telling Mama that they were getting married.

"You don't trust me," she said. "I'm hurt." She flipped on an outside light and opened the side door to the garage. "But since you mention it…"

She stepped outside. Jas set the pizza box on top of his car (coincidentally out of Caramela's reach), followed her through the side gate and down to the sidewalk. She stood thinking a moment, riffling through the second-hand spells in her mind, then found one that would work.

Amethyst knelt by the curb. With her finger, she drew a rune, a straight line with three lines branching off of it. It glowed an eerie purple for a moment, almost beyond the range of vision, then seemed to sink into the surface of the concrete.

Jas watched her. "That," he said, "is an old, old spell."

"I'm supposed to use a rowan wand to draw the runes, since rowan is a protection against enchantment. But I figured out that most stuff like that is just symbolism. All I really need is the right intent to set the magic." She stood, moved to the opposite corner of her property and marked the same lines. "And my intent here is to see the truth."

"You seem to favor old spells, from some of the magic I've seen you work."

Setting another rune into her driveway, she shrugged. "It seems a lot of wizards don't recognize the old magic, so it's harder to counterspell."

She moved to the opposite side of the driveway, then to her front walk, Jas drifting behind. Finishing one last rune, she stood and dusted off her hands. "I'm hungry now. Let's eat."

It was back into the garage then to collect the food and Jas' bag.

He put the pizza box on the dining room table and his duffle on a chair. Unzipping it, he extracted a bottle of wine and set it next to the pizza.

"I thought this might go well with dinner." He zipped up the bag again and picked it up. "Where shall I put this?"

"Oh. Yeah."

Leaving the plates and bowls she'd taken down, she led the way into the living room and down the hall. The nervousness was back.

Oh, come on, she told herself. *This was your idea.*

Besides, the thought of Jas in her guest bedroom was a lot more appealing than lying awake with wizard's senses strained for someone using magic.

She turned on the light in the bedroom across from hers. "Here it is."

The room was furnished with a Craftsman-style futon, an oak dresser and nightstand, and a wrought iron lamp with a stained glass shade. The shade was her handiwork and echoed the red and cream and tan pillows on the futon and the small Navajo rug on the wall. Probably a long way from the style Jas was used to.

Jas came to stand beside her. "It's nice. It looks like I'll be comfortable."

She ducked her head. "The hall bath is yours, too."

He left his duffle on the floor and followed her back into the kitchen.

She got out cutlery and napkins, trying to figure out why this felt so strange. Maybe because she'd wanted to slow things down, and here she was, having him stay with her. One more barrier falling she wasn't sure she was ready to let go.

Oh, well. Too late for that now.

"Your glasses are here, is that right?" Jas said behind her, opening a cabinet door.

She was amazed he remembered. When had he last seen them? A year ago? Certainly when Talys was still with her—she remembered him getting them down.

He took the glasses, hand-blown in garnet and purple, to the table and poured wine.

She finally found herself relaxing at dinner. The wine might've helped, but the fact was that it was nice to have the company. After they'd demolished everything (wizards actively using magic tended to eat a lot), she got up to clear the table. Jas stood, too, taking his plate and bowl and silverware to the sink and rinsing them.

"You don't have to do that," she said. "Go sit down. You're a guest, and guests don't do their own dishes."

He glanced at her and she instantly realized how it sounded: *You're a guest. Nothing more.*

And dammitall, wasn't that what she intended? That was why—hello!—he was staying in the *guest* bedroom.

She backpedaled anyway. "I mean, you're already doing me a favor just being here."

He opened the dishwasher and put the things in. "I don't expect you to wait on me, Amethyst."

"Huh. I thought women always waited on men way-back-when."

"This isn't way-back-when." He straightened. "Do you want to wait on me?"

There was something different in him. She suddenly realized she'd been seeing that difference since the party, but hadn't noticed it. The old, smooth charm was absent.

It shook her. He was showing her glimpses of himself, of the real Jas Harker. Earlier this afternoon, she'd seen real worry. Now, he was uncertain—maybe not sure what she expected of him while he stayed in her home. It made her warm to him more than the charm ever had.

She realized she still hadn't answered his question. She pursed her lips as if the long pause had only been for the appropriate answer.

"Maybe for tonight. After that, we'll see how it goes."

He nodded, and the uncertainty went away. "We'll make the bed, first. It's much easier with two."

"Okay," she agreed. "Besides, that futon is a bear to make into a bed by myself."

She started toward the bedroom, Jas following after.

"I've seen you make a desk into a bear," he said, "but you're right. Making a bear into a bed might indeed require help."

She looked back, frowning, wondering what the hell he was talking about. At the little quirk of his lips, she got it.

In the middle of the hall, she turned and planted fists on hips. "What did I do to deserve a joke that bad?"

"I thought it was rather clever."

She sniffed and opened the linen closet, taking out

sheets and pillows. "Did you hear the one about the new corduroy pillows?"

He glanced down at the pillows she handed him, which were, of course, not corduroy. "No," he said warily.

"They're making headlines." She continued to the bedroom, smirking.

In three, two, one…

He groaned.

Trading bad jokes while they made the bed made the task much less awkward than she'd been afraid it would be. When he stooped to knock-knock jokes, she decided to torment him.

"I'll just go slip into something…more comfortable."

The look on his face as she stepped into her bedroom and shut the door was priceless.

When she returned to the living room, Amethyst struck a pose in the doorway, hand on hip.

She wore sweats, purple slippers and a Proud Pitbull Mom jersey. Jas, wearing an old, faded, very comfortable-looking pair of jeans and a green plaid flannel shirt, looked her up and down.

He sent her a smoldering look. "Be still my heart."

She gave her hair an exaggerated flip and sashayed to the pellet stove to start a fire. Caramela flopped down on her bed by the stove, gave a groaning sigh, and put her chin on her paws.

The whole situation might've been unbearably fraught. How was it that they'd managed to find a way to make it comfortable, without ever saying a word about it?

Amethyst settled on the sofa and curled her feet

under her. It was strange. She *liked* seeing Jas in the chair, his socked feet crossed at the ankle on the ottoman, a glass of wine in his hand. And…

She could almost imagine being with him. Almost.

No, better not think about that. If she thought about that, she might think about snuggling with him on the couch, and then maybe kissing him, and then—

No. She couldn't think that way about Jas. Well, she *could*, but not with him staying in her house while they staked out a wizard of unknown intentions. Things were already complicated and confusing enough between them without adding sex. The complicated and confusing part needed to get straightened out first.

"So, what do you usually do in the evenings when you're at home?" Jas asked.

"Work, read, stream something on TV. Have people over sometimes. What about you?"

He took a sip of wine. "Much the same."

It sounded so ordinary she almost laughed.

Then he added, "When the one who hunted us was alive, I'd ride the magic, searching for signs of him." He took another sip. "That's how I found you. You lit up the sky like a fireball. What did you do, the first time you used your power?"

"This," she said, gesturing at the stained glass panel that took up most of one living room wall.

It was a forest scene, trees and ferns overhanging a stream and waterfall. It seemed to be illuminated by lights set behind it. It wasn't.

Jas stared hard at her as if trying to decide if she were

joking, turned to study the panel, then back to her.

"This was your first attempt at magic?"

"Actually," she said, "it was my attempt to prove I *couldn't* do magic."

He stood, put his glass on the coffee table and crossed to the panel. "Good God, Amethyst. I've looked at this before, but I never realized it was your first effort."

She squirmed a little. "Well, I'd wanted to make that window for a while. I had the design pretty well in my head. I figured if I could really do magic, stained glass would be the easiest thing to try it on."

He traced a solder line with a fingertip. "And the light?"

"I don't know where the light comes from. Of course, I imagined the way the panel would look lit from behind, and that's how it came out."

"And you didn't even believe you could do it." He shook his head then considered her. "You surprised me when I met you. I expected you to be much younger. Most wizards are when they first come into their power. It seems odd that yours came so late, particularly when your great-grandmother had power of her own. She must've realized you had potential."

"She did. Nani started teaching me when I was…oh, eight or nine, I guess. I hardly remember most of it. The uses of different herbs. How to close your eyes and see everything around you. How to reach inside yourself and touch your power." She cocked her head. "I did some of that when I created the panel."

He sat down on the ottoman, elbows on knees. "But

when I met you, it seemed you were trying very hard to deny your wizardry. And just now you said you were trying to prove you couldn't work the magic."

Amethyst swirled her wine, watching it spin in the glass. It was suddenly hard to talk. She took a sip.

"It's…probably not very interesting," she said.

"I don't mind listening, if you don't mind talking about it."

She nodded to buy herself a little time. She hadn't talked about it to anybody—Mama, Dad, certainly not the counselor they sent her to after Nani died.

"I was closer to Nani than to anyone else in the family. When she died, I…didn't take it well." Into Jas' waiting silence, she said, "There's a year I don't remember much."

"How old were you?"

"Thirteen."

"That's a vulnerable age for anyone, much less a wizard. With your powers stirring, in addition to all the other changes taking place…" He gave his head a grim shake. "A bad, bad time to lose your teacher."

The tension, the echo of old grief faded. All these years she'd thought there must be something seriously wrong with her to have fallen apart the way she had.

She remembered she was supposed to be explaining why she was pushing thirty before she realized she was a wizard.

"I don't know what happened, but Nani knew something bad was going on. She was working protective magic on both of us. I don't remember spells, but she taught me... I don't know. Something like camouflage, I guess. I'd close my eyes and pretend to blend in to whatever was around. Shadows, grass, furniture, whatever."

"That would help hide a wizard-child," Jas said. "Like a fawn lying still on the forest floor."

"Probably. And she told me if I ever heard of *el encantador*, a magician, stay away from him. And don't let him find out I could work the magic."

"Interesting," he said. "I wonder what she saw or heard. Possibly the same things I did—magic-wielders of all degrees vanishing, from those with only a single talent to full-blown wizards. That would be consistent with her warning to you."

"I wish—" Amethyst stopped, shook her head and pushed out a breath. "I was the one who found her. When I came in that day, the house reeked of magic, so thick it burned. I saw the look on her face. I knew whatever—whoever—she'd been afraid of had found her."

She took another sip. "I must've been in bad shape after that. I don't really remember. My parents took me out of school and Mama homeschooled me. When I was able to think about it again, I decided if magic couldn't save Nani, what use was it? Pretty soon I convinced myself that magic must not exist at all." She shrugged. "Up until around the time you met me, I was living my life just like everybody else, never even thinking about magic."

"Yes, I can see why you'd want to deny your magical heritage. And run from the slightest whiff of magic." Jas stared down into his own glass. "I was about to say if I'd found you then, I'd have taken the two of you under my protection. But the only way I could protect even myself in those days was to hide as thoroughly as I could. But I wonder…" he mused. "How might it have been if I'd taken you as an apprentice? Taught you what your great-grandmother couldn't."

"Jas! That's just weird."

He looked up. "But I didn't apprentice you. And I didn't know you as a child."

"Yeah, well, good thing."

He smiled. "Yes. A very good thing." He leaned back on an elbow. "What finally prompted you to use magic?"

She laughed, but it wasn't funny at all. "Talys showed up and announced that he was my familiar. It didn't help that he was inhabiting a car at the time. I figured I had to be going crazy, because despite what my superstitious great-grandmother had believed, we all know there's no such thing as magic."

"Of course not."

"So I went to see a shrink. Guess who that turned out to be?"

Jas looked puzzled for a moment. She could see when the answer hit him.

"The hunter? The one draining wizards of their power?" he said.

"Of course, I only knew him as the therapist who specialized in the treatment of delusional patients."

He gave a low whistle. "Clever."

"Talys thought so, too. He—Talys, that is—knew there was a problem, that wizards had been disappearing, but not how or why. I didn't know there *was* a problem. Other than a couple of whack jobs were trying to convince me that I was a wizard."

Jas gave a short laugh. "So you decided to prove them wrong."

"And got this big, beautiful stained glass panel on my living room wall to explain to friends and family."

"That must've been interesting."

"That's one word for it."

They sat watching the fire a few minutes. Caramela lay with her head to the side and the tip of her tongue slipping in and out in some dream.

"If I'd been honest with you then," Jas said, "if I'd told you I was a wizard, you still wouldn't have wanted anything to do with me."

"Probably not."

"Although I could've helped and taught you."

She snorted. "Jas, Talys offered to teach me. Korhonen, the wizard-slash-therapist, offered to teach me. I locked Talys in a storage unit, told Korhonen 'thanks, but no thanks' and ran as fast as I could."

Jas nodded. "Then I'm glad I didn't tell you what I am. I'd never have had the chance to get to know you."

Amethyst blinked. The whole world fell out from under her.

"I guess…" her voice came out in a whisper. She cleared her throat. "I guess that's right."

He studied her a long moment. "Would you have been better off not knowing me?"

She looked down into her glass again. It was empty.

She abruptly stood. "I'll get us more wine."

"Amethyst?" he said behind her.

She stopped in the kitchen doorway, but didn't turn. "No," she said to the kitchen. "I don't think I'd've been better off."

She escaped into the kitchen. She wanted to put her head down on the counter until her thoughts and emotions stopped flailing, but didn't want to take the chance of Jas catching her like that.

She moved around the kitchen with no idea of what she was doing. She'd spent a long time hating Jas for what he'd done, even longer being angry at him. Had it all been for nothing?

Well, no. Not for nothing. That binding had been a little more than lying about what he was.

But as if someone had turned on a light in a dark room full of scary shadows, she could suddenly see how Jas, wily as he was, might've boxed himself into doing something like that. Living for decades in hiding, losing at least one child to the predator, forced to avoid using most of his power, he must've been scared and desperate. And here came another wizard who might be an ally, who might stand with him...but she didn't want anything to do with magic.

The realization didn't make what he'd done excusable. But it made it more forgivable.

She looked down at the countertop. Ranged across it were a mug, two juice glasses, two tins of tea and a zester. Her kettle sat in the sink, overflowing under the tap. She turned off the water, gathering that at some level, she'd meant to make tea despite coming into the kitchen for the wine. She headed for the dining room table for the bottle.

"Amethyst," Jas called from the living room. "We have company."

Abandoning the wine, she made a U-turn. Jas stood in front of the ottoman, staring down into his wine glass once more. Amethyst glanced automatically at the front door. For an instant, she wondered why he was looking into his glass and not out the window, then she realized he was scrying.

She walked over. She had to stand close to see into the glass, close enough that her hair brushed Jas' shoulder. As she looked into the dark, reflective surface of the wine, his hand came to rest lightly on the small of her back. Watching the image of Balgaire walking Heather to her front door, she barely noticed.

"I thought you couldn't scry other wizards," she said.

"You can if they aren't warded." He slanted her a look. "Or if someone has placed a spell of true-seeing in their vicinity."

"Cool," she said, pleased with herself. That was the problem with knowing spells but not necessarily knowing their practical applications. But every once in a while, she got it right. "Wanna place bets on whether or not she invites him in?"

"I'd rather bet on whether or not he *goes* in."

She made a skeptical face.

"Watch," he said.

The image was tiny, shivering a bit with ripples in the wine, but she was still able to see Balgaire and Heather on

Heather's front porch, apparently talking. Amethyst tapped the glass.

"Where's the audio on this thing?"

"Under the circumstances, I didn't bother." The hand on her back gave two quick taps. "And you're ruining the video."

It was obvious that Heather was really laying it on. She stood close to Balgaire, a hand on his arm. He shook his head, touched her cheek and stepped back. The vibe was still friendly as they exchanged a few more words, then Heather opened her front door and went inside. Balgaire waited until the door shut, then strode back down the walk. Judging from the spring in his step, he was pleased. Just before he reached his flashy Cadillac, he turned to face Amethyst's house.

Balgaire stood a moment, then raised his hand in a salute.

"Bastard!" Amethyst burst out. "He knew I'd be watching!"

Jas nodded, eyes still on his scrying. When Balgaire climbed into the Caddy and drove off, Jas put the glass down.

"That answers that question," he said.

"He's coming back," Amethyst said. "He just made sure of it. And that cheery little wave before he left was to tell us he planned it that way." She plunked down onto the ottoman and hung her hands between her knees. "So much for my secret weapon."

"On the other hand," Jas said, "it will be easier to keep an eye on him."

"We might've avoided an argument if you'd thought about it that way earlier."

"I like to think I'm flexible."

"I'll admit, that's a whole lot better than saying *I told you so*."

"I'd never dream of it." He settled opposite her on the edge of the coffee table.

She sighed. "What do we do now? Set watches?"

"I doubt we'll see more of Mr. Balgaire tonight," he said. "But if you haven't already, you can set spells to alert you if anyone nearby attempts to use magic."

Despite what she'd told Jas this afternoon, she hadn't been so naïve as to assume that Balgaire would be easily gotten rid of. After all, that was the whole point of Jas' stay here. What she hadn't thought about was how long that stay might end up being.

CHAPTER 12

Drives Me Crazy

Amethyst woke to Caramela's soft *boof*. Early light filtered through the shades, painting the comforter and bedroom furniture in shades of lavender and blue. Ears up, head raised, the dog faced the bedroom door. For an instant, Amethyst wondered why the door was closed. The sound of the water running in the hall bath came, and she remembered.

Jas. That was him in the bathroom. She thought of him in the shower, water sluicing over the muscles of his shoulders and back, slicking down the black hair on his chest and belly and—

"No, no, no," she told herself, rapping her head to drive out the image. "You already have enough trouble. You don't need more."

She lay staring up at the ceiling, waiting for the throbbing down low to subside and trying to decide which was more dangerous: dealing with Balgaire on her own, or having Jas sleeping and showering a few feet beyond her bedroom door.

She sighed. Well, if nothing else, the kind of danger

she faced from Jas would be more pleasant. At least in the short term.

She nudged Caramela out of bed, rolled out after her and, in her pajamas, padded into the kitchen to let the dog out, put on a pot of coffee and turn on the hall furnace so Jas wouldn't freeze in the bathroom. It was cold this morning.

The coffeepot gurgling away, Amethyst stood looking out the patio door. The backyard was a well of blue light. With the granite-and-juniper wall of the Sandia Mountains rising no more than five miles away to the east, it would be a while before the sun broke the crest. Now, frost rimmed the blades of grass and Caramela's breath plumed on the air as she snuffled her way across the yard.

After Caramela finished her business, Amethyst returned to the bedroom to begin her own morning routine. And, incidentally, avoid any chance encounters in the hallway with a possibly towel-clad Jas, his hair damp and unruly, his pale skin gleaming—

And, dammit! She was thinking about it again!

She made up the bed, ruthlessly throttling any fantasies involving it. There were several. When she didn't hear any more noises from the hall bath or the guest bedroom, she decided it was safe to venture out.

The humidity from the shower and the scent of Jas' aftershave wafted from the bathroom as she passed it. The aroma of coffee replaced it as she neared the kitchen. A quiet pleasure washed over her at the smells, so different from every other morning.

Jas had set up a nice little workstation at one end of

the dining room table. Sitting open in front of him was a laptop about the thickness of a menu from a fancy restaurant. A portable printer/scanner sat to one side. To the other lay an ominous, matte-black cube bearing the Magus logo, a stylized 'M' resting on a green starburst.

Amethyst stopped in the doorway and pointed at the cube. "What," she said, "is *that?*"

"That," Jas said, "is a hyper-secure wireless modem."

She went on into the kitchen, got down a mug and, from the pantry, a bag of chocolate granules. "How come *I* don't get a hyper-secure Internet connection so I can work from home?"

He took a sip of the coffee she'd made earlier. "Because then I wouldn't see you as often."

Her mug hit the microwave turntable with a *clink*. "You are the most scheming—"

"You already knew that," he interrupted. "But doesn't admitting it count for something?"

She started the microwave, leaned back against the counter and thought about it. "I guess it does."

He closed the laptop screen and stood, coffee in hand. "Good. I was hoping it would."

A laugh unexpectedly bubbled up. She coughed to cover it. "Just for that, you can fix your own breakfast. You'd better get in here if you want to find out where everything is."

Only one night, and it no longer felt strange to have him here, eating meals with her, cleaning up afterwards, settling down in front of his computer to do whatever it was slumming CEO's did with their days.

How would it feel when they'd dealt with Balgaire, and Jas went back to his own house? She ignored the anticipating twinge of regret in her middle and carried her mug of hot chocolate back into her own workroom.

It shouldn't have made any difference having Jas out there in the dining room. Other than the occasional murmur of his voice on the phone or possibly a video chat, most of the time he was quiet. But she kept catching herself drifting out—to get a snack, check the mail, let Caramela out....

Well, okay, she usually did drift out of her workroom to do this or that, but it was different now. Now it felt like an excuse. And she was pretty sure she knew what it was an excuse *for*.

This time, Jas glanced up with the quirk of a brow and a half-smile.

"Restless?" he said.

"Um," she said as if caught. Which, in fact, she was. *Damn. This isn't going to work.*

And the reason it wouldn't work now was completely different from what it had been. But she sure wasn't going to tell Jas. He'd ask why, and she wasn't about to tell him that.

"Distracted," she said. "I'm not, um, used to having someone else in the house while I work. I feel like I'm neglecting you or something."

"Or something," he repeated.

"I feel like we should be doing something." *Oh god. Did I really say that? Please tell me it didn't come out like it sounded.*

He closed his laptop screen. "Forget about Balgaire. There's no point worrying about him until he makes his next move."

"I'm not worried about *Balgaire*," she muttered.

"You don't have to worry about me, either."

"I *know*." She folded her arms and looked out the kitchen window. "I'm sorry. You're going out of your way for me. I really do appreciate it."

"It's my pleasure. Which I'm sure you also know."

She gave him a sideways look. "Jas, you can't always be this nice. You're setting yourself up for a fall."

He laughed. "If you think I'm being nice by staying with you, you're giving me far more credit than I deserve."

"Okay, just don't let me take advantage of you."

"Please," he said. "Please take advantage of me."

Oh, yeah. He knew exactly what was going on.

She grinned. "Don't tempt me."

She came around the breakfast bar to where he sat at the table, bent and kissed him. "Thank you. Thank you for being here. Thank you for making it easy."

He looked somewhere between startled and taken aback.

"Amethyst, I'd make every day easy for you, if you'd let me."

Her hand still on his cheek, she smiled down at him. "I won't hold you to that."

He looked way more pleased at that than he should. Amethyst puzzled over it, trying to figure out why. Then she got it. She'd just implied that they had a future together.

Pretending cool, she headed for her workroom before she could say anything else damning.

✧✧✧✧✧✧

It was too much to hope that Balgaire wouldn't come back. So when the little spell she'd set to alert her to that eventuality scooted a piece of red glass from one side of her worktable to the other, Amethyst only sighed, got up and looked out the window.

Sure enough, there was Balgaire's screaming red Cadillac pulling up in front of Heather's house. Amethyst stepped back, out of sight. She stared at the clutter of glass and strips of copper foil and coils of solder on her worktable, thinking. Finally, she reached a decision.

In the dining room, Jas sat back in his chair, arms folded, eyes on his computer screen. From the intentness of his gaze and the pinch between his brows, she guessed he was using the screen as a scrying medium.

"I'm just going to step outside," she said, shrugging on her coat.

He raised his eyes to her face. "Are you indeed."

"Yep." She could see him wanting to get all male about the situation and restraining himself.

"You'll deny me every satisfaction," was what he finally said.

Leave it to Jas to turn it into a double entendre.

She grinned. "Not *every* one. But there's something I feel honor-bound to address, first."

He barked a surprised laugh. "Sometimes you're more

old-fashioned than I am."

"Just my conscience bugging me."

"Ah," he said. "I know better than to stand in the way of that."

It was an old argument. Jas liked to call it the Rey sense of What is Right. And then he'd shudder.

"Thank you," she said. "I know you'll be watching, so if things go south, please don't come out with magic blazing, okay?"

His eyes crinkled with amusement. "You're speaking to the man who avoided a far greater menace for more years than you want to know."

"Okay. Just so you remember." She leaned down, patted Caramela's side and told her, "Be good for Jas."

Heading for the front door, Amethyst shaped the magic in a hunter's spell, something that would leave her silent and unseen by her prey. Until she was ready.

Balgaire's Cadillac SUV sat parked at the curb in front of Heather's house. Amethyst wondered where he learned to drive and how he paid for a vehicle like that. Then again, wizards didn't seem to have a problem getting whatever they wanted—which was why Jas found her sense of right and wrong so entertaining.

She walked over to the Caddy ("SRX" according to the emblem), and leaned against one flaming red fender.

She could see Balgaire on the porch, ostensibly waiting to see if Heather would answer the door. But when he stepped away, he turned to look toward Amethyst's house. She waited until he was most of the way down the driveway before dropping her concealing spell.

He stopped short. "Ah, very good! Where did a young lass like you learn a spell like that?"

She cocked her head, thinking about her answer. "My great-grandmother's *compadre* was an old Pueblo Indian. He's been my mentor." She thought a little more, tapping her fingers on the Caddy's sheet metal—a soft *pap-pap-pap*. "He doesn't have much respect for Anglo *magos*. Says they want the magic all for themselves."

"We've known one or two like that ourselves, eh, lass?" Balgaire said, either ignoring or not getting the insult.

"What do *you* want, Dougal?" she said. "Because if you're looking for Heather, you wasted a trip."

"It's no waste when I still happen to see a lovely lady."

Amethyst snorted. "Does that line work on lovely ladies? Because it sure doesn't on me."

He grinned. "Modest, are you?"

"Just honest. Which is what you should be, too. If you've got business with me, bring it to me. Don't put Heather in the middle of it."

A calculating gleam came into his eye. "What's all this, when you yourself placed such a tasty morsel before me?"

A spurt of guilt went through her, but she didn't let her gaze drop. "Maybe. Or maybe I'm just not interested in vying with Heather for anyone's attention."

She thought she was being clever, but it must've been the wrong thing to say. He looked intrigued.

"Modest *and* proud," he said. "That's not a thing a

man sees much in women."

Spanish guys could be macho and sexist, but they usually knew better than to be so in-your-face about it.

"And no woman wants to be used." She pushed off the fender, not quite intruding into Balgaire's personal space, but almost. "Don't use Heather. If you like each other, fine. But no wizard games with her."

He drew himself up. "I've no need of magic to bed a woman I fancy."

"Good. And don't lead her on, either." This was hitting too close to home. Her temper rose. She throttled it with an effort.

"Are you her da, to be askin' my intentions toward the lady?" he said with a snotty little smile.

"I'm the wizard whose territory you're in, and if I find out you're messing with the civilians under my protection, I won't be happy."

The good-ol'-boy attitude fell away. "You're not what I expected, Amethyst Rey. I've not seen your like in a long, long while."

He studied her, looming a good foot over her, broad and tall and imposing in his kilt and boots. It was probably stupid, but she wouldn't give him the satisfaction of reaching for the magic, letting him know that he worried her. She just met his eyes, prickles running up her spine and into her hair like hackles rising.

"But I'll see you again." He nodded once. "That I will."

He tipped an imaginary hat, circled around to the driver's door and got in. She crossed her arms, watching.

The Caddy's engine started with a purr. One more salute, and Balgaire drove off up the street.

Jas looked up from his computer when she came back in. "Remind me not to get on your bad side," he said.

She filled a mug, plunked in the tea strainer. She was still hot enough to warm the water without magic. Okay, maybe not literally, but zapping heat into the water did help burn off a little of her temper.

"You've *been* on my bad side," she said. "For similar reasons."

What is it with you guys? she felt like saying. But that wasn't fair to Jas who, despite leading *her* on once upon a time, was at least willing to admit it was a mistake. And to go to great lengths to make amends.

She plopped into the seat next to his. "See? He did it again. Got me all fired up about what happened with you. It *can't* be an accident."

Jas sat back in his chair. "That assumes he knows our history."

Or he sees a man like you showing interest in a woman like me and just put two and two together. She was surprised at how depressing the thought was.

Jas was watching her. God only knew what her face showed. Scowling to hide whatever he might see, she took a sip of tea, steam laden with the scent of cinnamon and cardamom curling over her face, the same flavors running over her tongue.

When she got her emotions back under control, she said, "He's got a brain behind all the BS."

"I don't doubt he does," he said, either diverted or

willing to pretend to be. "But in this case, I'm not certain he intended what you think."

She sipped tea, running the conversation back through her mind. True, *she* had made the assumptions about Balgaire's intentions toward Heather. And that had touched something still sore.

"Well, what do you think he was up to?" she said.

Jas tapped the tabletop with one finger. "I don't think he expected any success from his flirtation."

Amethyst made a gagging noise.

"It still feels like he's testing," he said. "First the extent of your power, now the extent of your forbearance."

"Apparently I gave him the impression that I'm more forbearing than I am. If someone told *me* to back off, I wouldn't say, 'See you later, sweetheart.'"

He smiled. "Women sometimes have better sense than men."

"It's nice to know somebody thinks so."

"The misogynistic comment was all part of the testing. I think his parting shot was, too. Now he'll want to see how you'll back up your threat."

She carefully set her mug on the dining room table. The urge to throw something was almost overwhelming. She stood and paced to the patio door.

"You know, this is exactly the problem I've had with wizards from the beginning. Nobody takes me seriously."

Jas was silent behind her. After a moment, he said, "I take you seriously. I take you seriously enough to let you go out there and confront the man on your own. Despite the fact that I'd take great pleasure in simply putting a stop to his games."

He said it calmly enough, but she heard the current of anger that underlay his voice. She didn't quite know what to think about this newly-protective Jas. Was it simple possessiveness? Or concern about someone he cared for? The answer made all the difference in the world.

She sat down again, in the other chair this time. Jas slid her tea over. She curled her fingers around the mug, tracing the glossy ridges where the brown glaze shaded to purple.

"I really, really hate posturing," she said.

"It didn't sound like you were posturing out there."

"No, I guess not. Heather might be an annoying flirt, but she's my neighbor. And she can be pretty decent when she wants to be."

He nodded. "By the time we discover Balgaire's aim, I suspect he'll have learned to take you seriously." His eyes crinkled and one corner of his mouth quirked up in smile. "We all do, if we know you long enough."

CHAPTER 13

One Step Forward...

"Jas," Amethyst said, "you can't work from home forever."

He sat at his end-of-the-dining-room-table workstation, sipping from the coffee mug in one hand, clicking and scrolling with the mouse in the other. Today he wore a black sweatshirt that announced **BEZOS IS MY DARK LORD** in menacing, crackly white letters with a red Eye of Sauron over the Amazon smile.

He lowered his coffee. "Only three days, and you're already tired of me."

"Trust me," she said. "I'm not tired of you."

Heaven save her, anything but.

"That's very..." He let the pause draw out to suggestive proportions. "...promising."

Rolling her eyes, she took eggs out of the fridge, cracked them into a bowl and whipped them. "What's with the shirt? Please, please tell me Jeff Bezos isn't another wizard."

He got up and came into the kitchen. "Jeff Bezos isn't a wizard. Unless he's as far undercover as I am. I just admire his business acumen."

She put a pan on the stove and chopped some green chile. "Lucky for him, he's not a competitor."

"True." Jas came up behind her and slipped an arm around her waist. "Good morning, Amethyst." He kissed her.

Amethyst, stirring the green chile into the eggs, let her spoon hang above the pan and leaned into the kiss. Jas' other arm slid around her and the kiss became rather more than a morning greeting. Her own arms went around him and she melted into him.

His lips, warm and insistent, coaxed her mouth open. His tongue teased hers. She made a noise somewhere between a whimper and a sigh and ran her hands into his hair, still damp from the shower, pulling him down to her. Her nipples became two knots of excruciating sensation. His kiss became more eager, devouring, then he broke away and nibbled his way down her neck. She tipped back her head, eyes closed, breaths moving fast between her lips.

Why not? whispered into her mind. She wanted to, God knew. There were two perfectly good beds at the other end of the house. No reason not to, really. Was there?

There must've been, or they'd already be waking up in bed together. But she couldn't think what it was. Some reason…important enough…

Jas brushed back her hair and nuzzled the angle between her neck and shoulder. The sensation made her shiver and tighten in anticipation.

No reason, no. Just excuses. Justifications. Nothing to stop her from doing what felt so natural.

She felt him fumbling beside her. The stove. She reached, fingers tangling with his, and turned off the burner.

She ached for him. She'd gone to sleep last night aching, woken up this morning aching. She had *fantasies* about this, for godsake, where they spent the long winter nights loving, exploring, where she found out what it was like when a wizard's power was involved…

And then when her blood had cooled, she'd think, *And what about afterwards? What happens then?*

That was the real reason.

Jas' hands slid up under her sweater, a warm glide over her ribs. She found her own hands under his sweatshirt, moving across the contours of his back, into the dip where his muscles met his spine.

"It'll be…impossible…"

"Nothing is impossible for us," he breathed.

She panted. "Every day…together?"

"Mmm," he purred. His fingers found her bra clasp, effortlessly unhooked it. One hand slipped around to caress her breast. "Yes."

Yes.

But for how long?

"Jas. I'm not…not…a fling."

"No."

"I can't—"

He drew back, his eyes darker than ever, glazed with desire. "What?"

She struggled up out of her own desire like warm, caressing quicksand. "I don't— If you—"

His brows drew together. "You aren't still afraid of me?"

She was conscious of the heat of his hands on her bare skin, his thumbs inches below her breasts.

Frustrated, angry tears suddenly pushed their way up. "I'm an idiot. I'm a jerk."

She tried to extricate herself, but he held tighter.

"What's wrong?" he said. "Why would you say that?"

"Because—" She would not cry. She *wouldn't*. "Because you've been thoughtful, and kind, and caring, and I-I-I—" She took a breath, swallowed hard, pinched her eyes to seal in the tears. "And it's still not right."

His silence would've made her crumple, except for the way he still held her, his hands moving soothingly on her back. She opened her eyes to find him gazing seriously down at her.

"I'm sorry," she said. "I—I'm not—toying with you, I swear—"

He put his fingers over her lips. "No. I don't think that." He ran a hand through his hair. "But Amethyst, you're confusing me. I don't know what you want."

"*You're* confused!" she said with a bitter laugh. At least he knew what *he* wanted.

"Should I go back home?" he said. "Would that be better?"

"It's not *you*."

"Amethyst—" He gusted a sigh. "Making you unhappy is the last thing I want. But you have to help me here. Tell me what I should do. Because right now, I want to take you back into that bedroom and show you that whatever it is you're afraid of, you don't have to be."

She gave a shaky laugh. "I can't say I'd fight you all that much."

Tension went out of him. "I'm glad to hear that."

"But— I think—" She rested her forehead on his shoulder so she didn't have to look at him. "What I'm afraid of…I'm not ready to find out."

He was silent a long moment, probably puzzling. "You can't tell me?"

She laughed again, sheer tension. "Oh god, Jas. Do you really want to see me humiliate myself?"

"No." He held her away suddenly, sliding his hand into her hair, his thumb lifting her chin. "I never want to see you humiliated."

She swallowed again. "I know that. I'm just stupid. But—" She struggled to explain. "It's too important. To me. It's something…something I have to make sure I get right. Do you understand?"

Hell, she wasn't sure *she* did.

"I understand you're still worried about something. And despite what you say, it's something to do with me."

"No—"

"Yes," he interrupted. "I *will* find out, Amethyst. It's up to you how long that takes."

Amazing how gently he could say something that should sound threatening.

"Yeah, well, maybe it's *me*. Maybe I'm just really hung up."

"The evidence suggests you're anything but hung up."

"Maybe I got over it," she grumbled.

"And *maybe* you're changing the subject."

"Maybe I am." She abruptly became conscious of the state of her clothes, her sweater bunched up, her bra hanging down. "I'd better, um, put myself back together."

Jas gazed at her distantly, like a coyote deciding whether or not to pounce on that succulent rabbit.

At last, he stepped back, his hands falling away. "Today might be a good day for me to check in at the office."

It felt like her feet went out from under her on slick ice, knowing how much it would hurt when she hit the ground.

"Oh," she said. "Okay." She swallowed hard, willed her voice to be steady. "You'll stay for breakfast, won't you?"

"Amethyst—" he began, then let out a breath. "Yes. Of course I'll stay for breakfast." He waved in the direction of the bedroom. "Go ahead. I'll watch the eggs."

She slunk off to make herself decent.

✦ ✦ ✦ ✦ ✦ ✦

Breakfast was full of awkward silences and stilted conversation.

Amethyst made sure she had somewhere else to be when Jas left. When she came back in through the garage, the dining room table was back in its pre-workstation condition, Jas' conscripted end bare.

Her stomach fell. She put her purse in its usual spot on the dining room chair, absently greeted a wagging, happy Caramela and let her out to go pee. At last, Amethyst ventured back to peek into the hall bath and the guest bedroom, her heart beating far harder than it should.

The bathroom was tidy, but Jas' travel kit sat on the countertop. In the bedroom, the bed was made. There was no sign of his duffle, but a slip of paper lay on the dresser. A note? Her stomach dropped even further, her heart beat even harder.

She crossed to the dresser and unfolded the paper, a receipt from someplace called Darien's. *Chris Rivera*, it read in unfamiliar handwriting, along with a phone number. Wondering irrelevantly if the name belonged to a male Chris or a female Chris, she re-folded the slip and put it back exactly at it had been.

Her curiosity suddenly and unaccountably snuffed out, she left the room.

She wanted to curse herself, but didn't have the energy. Would it have been better to just go to bed with him? Heaven knew they both wanted to. And she *didn't* think Jas would do something to her once he had her in such a terribly defenseless position—nothing like that damned binding, anyway.

But she couldn't escape the gut-sure feeling that once she did cross that line with him, she would inescapably, irreversibly become vulnerable to him. And what then? While she stood there—or lay there, as the case may be— totally smitten, would he gloat over his conquest? She cringed at the idea. Or maybe he'd plot. Or maybe he'd…he'd—

Amethyst stopped short in the middle of the living room, staring out the window at the view of the yard and street outside, bits of trash impaled on the many-jointed cholla cactus across the street. Sweet Mary in Heaven. When had she started worrying about how their relationship might progress?

She plunked down on one end of the sofa and dropped her head in her hands. "I'm doomed. So doomed."

Caramela put her big, blocky head on Amethyst's knee. Amethyst dropped her hands and petted her.

"What do you think I should do?" Amethyst asked.

Caramela just looked up at her out of ale-colored eyes and wagged her tail.

"Go for a walk? You're probably right. Get outside, get some exercise, clear my head."

It might not solve Amethyst's dilemma, but it certainly made Caramela happy. She spun in tight little circles of excitement until they were out the door.

It was one of those winter days that tasted a little like spring…except without the wind. Though colder than it'd be in March or April, the calm, clear air made it more pleasant.

She'd just stepped onto to the sidewalk when Heather's Mini Cooper swung into the driveway. Amethyst stopped, raised a hand in greeting and gritted her teeth. She needed to have a talk with Heather.

Heather bounced out of the Mini dressed in an electric blue collarless blazer, black flounce-hem pencil skirt and blue pumps, just as traffic-stopping in business wear as everything else.

"Amethyst! You're just who I wanted to see. I have to talk to you about Dougal."

"About that," Amethyst said, stuffing her hands, including the one holding Caramela's leash, in her jacket pockets. "I owe you an apology."

Heather stopped short, her blue eyes widening. "Whatever for?"

"For foisting him off on you. I shouldn't've done that."

Heather blinked in astonishment, then laughed. "Oh, Amethyst, honey. I'm ever so glad you did! He's...he's..." Her gaze went far-off and dreamy. "He's not like any man I've ever known."

"That, I believe," Amethyst muttered.

"He knows just how to make a girl feel special. The way he treats me..." She closed her eyes and her enviable bosom rose. "Oh, my lord! If only you knew."

Amethyst knew. Oh, yes, she did.

She shifted her weight. "Well, I feel responsible. I mean, to be honest, he kinda seems like a player to me. I hate the thought that he might hurt you."

A rare serious look replaced Heather's raptures. "Dougal told me a few days ago you said the same thing to him."

"He did?" Heat ran into Amethyst's face. "I...ah..."

Heather touched her arm. "It was the nicest thing I've ever heard. No one's ever worried about me like that. Oh, they'll shake their heads and say, 'Too bad, you know how men are, but you know you can always get another one, sugar.' Like I don't even have a heart that can break like any other girl's."

I am such a bitch, Amethyst thought. "But Dougal—"

"Oh, I know he's, well, *retro* sometimes. But that can be nice, too."

"And he—"

"And of course I can see he has a roving eye. But so do I. There's nothing wrong with appreciating a fine specimen of the opposite sex." She gave Amethyst a quick hug. "Don't worry, honey. I'm not seeing picket fences yet." Her eyes sparkled. "Now your Jas, I think *he* might be seeing picket fences."

The ground went out from under Amethyst for the second time that morning. "What?"

Oh, come on, Amethyst, she told herself. *How many times has the man asked you to marry him?*

"Don't think I don't see the way he looks at you." Heather dimpled. "It's like I'm not even there. I can't say the same for many men."

Damned if Heather wasn't right. Jas *had* turned his back on her come-on, but Amethyst had just assumed that was for her own benefit.

"Um, well…" she said.

"I'll tell you, you'd better hang on to that one," Heather said. "Take it from me. There aren't many true blue ones out there."

'True blue'? Jas Harker? It boggled the mind.

She gave Amethyst a quick pat on the arm. "I'm so glad we got the chance to talk. Maybe sometime we can get together—all four of us."

Now *there* was a truly terrifying thought.

"Sure." Amethyst put on a smile and said before Heather could start making concrete plans, "I can tell you're in a hurry, so I'll see you later."

Heather gave a little cheery little wave that reminded her of Balgaire's in Jas' scrying and tippety-tapped to her front door in her electric blue pumps.

Caramela looked up at Amethyst, a curious wrinkle on her forehead. Giving her a reassuring pat, Amethyst made herself walk on, more confused than ever.

CHAPTER 14

Second Thoughts

J as wasn't coming back. Amethyst was sure of it now.

She sat by herself at the dining room table eating a stuffed baked potato for dinner and pretending the realization didn't make her stomach upset. It just meant she could have the other potato, the one in the fridge, tomorrow.

She looked at the bite of potato and cottage cheese and salsa and zucchini on her fork and realized it had been hanging there a good minute. The steam that had risen from the potato after she took it out of the oven was gone, along with the savory smell. She took the bite. It was barely lukewarm.

Idiot, she told herself. *Stupid, boneheaded moron. You can't keep rejecting a man and not expect him to eventually take it to heart.*

He hadn't even called to tell her. Not that she probably didn't deserve a brush-off that cold, but…

She really hadn't expected that from Jas.

You'd better hang onto that one, Heather had said. Oh, well. Too late now.

Caramela, lying beside her, stood up and whined at the laundry room door. Her heart suddenly beating hard, Amethyst put down her fork, listening.

The sound of a car's engine came from the garage. She leapt to her feet, her heart galloping now.

"Okay, be cool," she told herself.

The engine fell silent. Seconds ticked past in more silence. Amethyst made herself sit back down and pick up her mug. On the other side of the closed laundry room door, she heard the sound of the door to the garage opening. She stood again, carried the mug into the kitchen.

Jas opened the door and came in.

It was like the first time she'd seen him, black hair stylishly mussed, the little quirk to one brow, good-looking enough to make her stupid. His tie was loosened, pale green dress shirt rumpled, his suit jacket draped over one arm, distressed leather satchel in the other hand.

She took a sip of tepid tea to hide her agitation. "'Honey, I'm home,'" she said, deadpan.

He put his satchel on the chair and draped his jacket over the back. "Don't worry. I won't kiss you."

Kiss me, she thought. The way she felt right now, that was *so* not a good idea. Or maybe it was a great idea. She couldn't begin to say.

"Tough day at the office?" she said instead, topping off her mug with hot water.

He stripped off his tie. "There were a few things I needed to deal with. They took longer than I expected." He stood as if waiting for her reaction.

"So I guess we're off the buddy system," she said and

took another sip.

She could see his shields go up. "That's news to me," he said.

She searched for something to say that didn't sound accusing or whining, like, *So why leave me alone all day?*

"Oh," was all she could come up with.

"I already asked if it would be better if I went home. Have you decided it would?"

Not that she hadn't spent the last several hours thinking about it. Not that she'd come up with a satisfactory answer.

"If you'd be happier." She put both hands around her mug. "You weren't when you left this morning." She kept her tone neutral.

"I was under the impression that it was you who weren't happy. I thought you might need some space."

"You were mad at me."

His brows shot up in surprise. "I wasn't angry at you. Frustrated, yes. Confused, certainly." He studied her. "Why would you think I was angry at you?"

"Well…" She carefully set her tea on the counter. "You deserved to be. I— It wasn't fair to you."

He took a sudden step closer. "I don't want you to be *fair*. If you're thinking of going to bed with me out of some sense of obligation—"

She bristled. "I don't pay my debts with sex, Jas."

"Good. Because if you sleep with me, I expect it to be because you want to."

"Oh, don't worry, it will be."

Seething, she glared at him. He glared back. Finally,

he backed half a step, raked a hand through his hair.

"Are we arguing?" he said.

"Sounds like it to me." She crossed the kitchen, took his potato out of the refrigerator.

"Why are we arguing?"

"I think," she said, "it might be because you just accused me of being a whore."

He drew a quick breath, either of outrage or protest, stopped, let it out again. "Good God." He ran a hand down his face. "You know I don't think anything of the kind, Amethyst. I hope you know."

"I certainly haven't led you to assume so," she said nastily.

"No. No, you've been…cautious."

Another nasty comment occurred, but she refrained.

"Can I try again?" He took a long breath. "I don't want our relationship based on obligation, or guilt, or need, or anything so mercenary. Only on mutual respect. On genuine pleasure in each other's company."

Her temper crashed into a wall. She scowled at him. "You really know how to ruin a good mad, you know that?"

"High praise, from you."

She gave a disgusted snort and put his plate in the microwave. A laugh suddenly tickled at her stomach. She struggled to contain it, but it bubbled up despite her.

"Oh, Jas," she said, still chuckling. "We're impossible."

"What do you mean?"

"We're circling each other like two wary dogs."

One corner of his mouth pulled up in a reluctant smile. "Yes, we are."

She crossed the space between them, but didn't touch him. Even though she really wanted to. "I'm sorry about this morning. That was my fault."

"I hardly think you can shoulder all the blame for that."

"I guess not. But I'm sure we can both be grownups while you're here and keep from ravishing each other."

He looked thoughtful. "I'd much rather ravish each other. We'd be less distracted."

"Or maybe more."

"Mmm." He tipped his head in acknowledgement. "We might not even notice when Balgaire makes his move."

"That could be…awkward."

His hand had drifted to her hip. Hers was curled around his waist.

"Jas…"

"Amethyst?"

She gently took his hand from her hip and sighed. "We really are impossible."

"I wouldn't say that. Only that we should deal with Balgaire soon. He's becoming far too…." A smile hinted at the corners of his mouth. "…*distracting*."

"Ugh." She made a face. "There's a thought I could've done without."

"You don't find Dougal Balgaire appealing?" he asked earnestly.

She smiled sweetly. "When I talked to Heather earlier,

she suggested that the four of us get together sometime. I told her 'sure,' but she was in a hurry, so we didn't have a chance to pick out a date."

He gave her a narrow look. "That," he said, "is not true."

Amethyst raised her right hand. "It is absolutely true. Would I lie to you?"

"At the risk of starting another argument, you've demonstrated a willingness to use guerilla tactics to exact your revenge."

"Oh, you mean like whoever that was who called my mother to tell her we're getting married? That kind of guerilla tactics?"

"That was truly inspired, wasn't it?"

"You really are trying to pick a fight tonight."

"Never."

She pressed her lips tight, exasperated—

And realized how much more cheerful she felt than she had five minutes ago. Damn Jas. When had she started to enjoy sparring with him?

I'm crazy, she thought. *I've gone completely off the deep end.*

"What's that look?" he said.

"My potato's cold," she said, heading for the table to avoid answering him.

"Is it," he said.

She picked up her plate and turned to face him, silently daring him to ask why her food was cold.

That smile still teased corners of his mouth, but didn't get any further.

"Bring it here," he said. "I'll heat it up."

She considered the gleam in his eye, the lift to one brow, daring her right back.

"I don't doubt it," she said. "I don't doubt it for a minute."

CHAPTER 15

Snow Day

It shouldn't have been obvious. But watching Melodie's gaze travel around the living room, Amethyst was afraid it was. The tablet that wasn't hers, sitting on the round maple table by Jas' chair. The coaster he'd set his glass on last night after dinner… Every little thing seemed to have flashing neon arrows that said, 'Jas is staying here!'

Then again, it could be just her guilty conscience.

"I booked the one o'clock snowboarding lesson," Jas said, crossed to the coat closet and took out their coats—both their coats. "Give the day a chance to warm up."

Melodie shot Amethyst a look, her brows giving an upward twitch.

Nope. It wasn't just Amethyst's guilty conscience. Melodie knew. Amethyst met her look and gave a ghost of a shrug.

Jas, holding her coat, noticed the interchange. Most guys never picked up on subtle female communications. But of course Jas would be the one who did. She shrugged at him, too, and slipped into her coat, her puffy, rich purple cold-weather one.

Marl, Melodie's husband, certainly seemed oblivious, chatting about what a perfect day it was and how they'd hardly need coats. Or it might just be that he was laboring to keep the atmosphere light. So far, Melodie was keeping her promise to be civil. But she wasn't making an effort to be friendly, either. Amethyst was surprised to find herself a little squirmy about it. And they still had a 45-minute drive up to the ski area.

She drove her Subaru, Jas beside her, Melodie and Marl in the back. The city gave way to sparsely-vegetated granite slopes, then to low-rise woods of piñon and juniper, and those to towering pines as they climbed. Snow appeared, first only in the shade, then as a white blanket.

Amethyst had to admire Jas' composure. The mood, while not hostile, was definitely cool. But Jas stayed as pleasant and friendly as if Marl and Melodie were a couple he looked forward to getting to know.

The Sandia Peak ski lodge rose from the parking lot above its bright red double staircases. Skiers in equally bright gear trooped up and down the stairs, moved across the snowy landscape, rode the lift to the top of the ski trails.

As soon as they'd unloaded, Melodie grabbed Amethyst's arm.

"Let's go check it out," she said. "We'll see you guys up there."

Amethyst didn't have a chance to read the look on Jas' face before Melodie tugged her away across the snowy parking lot. Sighing, Amethyst let herself be towed up the stairs, into the lodge and through a door onto a side deck.

Melodie found a relatively private corner and rounded on her. "Tell me Jas Harker isn't living with you."

Amethyst raised her chin and crossed her arms. "Jas Harker isn't living with me."

"Amethyst, I'm your best friend. Do not lie to me."

When Melodie used her real name, Amethyst knew she was serious. "I'm not lying. He's not living with me. He's staying with me."

Melodie shook her head. "Ah, semantics. You gotta love 'em."

"It's the truth."

"Look," Melodie said. "I don't want to cause trouble—"

"Not much."

"—but a week ago you wanted to throw the man under the bus. Now he's living—excuse me—*staying* with you."

"You were the one who told me I'd better think twice before I shut him down."

"And I'm feeling a little uncomfortable about that now."

Ah-ha, Amethyst thought. She took Melodie's hand. "Don't feel guilty, Mel. It's not like you think." *Yet.* "We're having wizard problems. We discussed it, and decided this was the best way to handle them."

Melodie held up a hand. "Whoa, whoa, whoa. Wizard problems. What kind of wizard problems?"

Amethyst sighed. "Hopefully not the kind that put me in the hospital again. So you see why Jas doesn't want leave me on my own."

Melodie put knuckle to lip and studied her a long moment. "You know, every time I want to think the worst of him, he turns around and does something like that."

Amethyst grinned. "I know, huh? Leave that gorgeous place of his up in the foothills to camp out in my guest bedroom, help with the dishes and everything. He even gave ol' Heather the brush-off when she fired up the charm."

Melodie made a face. "And we all know how hard that is. So these wizard problems—"

"It's just some guy who keeps showing up. He's probably harmless, but I'm not willing to give him the benefit of the doubt."

"Okay. So…" She gave Amethyst a worried look. "Are you okay with it? The close quarters and all?"

Amethyst gave a rueful laugh. "I'm hopelessly confused. I don't think I can expect any better than that."

"Well, I guess I'll get to see up close and personal today if Jas is worth all the agony."

Amethyst hadn't thought about it that way. "I know it sounds crazy," she said slowly, "but I'm beginning to think he might be."

Melodie studied her again as if trying to decide if she really was crazy, then sighed. "He'd better be, for his sake."

Amethyst hugged her. "Thanks. You're the best kind of friend. There aren't many who'll ask if you're being stupid."

"Hey, you know me," Melodie said. "Anytime."

Amethyst laughed and went back inside, Melodie following.

They climbed the stairs to the main level of the day lodge. Brilliant sunlight reflected from the snowy slope outside poured through the tall windows. The day lodge was nothing fancy, just a café with the usual assortment of burgers, fries and fountain drinks, a rental shop and a bank of lockers lining a space filled with utilitarian tables. It was a busy place right now, people going in and out, sitting at the tables eating and chatting.

Amethyst and Melodie made their way out the doors. Skiers and boarders waited at the chairlifts, skimmed gracefully down the slopes. Amethyst made her way through them, finally spotting Jas and Marl at the lift ticket window.

"Okay," Amethyst said when the four of them met after their transaction there. "There's something I'd like to do before we get started."

She led them across the packed snow of a service road and out of sight around the corner of a building.

She faced Melodie and Marl. "I'd like to put an anti-bust-your-ass spell on us."

Marl exchanged a glance with Melodie. Jas just listened with polite interest.

"If you're okay with that," Amethyst added.

"I won't complain," Melodie said.

Marl pulled off his ski cap, ran a hand over his hair and tugged the cap back on. "I suppose it couldn't hurt."

He knew about her wizardry. When they were doing ordinary things together, he was okay. But the magical aspect of her life seemed to make him uncomfortable. Amethyst didn't really blame him.

"I'll do myself and Melodie first," she told him, "in case you decide to change your mind."

A lot of magic wasn't flashy. Protection spells and curses, come hithers and findings and bindings were all invisible to ordinary people—except for their effects. Of course, a wizard could perceive a spell in a variety of ways.

To Amethyst, this spell appeared as translucent, sky-blue fake fur that gave off a faint, chiming hum and a scent of sour apples and smoke, of all things.

Jas did a lot of gesturing when he worked the magic. Not her. She'd finally gotten to where she didn't feel like she was playing make-believe. Using gestures, especially around other people, only made her feel stupid. So she simply reached out with her power and tucked the spell around herself and Melodie.

"Done," she said.

"That's it?" Melodie held out her gloved hands, turned them this way and that. "I don't feel any different."

"You won't," Amethyst said. "And you'll still fall, because if I put a spell on you to keep you from that, it would be pretty obvious to anyone watching. But this one will keep you from crashing into things, or falling in a way that would hurt you." She crooked a mischievous smile. "Here, I'll show you."

She launched into a run, risky to begin with on the icy ground, heading for the snow fence on one side of the road.

"Wiz!" Melodie yelped.

Under ordinary circumstances, Amethyst would've piled into the fence and taken a header over it. Instead, her feet slipped, arcing out from under her and sending her into a twisting fall. She landed with a *poof* in the soft snow alongside the road.

She got up with a flourish and brushed the snow from her pants. "Ta-da! Just like water skiing."

Jas shook his head, smiling.

"Okay, I'll take some of that," Marl said.

"Coming up," Amethyst said and worked the spell on him, then the four of them trooped back up the road to the ski school.

Amethyst liked to think herself athletic. She hiked. She skated, and she'd thought skating would give her an edge in learning to snowboard.

No. She fell on her butt a lot. She fell on her face. Thank god for the spell, but it didn't do anything to get the damned board back under her and get back upright after she fell. It was embarrassing, especially when little kids zipped past, squealing, like they were riding Big Wheels in the street. She consoled herself by considering that it was only their lower center of gravity.

Jas, however, was skimming around smooth as an ice cube down a greased glass chute, all cool in his rainbow mirrored goggles and helmet and dark green snow pants.

The instructor, an Anglo guy with a fashionable three-day's growth of beard who looked maybe all of 20, clapped his gloved hands together.

"Good job!" he called as Jas glided down the beginner's slope. "You're a natural."

Amethyst, on the other hand, landed on her butt again and did a quarter turn on the snow before coming to a stop. Jas dug in the edge of his board in a crunching, squeaking stop by her, then laughed as he pulled her up.

"That was a fine fall," he said. "I'm impressed."

She gave him a withering smile. "Why, thank you, Jas."

With a wave, he glided off again. Amethyst raised her goggles and narrowed her eyes. Melodie came wobbling up beside her.

Jas might be the classic smooth operator, but he wasn't *that* smooth.

"He's cheating," Amethyst said.

Melodie set hands on hips, puffing. "What do you mean?"

Amethyst nodded her head after Jas. "He's using the magic."

Of course, any wizard would maintain spells of protection, of deflection and bafflement. She could see the magic at work around Jas, but it wasn't easy to tell what it was doing unless you actually saw the effects. And the effect here was that Jas, who supposedly didn't know how to snowboard either, wasn't having the same problems the rest of them were.

Amethyst dug through the spells she knew, looking for just the right one.

It was a little like the true-seeing spell she'd set around her house. But instead of breaking illusion, this disrupted luck spells and come-hithers. So if Jas was calling just the right conditions to let him board with ease...

She gave a slow, one-sided smile and told Melodie, "Watch this."

She shaped the magic and tossed the spell at Jas.

His head snapped around when the spell hit him. Amethyst smiled and waved. He began a slow rotation, then somehow got going backwards down the slope. The edge of his board caught in the snow and he flipped head-over-board. His hat, his goggles and one glove flew and he landed sprawled on his back on the snow.

Amethyst laughed and smacked her gloved hands together. "Yard sale!" she called.

Melodie took off a glove, put her fingers in her mouth and whistled. Amethyst scootered over to Jas, braced hands on knees and bent over him.

"That's what happens when you make your date look bad," she said.

Still on his back, he frowned up at her. "You have a mean streak, Amethyst Rey."

"I prefer to think of it as mischievous."

She offered her hand. He took it and gave a yank. She yelled and went sprawling on top of him, their boards clattering and legs tangling.

"You aren't trying to start another duel, are you?" he said into her ear.

"Are you asking for a rematch?" She tried to push herself up, but he wrapped an arm around her and held her.

"Only if it's for the same stakes."

The stakes last time had been marriage.

"You never give up," she said.

"Of course I don't."

"Hey, you guys," Melodie called. "There're kids around!"

Jas laughed and let her go. "Later."

A shiver went through her, but Amethyst said, "You *wish*." She pushed off of him.

CHAPTER 16

Over the Edge

A golden afternoon abruptly turned to blue shadow on the east face of the mountain. Amethyst's breath puffed white on the air as she beeped the locks to her car and they all climbed in.

"What happened?" Marl asked Jas. "You started off great."

Jas pulled out his seatbelt and buckled it. "I suppose it must've been beginner's luck."

"It was *some* kind of luck," Amethyst said.

He slid her a look.

She smirked. "Too bad it didn't last."

Melodie snickered in the backseat, then coughed into her hand when Jas slid *her* the look over his shoulder.

Marl reached forward and clapped him on the shoulder. "Let me give you the benefit of my experience," he said. "You don't want to get these two going."

"Hey!" Melodie punched him in the arm. Marl grimaced and clutched his arm as if mortally wounded.

"I'm beginning to see that," Jas said.

Amethyst grinned and backed out of the parking

space, snow and cinders crunching under the Subaru's tires. "What do you think about hot food someplace warm? Maybe at Greenside? It's close, and I'm hungry."

"You're always hungry," Melodie said.

"Well, magic does that," Amethyst said and pulled out of the parking lot.

The day had been warm enough to melt the snow a little. But the temperature plummeted when the sun went down, and ice formed quickly, too. Amethyst didn't worry about the drive back down the mountain. Her Outback was bulletproof on ice. Most of the time, she couldn't even tell the roads were icy.

It was like that now, tilting the wheel left and right as she guided the car around switchback curves.

She groaned when they caught up with another car. "Here we go."

Melodie leaned to peer past her shoulder out the windshield. "It's going to be a lo-o-o-ng drive to the highway."

Amethyst grunted. It was.

The white sedan—Sonata, she could clearly read on the rear nameplate—wasn't an SUV, or a Subaru, or anything else that looked like it might be able to reasonably handle the fast-freezing mountain road. The driver was right to be cautious, but there also wasn't going to be any passing going on. Sighing, she downshifted so she didn't have to keep putting on the brakes.

Another, sharper curve came, and the Hyundai's brakelights flared. The car suddenly swung around, front wheel spinning, snow and ice flying in a white cloud. Marl and Melodie shouted from the backseat.

"Shit! Oh, fuck!" Amethyst yelled.

She reached out both hand and magic. The same instant, Jas did the same. But the car was already gone, disappeared over the drop-off at the edge of the road in a cloud of snow.

The antilock brakes stuttered the Subaru to a stop. Amethyst punched the emergency flashers, flung out of the car and ran back to the spot the Hyundai had gone over the edge.

Except for the click of the flashers and soft mutter of the Outback's engine, it was silent. A trail of broken branches, uprooted rocks and gouged snow showed the path the car had taken down the slope. Somewhere down there, something cracked. Beside her, Jas and Melodie and Marl looked down, too, Melodie cursing softly under her breath.

Marl held his phone. "No signal."

Jas closed a hand over it, pushed it back at Marl. "Now you have one. Call and come on."

He started scrambling down the slope.

Marl gave his phone a disbelieving stare, punched in 911 and handed it to Melodie.

"Someone will have to watch for the paramedics. And other drivers." His gaze flicked between Amethyst and Melodie.

"Okay," Melodie said and put the phone to her ear.

"Mel," Amethyst said. "Don't let anybody else come down there." She waggled her fingers as if casting a spell.

"An accident on the Crest Highway," Melodie said

into the phone. "The car skidded and went over the edge." She gave Amethyst one firm nod.

Marl scrambled through the snow in Jas' wake, Amethyst right behind him.

It wasn't an easy descent, clambering over rocks and broken trees through the snow. Snow crept cold over the tops her snow boots. She hadn't taken time to grab her gloves, so her hands were positively painful from hanging onto frozen branches and roots and rocks. Belatedly, she called a spell of warmth into the air around her and Marl where he puffed a few yards ahead. She shaped the magic into a come-hither like Jas had used while snowboarding. Something to keep them from taking the fast way down the slope.

She smelled gas and antifreeze before she saw the car. Then there it was, broad, black scrapes along the white paint, the sides caved in, axles broken, hood buckled, bumper wrapped around a tree. She cursed again and skidded to a stop by Marl and Jas. A child's scream cut the air, and she went colder than any amount of freezing air could make her.

Jas flashed a look back at her. "You're here. Good. Come help me."

He suddenly looked very much a wizard, forbidding and formidable. She instantly moved forward.

"I'll get the child out," he said. "You help the parents."

"Mommy! Daddy!" the child screamed, increasingly frantic.

Marl was quickly by the shattered back window.

"Sweetheart? Sweetheart, listen to me now. We're going to get you out of the car. We're going to help your mommy and daddy, too, okay?"

The child's screams turned to terrified sobs.

"Keep talking," Jas said. "I'll be making a great deal of noise."

Marl kept talking, soothing words in an upbeat voice though his face was strained. He had two daughters. They were both teenagers now, but Amethyst knew he'd had to deal with his share of crises.

Jas narrowed his eyes and put his hands on the car's rear door. The magic leapt, answering his power. The car's caved-in door screeched and howled, twisting out of the bent frame. Amethyst turned to the driver's door and did the same. The car shuddered and the child inside began screaming again.

The airbags had deployed, so all Amethyst could see was a wall of floppy white fabric and a scattering of broken glass. The driver's door bowed outward, welds popping, plastic cracking. Marl, his eyes round, kept up his reassuring patter. With a squeal and thunk, the door wrenched free.

Amethyst jumped back as it burst open, then turned the force she'd called to the airbags, tearing them away to get to the people in the front seats. At last, she saw them.

"Oh, god, Jas," she breathed.

He glanced toward the front seat. So did Marl. His mouth went flat and grim.

"Take care of them," Jas told her.

"How?" she said, a desperate note to her voice.

"You were trained by a healer. Heal them."

"That was a long time ago!"

"Amethyst," he said.

She turned, and his black gaze snagged her.

"Like this," he said.

As he had at the party, he reached out to her through the link they shared. She'd originally forged the blood-bond to protect them both from another wizard. She hadn't been happy when she realized that neither of them could undo it, but the link had proved useful more than once.

It was useful again now. It was like he caught her hand and gave her exactly the tool she needed when she'd been fumbling through spells for something that would work.

Ignoring the blood, the terrible smell of it, the warm, slippery feel of it under her fingers, she touched the driver, a man.

She could almost hear Nani's deep, strong voice, feel her callused hands on hers. *Close your eyes and open your mind, mijita. Do you see me? Now look inside of me, see the life moving there...*

Amethyst opened herself again to the magic, that ether that permeated and emanated from everything. It was like looking at some weird, multi-sense CAT scan, a swirl of color and sound, flavor and scent. The wrongness of the man's wounds crackled and squealed with throbbing yellows and pulsing white that gave off a sharp, hot, sick smell. Above all the iron taste of blood lay thick and choking on her tongue.

She moved her hands to the wounds, drawing the magic with her, smoothing away the sharpness, cooling the hot colors, damping the whine of distress and pain. The man, slumped against his seatbelt, turned his head and groaned. She stripped off her jacket and covered him then called a spell of warmth into the car.

There were broken bones, but she couldn't fix those using only magic. Could she? Maybe she could, but her gut told her it would take time, and there was still the woman slumped in the passenger seat, who she somehow had to reach without clambering over the injured man.

Marl's voice spoke, and Jas'. The child was crying for Mommy and Daddy again.

"Don't worry, sweetling," Jas said. "My friend Amethyst is making them feel better."

He leaned into the car, extricated the child from the car seat. She was a little Spanish girl maybe three or four years old with a bob of dark hair and terrified eyes. Her face was wet with tears and snot, but otherwise, she seemed okay.

Melodie came skidding down the slope, panting hard. "There's an old retired Marine up there. He can barely walk, but had a ton of emergency gear in his trunk. He's directing traffic."

Jas glanced at Amethyst then flicked his gaze to the parents slumped in the front seats. Melodie followed his gaze and her face went pale. Amethyst moved to block the sight as Jas handed the little girl to Marl, but she twisted, stretching out her hands toward the car.

"No! MommEEEEE!"

Marl joggled her and patted her back, trying to calm her. Melodie quickly turned away from the car and did the same.

"We'll take care of them, I promise," Jas said. "Mister Marl is going to take you to meet the firemen now."

"Do you like firemen?" Marl said. "They'll have a big yellow truck and I bet they'll let you play with the siren. There it is now. Do you hear it?"

Sure enough, a siren echoed across the slopes, then faded again. Still a way off, then.

The little girl shook her head hard, her dark hair flying. "I want my daddy!"

"Shh," Jas said and laid a hand on the child's tousled hair.

She suddenly quieted. Her big, dark eyes turned to him.

The magic rippled—Jas must've used a calming spell on the little girl.

"Watch," he said.

He half-turned from her, looking over his shoulder with a mysterious smile as if hiding something. Whether it was Jas' spell or the distraction of his behavior, the child watched him curiously. He turned back, hands cupped in front of him. He opened them with a flourish and butterflies flew out, a fluttering, sparkling rainbow of color, as if their wings were dusted with glitter.

The little's girl's mouth went round. She held out her hands and a bright pink butterfly lighted on the sleeve of her jacket. She reached out a chubby finger to touch its wings and it fluttered away, circling her head.

Marl, watching the display, looked equally wondering. Melodie was more used to magic by now. But her gaze on Jas was thoughtful—and maybe a little surprised.

"Do you like kittens?" Jas asked the child in a kind and gentle voice Amethyst had never heard him use before.

"Bunnies," she said shyly.

Jas nodded solemnly. "I have something to show you, but it's a secret. Can you keep a secret?"

The little girl stuck her fingers in her mouth and nodded.

"All right."

He turned away again. This time when he turned back, he held a baby bunny so white it looked like a stuffed animal.

"Oh!" The little girl stretched out her hands for it.

Jas unzipped her jacket to make a pocket, then tucked the bunny inside. A real bunny probably would've squirmed and kicked, but this one snuggled under her chin, its white whiskers brushing her neck.

She curled her little hands over it and smiled. "Soft!"

"Yes," Jas said with a smile that turned Amethyst's insides into mush. "This is a magic bunny, only for you. No one else will be able to see her. She'll stay with you to keep you from being afraid. Are you afraid now?"

The little girl hugged the bunny and shook her head.

"Good." Jas touched her hair again. "Now let Mister Marl and Miss Melodie take you to see the firemen. Your mommy and daddy will come soon."

"Hold onto my neck, sweetheart," Marl said, "And

don't hug your bunny too tight. You don't want to squish her."

"Shh! She's secret!" the child said, hooking her little legs and one arm around Marl.

Marl gave Jas an approving nod then started back up the slope, the child's dark head tucked behind the collar of his jacket. After one last, speculative look, Melodie followed.

Amethyst quickly crawled into the backseat of the car to reach the woman in the passenger seat.

Jas leaned in the open doorframe. "How are you doing?"

"I don't know," Amethyst said. "Check me."

He touched the driver's neck. The man had subsided into unconsciousness again.

"Good," Jas said. "I'll work on the pain…"

Amethyst dived into the magic once more. The woman had injuries to her chest from slamming into the seatbelt. Something was also wrong in her head and neck, probably from the airbags exploding into her.

Amethyst hissed between her teeth. The magic was one big roil of wrongness. She dragged her coat off the man and onto the woman. Very gently, she laid her hands on either side of the woman's head and used the magic to knead out the knots of swelling and bleeding. Jas' spells soon wove with hers, complementing them, touching what she hadn't.

Amethyst, Jas' voice whispered into her mind through the link.

She blinked her way out of the magic. Voices came

down the slope, the crunch and crack of several sets of feet scrambling through the snow and over broken branches. The light had dwindled, deepening to true dusk.

Amethyst backed out of the car. Jas steadied her when her feet touched the snow.

The bobbing beam of a flashlight appeared upslope, an EMT behind it. Others came after with stretchers and cases of medical supplies. Jas pulled Amethyst back, out the way as the EMT's, bundled in cold weather gear, crowded the trampled snow around the car, ducked inside and went to work.

"What's been done?" one of them asked, a black man a little shorter than Amethyst.

Amethyst realized both she and Jas were bloody to the elbows, both of them coatless. Jas must've covered the driver with his.

"We got the little girl out," Jas said. "We put our jackets over the parents and tried to stop the bleeding."

The EMT nodded once and turned back to the car. He paused, staring at the bent car doors.

"Bradley!" One of the others called out. He raised his head and hurried away to help.

Jas touched Amethyst's elbow and tilted his head toward the slope. Right. Time to go before people started asking questions. Like, how did those doors get pulled off the car?

She turned and began the scramble up the snowy slope, now slippery and icy from trampling feet. Her stomach felt sucked to her backbone and she was so hungry she was shaking. She shook from the cold, too.

Obviously healing magic, at least *this* healing magic, was big medicine—literally. Still, she called another spell of warmth. Hypothermia wouldn't be any easier on her.

She slipped a couple of times climbing over rocks, but Jas gave her a push from behind, propelling her upward. After snowboarding all afternoon then clambering up and down that slope, the muscles of her thighs trembled and burned.

"Almost there," Jas panted behind her.

She could see the red and blue strobe of emergency lights across the trees above. Radios squawked. She more or less clawed her way up to the road, then someone caught her arms and pulled her up the rest of the way. More emergency personnel pushed past her, going down the way they'd come up.

Vehicles now filled the winding lanes—other cars, three Bernalillo County Sheriff's SUV's, a fire truck and an ambulance. Headlights and flashlights striped the gathering darkness. Someone threw a blanket around her shoulders and she was drawn into the boil of noise and activity around the scene. Alarm rose in her and she looked around for Jas. He was right behind her, a blanket of his own around his shoulders.

He caught up and put an arm around her. "Doing all right?"

She shook her head. "Jas, those people were hurt so bad—"

He pulled her closer. "They'll make it. You made sure they will."

✧✧✧✧✧✧

Dinner at Greenside was out. By the time they'd finished with the sheriff's deputies and the ambulance had driven off, lights flashing and siren howling, it was too late to get to the restaurant before it closed. Besides, between the blood she and Jas were wearing, and everyone's wet socks and pants and snags and tears from the scramble up and down the mountainside, they would've alarmed the staff and other diners.

Jas placed an online order at Applebee's. They swung by the restaurant to pick it up, bag after bag of steaks and grilled chicken and pasta and baked potatoes and boneless buffalo wings and molten lava cakes for two magic-depleted wizards and two meals for two hungry civilians. They took it all back to Amethyst's house.

Surprisingly enough, there wasn't much talk. Exhaustion, Amethyst thought. At least that was her excuse. Marl and Melodie stayed only long enough to eat.

Melodie hugged her hard before they left, whispering in Amethyst's ear, "He's worth it."

Amethyst hugged her back, tears starting in her eyes. She had no idea why.

She shut the front door, crossed the living room and dropped onto the sofa. Caramela crawled up next to her and snuggled close. She'd sniffed Amethyst all over when she came home, then shadowed her after that, knowing that the smells of blood and distress meant something bad had happened.

"We didn't even get their names," she said to Jas.

"We'll never know if they're okay."

He sat down on her other side and put his arm around her. "It won't be hard to find out. I'll keep track of them."

Of course he could. She should've realized.

Amethyst leaned her head on his shoulder and tucked an arm around his waist. "Thank you."

He kissed the top of her head. "Of course." He just held her a moment, then jiggled her shoulders. "You did well. I'm glad you were there. It would've been difficult to take care of both the parents and the child."

"I don't feel like I did well." Doing well would mean those people could've carried their daughter out of there themselves.

His hand kneaded the back of her neck. "They'll heal. It takes more time than we had for more. That was a bad wreck."

Sighing, she nodded against his shoulder. She watched the flicker of flames in the pellet stove and stroked Caramela's soft fur.

"You must've been a good dad," she said at last. "How many kids have you raised?"

He chuckled. "More than you want to know."

Strange, how she'd never thought of Jas being a father. Even at the age he looked, he could already have half-grown kids. But no, that wasn't right. He'd said he hadn't had kids in over a hundred years.

"We're both tired," Jas said. "We should go to bed."

She'd showered and scrubbed and taken all the bloody clothes straight to the laundry room sink, but she still couldn't get the smell of blood out of her nose, still couldn't get the feel of it, warm and slick, out of her mind.

"You go ahead," she said. "Caramela and I will sit here for a while. I don't think I can sleep right now."

"I'll sit here with you then, if you don't mind."

Amethyst watched the fire a moment. "I'd like that."

Tucked against warmth of Jas' side, the scent of his soap and freshly-washed skin in her nostrils, she let the rise and fall of his breathing lull her. Finally, she drifted to sleep.

She half-woke once when the pellet stove ran out of fuel and turned off, and again to Jas' soft snores. She shifted on the sofa, meaning to wake him so he could go to bed. He murmured her name and stretched out, pulling her with him. She hesitated, then nestled her face into his shoulder and went back to sleep.

When Amethyst woke in the morning, Jas was still holding her in his arms.

CHAPTER 17

Revelations

"So," Amethyst said. "I've been thinking."

Her back to Jas where he sat at the breakfast bar, she was making cream gravy to go with the biscuits in the oven. After he held her all night, she figured he deserved Anglo food. No green chile in anything.

"Mmm?" he said.

She glanced over her shoulder. He was absorbed in something on his phone—texts or emails or something. That made it easier.

She wet her lips and turned back to the stove. "I think I'll drive up to San Cristobal to see my mom and dad. I wondered if you want to come." She was proud of how casual she sounded. "Of course if you have stuff to do at home," she rushed on, "I totally understand—"

"I'd be glad," Jas broke in, looking up from his phone, "to go visit your parents." He tilted his head as if considering. "But first I'd like to know if your father will lecture or interrogate me this time."

Amethyst grinned. "Your guess is as good as mine.

But since you told them we're getting married and here it is two months on and no date, my money is on interrogation."

He nodded. "Are we?"

"Are we what?"

"Getting married."

She scowled. "Not yet."

Jas clutched his chest. "Not *yet?* Good God. I had no idea I'd made so much progress."

"Yeah, well, before you started making smart comments, I was going to keep my dad busy."

He looked innocent. "The subject will certainly come up. I'll have to tell your folks something."

"You were the one who thought it was such an inspired idea. I'll let you figure it out."

He gave his best evil wizard smile and rubbed his hands together. "*Ex*cellent."

She ignored that. "Since it's a long drive, I usually stay overnight. Especially this time of year."

"Will we have to share a bedroom?"

"You want to discuss the subject with my dad?"

The evil wizard smile shaded to sly. "If we're sharing a bed, the question of marriage might not come up."

That stopped her. For one thing, it wasn't a bad strategy. For another...

Well, last night had been pretty nice.

"You have a devious, designing mind, Jas Harker."

"Thank you," he said modestly.

"Unfortunately, you're outsmarting yourself. Because then the question won't be *whether*, but *when*."

"Are you so certain I'm outsmarting myself?"

She turned and folded her arms. "Am I certain you wouldn't use my family to pressure me to marry you? Well, yes." She leaned forward. "Right?"

He held up his hands in surrender. "Absolutely."

"Good." The oven timer beeped and Amethyst took out the biscuits. "Just so you know, my dad and mom think you're a garden-variety corporate magnate. They do know what I am, but I'll leave it up to you to tell them you're a wizard...or not."

And under the circumstances, she'd be very curious to find out if he'd tell them. After all, it was a pretty big secret for an aspiring son-in-law to keep.

❖❖❖❖❖❖

Highway 68 on the way to Taos wound along the upper reaches of the Rio Grande. In the summertime, the kayaks and inflatables of white-water rafters dotted the river. Now, the water ran unmolested between the steep, snow-splotched slopes of its canyon before the road climbed up to the sagebrush flats around Taos. The view seemed to go on forever here, from the dark gash of the Rio Grande Gorge away on the left to the white-capped Taos Mountains ahead.

"Do you have other family in this part of the country?" Jas said, relaxed in the Outback's passenger seat, apparently taking in the passing scenery.

Amethyst rolled her eyes. "You can't make a random prank phone call without getting a Romero or used-to-be

Romero or married-to-a Romero."

"I assume you speak from personal experience."

"I'm taking the Fifth on that one."

"Does anyone else have special abilities? I haven't sensed anyone using the magic for a long time, so I suppose any talent must be subtle."

"Maybe," she said. "My cousin Martin has a way with animals. He's a vet tech, and no matter how scared or crazy the animal is, he can calm it down. My Auntie Cecelia can make anything grow. She owns a flower shop in Taos. My cousin Isabella... Whoo. She'll give you a run for your money in the looks and charm department."

Amethyst slanted him a glance. "We could stop by and say hi when we go through Taos, if you'd like."

"That sounds like a trick question," he said. "Would I like to meet your lovely, charming cousin? Any way I answer that will get me in trouble. I'd much rather meet your aunt. That sounds safer."

"Are you kidding?" Amethyst said, horrified. "If I go see Auntie Cecelia with you in tow, we might as well set a date right now. Because by tomorrow morning the whole Romero clan will be expecting a wedding."

He smiled.

"Don't even think it," she said.

He put a less alarming expression on his face. "Then I would be happy to meet your cousin Isabella."

Taos, tourist hot spot that it is, was invariably congested. Amethyst had always dreaded this part of the drive when going home for the holidays. Weekends were usually pretty bad, too. The closer you came to the plaza, the slower the traffic got. They idled their way along the narrow, two lane street past adobe storefronts and galleries, past arched gateways in courtyard walls still sporting strings of electric *farolitos*, New Mexico's traditional paper-bag lanterns, left over from Christmas.

Past the plaza, they gained a couple more lanes. Newer buildings lined the road, still adobe, most with colonnades supported by peeled posts topped with carved corbels. One was an attractive building with French doors and dark blue-pained vigas and trim set behind a dormant garden of native landscaping. An elegant sign in midnight blue read *Enchanted Circle Realty*. Amethyst turned onto a side street and pulled into the parking lot behind the building.

Jas gave her a glance she couldn't quite read. "Your cousin is a realtor?"

Amethyst gave a short laugh. "My cousin is *the* realtor in Northern New Mexico. Sotheby's in Santa Fe has been trying to lure her away for years." She shrugged. "Isabella says Taos is more her kind of town. Santa Fe is too trendy, I guess." Plus another hour and a half down the road.

She parked and turned off the engine. "Let's go see if she's in."

"If she's that successful, she's likely showing property."

It wasn't like Jas to look for roadblocks.

"You can wait while I go check, if you want."

"No," he said and opened his door. "I'll come."

The office was just as elegant inside as out, the kind of place that catered to high-end clientele. The receptionist glanced between Amethyst and Jas, Amethyst in jeans and a sweater, Jas dressed just as casually, but somehow still exuding importance. Amethyst was just about to give her name when Isabella came from the back.

Amethyst hadn't been exaggerating about her cousin's looks. Her adobe rose complexion was a little darker than Amethyst's own, her dark hair a few shades lighter with coppery overtones. Like Heather, she had a drop-dead figure despite having had three kids. She could look fantastic in a housedress, if she even owned such a thing. Smoky, jade green eyes grabbed and held you, if the rest hadn't already.

She'd been speaking to the receptionist, but stopped short.

"Amethyst!" Isabella ran and flung her arms around her. "How are you? I haven't seen you in ages. What've you been doing?"

Amethyst hugged her back. "I'm fine, still doing glass, a little computer work on the side. We're on our way to Dad and Mama's and thought we'd stop by."

At the 'we,' Isabella refocused, taking in Jas in one brief, appreciative glance.

"This is Jas Harker," Amethyst said quickly, wondering what to call him. 'Friend' seemed a little insulting. 'Boyfriend,' besides sounding juvenile, was more than she wanted to admit.

Her cousin held out a hand to Jas. "Isabella Ochoa." She frowned. "But I think we've met already." The frown smoothed away. "Yes, that's right. You purchased that property on the southeast corner of the plaza…was it last year? No—year before last, am I right?"

"Exactly right," Jas said, shaking her hand. "You have an excellent memory."

Isabella laughed. "I have to, in this business." Her gaze flicked to Amethyst, a spark of speculation there. "Auntie Tonia and Uncle Alex are wonderful people," she said to Jas. "Have you met them?"

"Actually, I have," he said. "And you're right, they're good people."

The talk turned to the property Jas had bought, how the real estate business was in the Taos area, but Amethyst paid only half attention. Her logical brain was click-click-clicking through the earlier conversation.

At last, Isabella got a call. Amethyst hugged her goodbye, promised to keep in touch and went back out to the car with Jas.

She buckled her seatbelt then rounded on him. "You!" she said. "You were *stalking* me!"

No wonder he was making excuses not to go in and see Isabella after he realized where they were going.

He snapped his own seatbelt. "You weren't speaking to me at the time. I had to do something."

"I wasn't speaking to you because you were one damn despicable excuse for a human being! Even if you are a wizard."

"Yes, you did tell me so once or twice."

She sat there, trying to decide if she was furious or flattered. "What did you expect to accomplish?"

He raked a hand through his hair. "Honestly? I don't know. I told myself I wanted to learn more about you, find out if I could possibly repair the breach between us. I suppose I also hoped you'd hear how I'd benefited your relatives and perhaps think better of me."

And what was she supposed to say to that admission?

She sighed. "Well, Jas, so that neither one of us is embarrassed, what other members of my family did you insinuate yourself with?"

"I didn't *insinuate* myself. I did honest business with them."

"Okay," she said patiently. "How many?"

He was silent a moment, either counting or not wanting to answer. Neither possibility was encouraging.

"I bought that flower arrangement for you—do you remember? When you were in the hospital the first time?—at Flores de Taos. You're right. Your aunt is quite... inquisitive."

Amethyst closed her eyes. Well, if anything was going to hit the fan from that, it would've done it a long time ago.

"I hired your uncle the architect in Santa Fe to design a small guest house. I visited the animal shelter in Los Alamos, where your second cousin works as an administrative assistant, to make a donation. I had questions for Santa Fe County Planning and Zoning, where another cousin works—"

Amethyst held up a hand and he stopped. "Jas, that's either pathetic or seriously creepy."

He sat staring out the windshield for a long moment, then turned and met her eyes. "I knew I'd made a dire mistake with you. It took a while, but I finally decided my best ally was time, no matter how hard it would be to wait."

"That was quite a leap of faith, I'm here to tell you."

"Yes," he said. "But all I could do was give you space and hope you'd eventually decide to relent."

She sat silent, touched, imagining him then, hopeful, despairing...

He reached over and took her hand where it rested on the gearshift lever. "Amethyst, I'm sorry. Things were so different then. I'd never do anything like that to you now."

She turned her hand over, closed her fingers around his. "I know. But you'd better be ready for gossip. If all those people ever get together and talk—"

"When the subject comes up, I suspect I'll be the object of knowing smiles rather than gossip. In either case, I'm willing to bear it."

Dammit! Why did he have to keep saying things like that? She was sitting here turning into a puddle of goo.

"I sure hope so," she said. "Because I think you'll be getting your share of both."

Giving his fingers a squeeze, she let go and started the car.

CHAPTER 18

Coming Home

Dad's blue heeler, Caballero, came yammering out the moment Mama opened the front door. No matter how many times Amethyst saw him, she had to calm the dog's suspicions anew. Heelers were like that.

Fortunately, Caramela headed him off at the pass. She bounced out of the backseat, her whole back end wagging furiously. Caballero stopped, whuffed and sniffed Caramela. She gave him a play bow, then the two dogs raced off around the side of the house, play-biting and throwing their butts at each other.

Amethyst crunched across the gravel driveway, clumped up the porch steps and hugged Mama.

Mama held out a hand to Jas. "Jasper. It's good to see you again."

Although Mama was smiling, there was a certain reserve there.

Uh-oh, Amethyst thought. It might just be the whole potential marriage that went *poof*. But she had a bad feeling that it had more to do with her history with Jas.

This time, Jas didn't seem to pick up on it. Or if he had, he was pretending not to.

Amethyst was beginning to wish she hadn't been quite so frank in her opinion of Jas' actions once upon a time. Now, she didn't enjoy seeing him put through the gauntlet.

The back door squeaked open and thumped closed. "Tonia?" Dad called from the kitchen. "Did I hear Amethyst's car?"

He came into the living room, not a big man, but solid, Amethyst's compass through every storm.

He crossed the room and hugged her. "Thistle! It *is* you!"

Her parents had purple nicknames for her. Thistle had always seemed perfect, not only because it was a play on her real name.

"Don't you have it backwards?" he murmured in her ear. "Aren't you supposed to bring the young man home to meet the parents *before* announcing the marriage?"

Her face went hot and her gaze darted to Jas. "Um…"

An ordinary man wouldn't have heard. Jas, being a wizard, did. He caught her eye, the ghost of a smile on his lips.

Okay, *now* she wasn't going to feel bad turning him over to Mama's tender mercies.

"I'll explain later," she murmured back and let Dad go.

Mama ushered everyone into the kitchen for tamales and pinto beans. The food did a lot to lighten the mood.

The beans had just a touch of bacon flavor and plenty of spice to keep them from being bland, the way beans could so often be. And the tamales were, as usual, delicious, the corn masa light, the pork filling tender and spicy with red chile.

Jas helped clear the table when they were finished. Amethyst took a plate to the sink and gave him a significant look: *don't lay it on too thick.* He only cocked a brow and took the plate from her.

"Have I shown you my latest project?" Dad said, refilling coffee cups. "I bought a laser setup for wood burning."

"Cool!" She turned to Jas. "Want to see it?"

He gave a little wave. "Go ahead. I'll stay and talk to your mother."

Amethyst hesitated. Jas had joked about Dad lecturing him, but she hoped he knew Mama could be far more daunting.

"I'll wash," Mama told Jas firmly. "You dry." She held out a dishtowel.

Amethyst looked at the dishes, most of which would be going into the dishwasher. But Jas was a big boy, and the fact was he'd gotten himself into this situation. He'd have to face the music sooner or later. With a helpless shrug, she followed Dad out the back door.

Caramela and Caballero trotted beside them on the way to Dad's workshop, out back. Sagging, ankle-deep snow piled along the north side of the building. Windows lined the south wall, so even without the space heater Dad used in the wintertime, it usually wasn't freezing inside.

Caballero flumped down on his bed in the corner. Caramela found a rectangle of sunlight to curl up in. Pit bulls love sunshine.

Dad folded his arms and leaned against the workbench cluttered with hardwood blocks and glue, drill bits and clamps, making no attempt to show her the laser wood-burner on a stand nearby.

Uh-oh.

"So what's the deal?" he said. "I don't get a real happy feeling when a man tells me he's marrying my daughter and I find out she's already told him no."

"Isn't that the way they used to do things?" Amethyst said, trying to joke.

Dad wasn't having it. "Things aren't done that way *now*. I know he has money and power and is probably used to getting whatever he wants. But if he thinks he can just railroad the daughter of a lowly mining engineer—"

"Dad." She crossed to him and put a hand on his arm. "That was just a practical joke that got out of hand. Nothing worse."

He eyed her, obviously not convinced but waiting to hear what she had to say.

"I did some magic stuff to him to torment him because he was doing his high-handed CEO shtick," she said. "He thought he was tormenting me back."

Dad looked somewhere between confused and angry. It was an odd look. "He asked you to marry him to torment you?"

"No, no," she said quickly. "He really does want me to marry him."

Dad nodded slowly. "Your mom said you don't even have that kind of relationship with him. Since you brought him here, I assume things have changed."

Amethyst puffed out a breath. "Yeah. They have."

"And?"

"And I thought it might be nice for you to have a chance to get to know him better."

His frown disappeared. "Are things that serious?"

Were they? Maybe they were. "I…really like him a lot. I enjoy spending time with him. I enjoy being close to him…" She trailed off.

"Sounds like there's a 'but' in there."

Amethyst brushed powdery sawdust off the workbench. "He's rich. He's handsome. He's great company. I imagine the pool of marriageable candidates must be pretty deep and wide for someone like that." She looked out one of those big, sunny windows, across Mama's sleeping garden to rolling land cloaked with sagebrush and dotted with junipers. "Like you said, he can have whatever he wants. Why me?"

"That something you should ask Jas."

"Are you kidding? I'll either hurt and insult him, or else I won't get a straight answer."

"If you're afraid you'll hurt and insult him, I think you already know the answer."

She snorted. "I wish."

Dad paced away. "You probably know I had this discussion with him a while back."

"About my magic." She hesitated. "Can I ask how it went?"

Dad glanced at her. "Let's just say that we agreed that neither one of us wants to see you unhappy."

Dad would be assuming the same thing Mama had: that Jas wanted her for her magic. Of course, he had his own. But it was Jas' place to tell Dad that.

"That's good to know, anyway," she said. And oddly enough, it was.

"I have to admit," he said. "I don't understand what's going on between you two. Jas has obviously been interested a long time. But I get the feeling he's pushing you."

This time it was Amethyst who paced the shop. "Sometimes it seems that way, I guess, but..." She shrugged. "Not really. We had sort of a rocky start. We've been in the process of smoothing things out. Jas just thinks they're smoother than I do."

Dad laughed at that. "I bet he does. But if he's serious, if he really cares for you, he'll give you the time you need."

"He has been, Dad. I know how weird it must look, but I just want you and Mama to know that he's...okay."

"That's a ringing endorsement," he said dryly.

"All right, more than okay," she said. "That's why we came, even though Jas figured he'd get grilled."

Dad's brows shot up. "*Did* he? That says a lot for him."

Something in Amethyst's middle unwound. "I thought maybe it did."

"As long as we're talking about grilling, Jas should be about medium-well by now. We'd better go pull him off the coals."

She grinned. "He was worried about you. I didn't warn him about Mama."

They found Jas still in the kitchen with Mama. Yes, Amethyst was more used to him being a regular human being now, but the sight of him with a dishtowel over his shoulder almost made her laugh.

She pulled her phone out of her pocket and snapped a picture of him. At the flash, he turned and frowned.

"I'm posting that on Instagram," she said. "'Jas Harker, CEO of Magus Corporation, at home with the in-laws.'"

Dad stopped like she'd slapped a staying spell on him. Mama gave a little gulp of shock.

Jas's lips turned up in a slow smile. "Be my guest. As long as you post it with that caption."

Oh. My. God. She *couldn't* have said that.

"Ha," she said. "Joking."

Now it was Mama who frowned.

Jas snapped Amethyst with the towel.

She yelped. "I can*not* believe you just did that."

She snatched the towel from him and snapped him back. It didn't snap as well when she did it, though.

"Okay, kids," Dad said. "Settle down." He cast Mama a meaningful glance.

It seemed like a good time to make herself scarce before Mama got the bit in her teeth about that in-law comment. Jas might get the bit in *his* teeth, too, but him, she could handle.

"I want to show Jas around the neighborhood," she

said. "As long as you don't feel like I'm deserting."

Dad made a shooing motion. "Go ahead while it's still light."

"We won't be long."

She grabbed Jas by the hand and hauled him out of the kitchen and to the front door. He took their coats from the coat tree and, as usual, held hers for her. Mama watched from the kitchen doorway. Amethyst gave her a little wave and stepped outside.

Caramela and Caballero joined them as they crunched along the gravel driveway toward the road, although Caballero stopped at the end of the drive.

Jas let out a breath. "I've managed hostile takeovers that were less tense than that conversation with your mother."

"Hey, I tried to get you to come with me," she said. "Besides, I didn't hear you arguing when Dad hauled me off."

"I didn't expect your mother to quite so formidable."

"Yeah, you thought you'd just turn on the old charm and she'd be putty in your hands."

"Something along those lines."

She gave him a sharp look. "Tell me you didn't use magic on her."

Jas didn't answer.

"Jas."

"Some," he said.

"Some?" she said, her voice rising.

"Only a luck spell." He glanced aside at her. "You and your father came in at an opportune moment. Your comment about the photo was even better."

She stopped. "You *made* me say that?"

No wonder she blurted something so damning!

He put a hand on her back. "Calm down. I didn't make you say anything. You only said it at a convenient time."

She started walking faster than before, forcing him to lengthen his stride to keep up.

"Amethyst—"

"When I start placing wards on my mom and dad," she interrupted, "I'll let you explain why."

He gave a long-suffering sigh. "I will. When the time is right."

She grunted. "The correct answer is, 'You don't need to place wards on them.'"

"You don't need to place wards on them," he said. "Is that better?"

She walked on, hands in pockets, Caramela trotting on one side, Jas striding along on the other. After a minute, a laugh pushed up.

"I would've loved to see Mama corner you. I can picture it now." She took her hands out of her pockets and framed an imaginary view. "Smooth, charming Jas, backed up against the kitchen counter, stammering as he tries to explain exactly why we don't have a wedding date yet."

"I did *not* stammer."

She grinned. "I bet you did."

He slanted her a look. "Perhaps a bit. Once."

"Oooh. Only once. You *are* cool."

He reached over and took her hand. "Stop gloating

and show me the neighborhood. It's been a long time since I last visited."

"That's right," she said. "The D.H. Lawrence Ranch. I didn't even think about that. You came here to hang with all the artsy people then?"

"It was as good an excuse as any to nose around, see if I could discover who was using magic up this way. Of course, I had no idea I was so close." He walked along, swinging their linked hands. "Or that this place should become so important to me."

A prickle ran up her back. Talys had told her a long time ago that things were seldom random when it came to magic. And now, to learn that Jas had visited her old home seventy years before she was born, when he knew even then that he was looking for something…

San Cristobal was a tiny place, a handful of dwellings—old adobes, singlewide mobile homes and tumbledown houses along the gravel roads that ran the length of the San Cristobal Creek valley.

"My dad took me to fly radio controlled airplanes in that field." Amethyst nodded at a pasture on the other side of a barb wire and juniper post fence. "See those trees over there?" She pointed to a line of skeletal cottonwoods sketching their branches against the brilliant blue sky. "The creek is over there. In the summertime, my cousin Ricardo would come visit his grandmother. That's her house there. We'd take his grandma's Tupperware bowls to the creek and catch tadpoles."

"What?" Jas said with feigned surprise. "No Barbies or tea parties?"

"Barbies. Ugh. Bo-o-o-ring. We'd play Ouija Board or have séances in Lucy's barn or make witch's brews in mud puddles."

"I can't imagine that went over well in Catholic families."

"Our moms and dads only knew about the Ouija Board."

"What did you call during your séances?"

"Spirits, of course."

He frowned. "Amethyst, if you'd been my apprentice, you wouldn't have been doing any of those things."

She glanced at him, startled. "Well, I wasn't, and I did, and I didn't get into any trouble."

He shook his head. "What made your great-grandmother decide to train you?"

"I'll show you."

They walked on up the road. A rabbit bolted from the weeds along the bar ditch, and Caramela shot after it. Amethyst called her, and after a few strides, she stopped, looked longingly after the rabbit then came trotting back.

"My brother Alex and I were playing with a snow saucer on that hill over there," Amethyst said. "Nani came along to keep an eye on us.

"Alex rode down a steep part of the hill. I was still pretty little, so I picked a spot that didn't look so scary and off I went. Only problem was, the spot I chose angled into the trees. I hit a hump in the snow and went airborne. I sailed so close under a tree branch that it scraped my hat off, then I went bumping through the trees, screaming all the way. All of a sudden, I made a half circle in the air, slowed down and landed gently on the snow. It was like a giant hand caught me and set me down. When I opened my eyes, I'd stopped about a foot from an iron pipe."

Jas' fingers tightened on hers.

"About that time," she went on, "Alex came pounding through the snow, his eyes huge and his face paler than I've ever seen it. Nani was right on his heels. She looked at that iron pipe and hugged me so tight I couldn't breathe. '*Mijita, gracias a Dios tu tiene mágica,*' she said."

"'Thank God you have magic,'" Jas translated. "You definitely wouldn't have been holding séances if you'd been in my care. That's an impressive feat for a child, even one trying to save her own life."

"To this day, I don't know how I could've done it without knowing any spells."

"Spells are only a way to shape the magic to your intent. You didn't need to know spells. You knew only that you had to keep from hitting something. So you didn't."

The back of Amethyst's neck prickled. "I hate to say it, but I think you're right. I probably shouldn't have been messing around with séances and Ouija Boards. If something like that thing Balgaire called had come crawling out of one of our bedroom closets, I would've gone off magic a lot sooner."

"No doubt."

Jas slid an arm around her, tucking her against his side. He was warm and smelled faintly of pine needles, as if he'd been carrying a Christmas tree the last time he'd worn this coat. About the only thing she could do was put her arm around his waist, feeling a little self-conscious about it. But only a little.

"This place reminds me of the village I grew up in," he said. "Only because it's small, and isolated."

She perked up. Jas so rarely talked about his past. This was the first she'd heard about his childhood. "Really? Where was it?"

For a moment, she thought he wouldn't answer.

At last, he said, "Virginia."

"Ah-ha. So you're Welsh."

It was Jas' turn to be startled. "How did you know?"

Amethyst wiggled her fingers. "Magic."

A look of alarm crossed his face.

"Joking," she said. "I heard of Dark Welsh somewhere, and remember reading that a lot of Welsh and Cornish people immigrated to Virginia to work in the mines. Since Anglos with black hair and eyes aren't exactly common, I thought maybe you're Welsh. "

"Good deduction." He walked on with her a few more paces. "In fact, my great-grandfather was a Welsh bard."

"Holy crap, Jas. A bard, as in Merlin?"

When were there still bards? In the Middle Ages? In Roman times? Something to check out later.

"Not quite so renowned."

"Is he the one who trained you?"

Jas gave a started laugh. "I'm not *that* old. No, my mother's uncle trained me."

"Sounds like wizards are thick in your family tree." Which seemed curious, since Jas had mentioned only one wizardly child of his own…but out of how many? "What about your mom and dad?"

"They were ordinary folk, although my mother possessed foreknowledge. She made my father quite a prosperous man."

"Hah! Wheelers and dealers from way back, huh?"

"Perhaps," Jas said, not smiling. "But that's enough ancient history for now."

"Just one more question—how ancient?"

He shook his head. "No, sorry."

"Not fair. I'm telling you about my childhood."

"I'll tell you about mine. When the time is right."

"I know when that is," she muttered. About the time she said 'yes.'

They walked on, Caramela following her nose into and out of the weeds along the roadside. The air was calm and cold and still, the only sound the distant whine of a jet overhead. The scent of piñon smoke spiced the air. An overgrown track branched off on the right, leading toward a juniper-dotted slope. A rusty metal farm gate sagged open, bound in place by dead weeds.

Amethyst stopped and looked down the track. "My Nani's house is there."

Jas looked too, but the only thing visible from here was a corner of adobe wall and corrugated metal roof beyond the bare branches of ancient apple trees and brushy native plums.

"Will you show me?" he said.

She stood for a long moment. "You go ahead. I'll wait here."

She felt his gaze on her, but didn't meet his eyes.

"Does anyone live there now?" he said.

She shook her head.

He was silent, his arm still around her. "Then let's go take a look," he finally said, drawing her toward the drive.

She set her feet. "No, Jas. I don't— I can't—"

He stopped and let her go, though he stood very close. She still wouldn't face him.

"When you live a long time," he said quietly, "the past spools out behind you, longer and longer. The hurts and fears of life can accumulate, leaving you unable to move in any direction for fear of encountering something that once gave you pain. When your life is very long, the way ours is, you have to face your hurts and fears or your past will trap you."

Something in her shifted, an old wound scabbed over but never quite healed. She finally looked up, into that dark, compelling gaze of his. Her heart beat too fast, making it hard to breathe. Swallowing hard, she took a long breath anyway.

"Okay," she whispered. "But I can't guarantee...how well I'll handle it."

He put his arm around her again. "You'll handle it fine."

How many times had she tried to walk down this overgrown drive, to see the house where she'd spent so much of her young life? The winter afternoons making biscochitos and sweet tamales, the summer ones hanging herbs and weeding the garden, digging bulbs in the fall, re-plastering the adobe in spring. Years and years of happy memories with her Nani—except one.

Her heart beat harder with every step. Jas looked around with simple curiosity. Amethyst forced herself to do the same. Kochia and tumbleweeds and dryland brush had overtaken the orchard and gardens. A splintering, peeling gate stood open in an adobe wall fast slumping into its constituent mud. Withered leaves stood in drifts inside the courtyard, the house's narrow windows gazing out on abandonment like blind, sorrowful eyes. Caramela stopped outside the gate and whined, but Jas drew Amethyst on.

He stepped up on the narrow front stoop and reached for the doorknob. He jerked back, his arm around her tightening.

His mouth went to a flat line. "Yes, I can see why you haven't wanted to return here. Let's see what we can do about it."

He called a spark of magic. The door swung open under his hand.

Amethyst squeezed her eyes closed, but still saw the room as she'd seen it that day seventeen years ago. Nani lying sprawled on her back on the living room rug, her mouth and eyes wide open, her fingers crooked into claws. Around her a circle of candles collapsed into puddles of wax on the scorched floor, bunches of protective herbs scattered as if by a contemptuous wind. And magic—

Oh, god, the magic so thick and hot and acrid it had burned her nerves and seared terror and agony into her wizard's senses.

Her eyes popped open. The magic was the same, just

as toxic and searing, still echoing Nani's last, terrible moments. She took a long, shaking breath, gritted her teeth and forced herself to stay where she was and look around the room.

Someone had cleared away the herbs and candles and the hardened puddles of melted wax, but the scorch marks remained. Except for an enormous, carved armoire that everyone else in the family had hated, the furniture was gone. Where, she didn't know. She hadn't seen it in anyone else's home, so maybe it had been donated. There was only the coolness of an abandoned house, the musty, earthy smell old adobe homes had and the putrid roil of magic.

She realized Jas still held her hand, his fingers laced tightly with hers.

"All right?" he said.

"No."

"Perfectly understandable," he said calmly. "But we can make things right here. Would that help?"

She concentrated on breathing, in, out, nice and slow.

She was thirteen years old again, her Nani dead there on the floor in front of her while she screamed and screamed—

No. That was gone, past. She'd put an end to the one who'd done that. She was a wizard now.

She was a wizard.

"Yes," she said tightly. "I think so."

"Good."

He pulled her inside the house, took her other hand and turned her to face him, away from that spot on the floor. Over his shoulder, she could see light through the kitchen doorway, the kiva fireplace in the corner with soot sketched on the plaster above its mouth.

"The magic has been tainted by what happened here," he said. "We'll work a healing spell, much like we did yesterday. Healing the magic is more difficult than healing a wound, so we'll need to work together."

She nodded, braced herself and slipped into the magic.

Open to it, it was much worse. But Jas was there with her, a spot of calm, cool green, like a forest pool. She plunged the dancing, purple flame of her power into it, followed his lead into a spell that seemed a combination of banishment, healing and reversal.

It was nothing like any spell she knew, and she wondered if it were some creation of Jas' own. The violet and green swirl of their combined powers pushed outward, displacing the pulsing boil of old evil, drawing in its place the vibrant harmony of life all around. In came the sleepy energy of winter, the slow flow of sap beneath bark, the bright black gleam of a raven's eye as she searched a pile of leaves for interesting tidbits, the crackle of ice crystals as the day's melt began to re-freeze.

Her heart slowed and the tightness in her chest eased. The pain that had lodged under her heart unwound like a cramp finally easing. At last, she opened her eyes.

The room was exactly as it had been...what, two minutes ago? Ten? Twenty? But the aura of terrible wrong was gone. Now it was just an old house long unlived-in, sad and lonely but nothing worse. Caramela had made her way inside and circled the living room, sniffing intently.

She and Jas stood close, separated only by their linked hands. She let go of his, put her arms around him and hugged him tight.

"Thank you."

He put his arms around her, cupping her head with one hand. "Now the power your great-grandmother filled this house with can shine once more. Someone might want to live here again. Or perhaps use this space to create beautiful things, like you do."

She nodded against his shoulder, grateful for the warmth of his embrace, grateful to be able to stand here, to remember all the love and joy and knowledge Nani had given her.

"Would you like to see the place?" she said.

He released her, trailing one hand down her arm to capture her hand. "Yes. I imagine it holds a great many memories."

"It does." She pulled him into the kitchen. "There used to be a big, heavy butcher block table here. Nani would spread out all her dried herbs…"

Reminiscing, visiting empty rooms she hadn't seen in 17 years, she lost track of time. They walked back to Dad and Mama's with the sun spilling apricot light the length of the valley. The aroma of green chile and baking potatoes met her when she opened the door. Oh, and Caballero barking up a storm, of course.

"We're back," Amethyst called.

Dad came out of the kitchen. "You were gone a while."

Mama, wearing an apron, came out behind him.

"We walked up to Nani's house," Amethyst said. "I showed Jas around."

Both Mama and Dad just stared at her.

Finally, Mama said cautiously, "You showed him the house? You mean…inside?"

Amethyst took a long breath. "Jas convinced me it was a good idea. It's…better now."

Their disbelieving gazes switched to Jas. She could see him ticking up points with them like a big win in some videogame.

Right now, it pleased her. She'd think about the long-term consequences later.

CHAPTER 19

Surprise Attack

Amethyst thought for sure Jas would press his advantage.

He didn't. After spending the night (yes, in separate bedrooms), they had a pleasant breakfast of eggs with green chile, pinto beans and tortillas with Mama and Dad. When they got back to Albuquerque a little after lunch, Jas took himself off to the office.

Tapping her foot, she frowned at the front door for a minute after he left. "I'm getting that hunted feeling again," she said to Caramela. "It doesn't make sense. He should be moving in for the kill, not giving me a smile and a sweet kiss on his way out the door."

Unless that trip to the office was actually something else, and she'd walk all unsuspecting into some restaurant or whatever in the next couple of weeks to find her family and friends dressed in their wedding best shouting, "Surprise!"

The thought should've been horrifying. What was *really* horrifying was that it wasn't. Not completely, anyway.

Well, if he did have some nefarious plot afoot, there

was nothing she could do about it. Other than make sure she didn't dress up to go anywhere.

She sighed, shook her head and went down the hall to work on soldering that fall aspens window.

She was laying the umpteenth bead of solder to the beat of her drums and Indian flute playlist when the drumbeat got unusually loud and aggressive. She dialed down the volume, but the pounding remained just as loud and just as angry. Caramela barked, jumped up and shot out of the room, slamming her butt into the doorframe on her way through—the pounding was coming from the front door.

Amethyst snarled a curse, snapped up a ward and a barrier spell and stomped into the living room, the pounding at the door growing ever louder. Caramela was about as pissed as she was, jumping and barking at the door as it shook in its frame. With the barrier spell in place to hold Caramela back as well as protect both of them from whatever—*whoever*—was outside, Amethyst jerked open the door.

Balgaire stood there, red-faced, henna-colored brows knotted, seeming bigger and more imposing than ever. He tried to push through the door, then hit Amethyst's spell. With a curse and a sharp gesture, he called magic that tried to thrust hers away. She pulled up more power and pushed back.

Caramela was barking in earnest again, ears back and teeth on full display.

Balgaire's livid gaze fastened on her. "Shut yer yap, ye goddamn mongrel!"

He raised his hand, magic swirling around him. Fury and fear shot through Amethyst. She called enough power to turn the moisture in the air to glittering ice crystals and hurled a fending at Balgaire that slapped him flat on his back and sent him skidding six feet down the front walk. Amethyst strode out after him, drawing power as she went. The smell of ozone unfurled around her as she sucked energy from the atomic bonds in the air.

"You hurt my dog, you sonofabitch," she said, "and I will gut you alive."

Balgaire shoved to his feet, fast and agile for such a big man. "Will ye now?" he said, low and silken. "All else you've done, and you still haven't had enough, have you?"

Magic coiled around her, a seething dragon on a golden leash. "What the hell are you talking about? What've I done?"

"Don't play coy with me, girl."

She faced him, trembling with rage. Rage was good. It kept her from being afraid. "You come pounding on my door, threatening me, threatening my dog. You goddamn sure better be ready with a good reason, or you'll find out firsthand why I'm nobody to *fook* with."

"You want reasons, do you?" He straightened his kilt. "I'm mindin' me own business, drivin' down the street and the bobby comes with his bright lights flashing and pulls me out of the car, none too gentle about it. Why, now, d'ye think he'd do that? Because my car—*my* car—was reported as stolen."

His brogue was so thick Amethyst had trouble understanding him.

"And then," he went on, "after more ill-mannered treatment than I'm willing to forgive, come to find my driver's license has been revoked!" He glared at her, breathing hard. "So off I go to the office where such things are handled, and what do I find there? Why, that my license was revoked because I've not paid for the keeping of my three wee bairns!"

"That's what happens to deadbeat dads around here," Amethyst said. "Why're you blaming me? *I* didn't knock up a bunch of girls."

He clenched his fists, turning red again. "Any bairns I sired are all dead and buried long ago. And now," he said, "now my wee plastic card won't work because my money's frozen!"

She frowned, translating that into *frozen assets*. "Look, Balgaire, I don't know where your problems are coming from—"

"I'll tell you where they're coming from. It's a curse! D'ye think I don't know the stench of a curse when I smell one? I come here, I offer you no harm, and you—"

"I did *not* curse you."

Over Caramela's barking at the front door, the sound of a car's engine echoed up the street. Jas' green Infiniti crested the little hill. She never thought she'd be so grateful and so horrified at once to see him.

"Ah, now, here's a treat." Balgaire sneered. "Your fine laddie, come to your rescue."

Jas pulled into the driveway, took off his sunglasses and stepped out of the car.

"Jas—" she began, because the way he looked,

Balgaire was about to end his existence as a large, smoking hole in her front walk.

"Ah, Mr. Balgaire," Jas said as if she hadn't spoken. "I see you got my message."

Balgaire's sneer fell away. "*Your* message."

"That's right. You don't suppose Amethyst was responsible for your recent troubles, do you? It's not her style, I assure you."

Balgaire's eyes narrowed, turning shrewd. "Who else could lay such a curse, now tell me that?"

Oh, shit, Amethyst thought.

Jas laughed and shook his head. "It's no curse. Simply the manipulation of data. Let me tell you a story about the last wizard who meddled with Amethyst. Currently, he's in Sardinia hoping to evade my notice. Unfortunately for him, computers, cell phones and networked surveillance cameras make that extremely difficult in most places, and I'm told that magic's effectiveness on electronics isn't particularly consistent. Since he's wanted by both the local and international police for child prostitution and trafficking in child pornography, I doubt he'll find refuge anytime soon."

Amethyst found herself staring at Jas in utter astonishment. Balgaire glanced at her as if to gauge her reaction. She blinked and pretended cool.

Jas smiled, an expression that made the hair on the back of her neck prickle. "Consider yourself fortunate that I decided to merely send you a warning." He paused. "For now."

"That's how it is, eh?" Balgaire said.

"That's exactly how it is, Mr. Balgaire." There was no trace of a smile on Jas' face now.

The two stared at each other, definitely some male thing going on.

Balgaire gave one of his stagey little bows. "Then I beg your pardon. Dinna mean to go stepping on any toes." He turned to Amethyst. "Miss Rey, my humblest apologies to you. And to your poor, faithful dog. I hope you'll find it in your heart to forgive a mistaken man."

Amethyst waved a hand. "No problem." *Not much.*

Balgaire got into his ill-fated Caddy and drove off quite calmly.

Amethyst let out a breath, slumped and dispersed the magic she'd gathered.

Jas crossed to her and took her in his arms. "Sorry about that. I misjudged my timing. I expected him to be detained by the police a bit longer." He rubbed her back soothingly. "You'd collected a great deal of power. How far did things go?"

She laughed weakly. "About thirty seconds more and I think they would've gotten pretty colorful."

He squeezed her tighter. "I could've been here more quickly—"

"If you used magic," she finished for him. "I'm glad you didn't. I'm still not sure he's not trolling you."

"It's entirely possible."

Well, now she knew what those trips to the office were for. Not to avoid her. Not even for surprise wedding arrangements.

"You know," she said, "you're pretty scary when you

want to be."

He rubbed her back a little longer. "I hope I don't scare you."

She thought about the possibilities of a wizard who could also do what Jas did with databases.

"I realized a long time ago that you had your chance to wreck my life while we were…"

"At odds," he said.

"At odds," she agreed. "And you did something else, instead. I guess it could be easy to be afraid of you. But I'm not."

She felt a subtle tension go out of him. "Good. Don't ever be."

❖.❖.❖.❖.❖.❖

B algaire seemed to be well and truly gone. Jas seemed to think so, anyway. He'd gone in to the office every day so far this week. She wondered if Balgaire was still seeing poor Heather. If he was, he was doing it somewhere else.

Amethyst tackled some housework, the noise of the vacuum cleaner filling the house's unaccustomed quiet. It wasn't lonely without Jas around—of course it wasn't. She'd just gotten used to him being there. Even though it had only been a week.

If Balgaire really *was* gone, what now? She didn't see things quietly going back to the way they had been. No, she had a strong suspicion there would be some impending decisions about living arrangements. And despite everything, she wasn't sure she was ready for that yet.

When the house was as clean as unease and fretfulness could make it, she put the cleaning rags in the laundry hamper and went out to check the mail.

She unlocked the box and pulled out a thicker stack than usual. Flipping through the assortment of bills and junk, she came to a hand-addressed envelope. Opening it, she found a thank-you card.

Ms. Rey, the note inside read. *I want to thank you and your friends for everything you did for my family after the accident last weekend. The people in the Emergency Room said what you did for my sister and her husband before the ambulance came saved their lives. They're both still in the hospital, but the doctors are amazed how fast they're healing.*

I was worried about my niece Ali after such a bad experience, but she's doing so good. All she talks about is the man who showed her magic tricks and gave her a bunny when she was crying. When she thinks nobody is around, she pets and talks to her invisible bunny and promises it that Mommy and Daddy will be better soon. Her Mama pretended to hold the bunny last time we visited. Ali told her it was magic and would keep her from being scared.

Please tell your friends how grateful we all are that you were there to help. I don't know what would've happened if you weren't.

Sincerely,

Estella deVargas

Amethyst swallowed hard and slid the card back into

its envelope. What would Jas say when he saw it?

A flicker of magic teased her fingers. Frowning, Amethyst shuffled past the electric bill and a mortgage refinancing offer to a card about the size of a large postcard. She paused long enough to check her wards then pulled it out, tucking the rest of the mail under her arm.

The card, oddly enough, was unaddressed. She flipped it over. The other side was densely written in a bold, loopy, old-fashioned-looking hand. Her eyes went straight to the bottom, to the signature: *Dougal Balgaire.*

Her heart lurched and her breath hissed through her teeth. She reached for the magic, ready to turn the card to ash, but the words "beg" and "beseech" leapt out at her. Curiosity got the better of her.

Miss Rey, it read. *I beg your indulgence. I've long wished to approach you about a matter of some importance but haven't been certain of the wisdom of such an action. In trying to settle my mind, I fear I've alarmed you and perhaps made you consider me an enemy. Allow me to assure you, nothing is further from the truth.*

In light of my recent difficulties, I hesitate to impose upon you again, but find I must. I hope I don't presume too much in stating that you will find what I have to impart of as much consequence as it is to me.

I beseech you for a meeting in person (and in private) that I might lay my case before you. I know I ask a great deal, but I give you my word of honor that you will in no way be subject to harm or duress of any kind.

If you are so good as to accede to my request, you may write the time and place of our meeting on the back of this card and I will receive the message.

Your most humble servant,

Dougal Balgaire

Card in hand, Amethyst leaned against the garage door, baffled, surprised and more curious than ever. On one hand, Balgaire's persistence finally made sense. On the other, what the hell did he have to say that he thought was so important—and that he didn't want to say in front of Jas?

She paced partway up the front walk and back. Balgaire put his request for a meeting in terms of a plea, but after everything Jas had done to him, here he was— *again*. If she ignored or refused this appeal, history suggested that whatever was going on would only escalate. And if it did escalate, she had a bad feeling Jas' restraint wouldn't last.

Dammit! Why couldn't these wizards just leave her alone? She flicked the card with a fingernail and rubbed her forehead. The most reasonable course was to just deal with Balgaire and get it over with. Sure, he could promise all day that he wouldn't do anything, but words were cheap…

She stared at the card, narrowing her eyes. Words might be cheap, but she could find out what lay behind them.

She didn't like working magic where anyone could see her, but damned if she'd take an encorcelled card into the house, inside her wards. Slipping the rest of the mail under the garage door's weatherstripping, she held the card in both hands and reached for the magic.

It was a subtle thing, not so much a spell as opening her wizard's senses to the energy surrounding and permeating the card. Impressions of those who had handled it flitted past, too brief and casual to leave much impression. The one who had written and cast a spell on it, however, was a whole different matter.

An aura of determination and desperation muttered like a distant thunderstorm, and a wish almost audible: *She must believe me. She must.* And, crackling in the background...fear.

Amethyst withdrew from the magic and stared at the card a little longer. Of course, the aura she sensed could be another spell meant to deceive. Only one thing convinced her it wasn't: the fear emanating from it.

She turned the card to the blank side, conjured a pen to her hand and clicked it, thinking.

Meet me at the dog park at Eubank and I-40, she finally wrote. *Half an hour.*

Touching a thought to the card, she reduced it to a burst of bright white light and a column of superheated air.

CHAPTER 20

Crash and Burn

Balgaire's red Caddy sat in the lot near the dog park and softball diamonds. Amethyst did her best to ignore her suddenly dry mouth and the increase in her heart rate.

'In private' be damned. She should've brought Jas. She set her jaw. No, she shouldn't. Oh, he'd back her up, no question about that. But running to him for help—*again?* The thought made her cringe. It seemed so…what? Weak? Presumptuous? Or maybe she was afraid of setting some kind of precedent. Or taking advantage of him. Or putting *him* in danger, too.

She pushed her hands deeper in her coat pockets and tucked her chin into her collar. Too late now. If Balgaire decided to try something, he'd have more than just Amethyst to contend with. He'd also have to shield his actions from all the cars passing on the freeway and on Eubank, not to mention the people at the park.

The man himself stood chatting, naturally, with a couple of young, attractive women at the small dog park. Poor Heather. Amethyst shook her head and sauntered over to the fence around the big dog park.

Balgaire shortly detached himself from his impromptu fan club and made his way over to join her.

"Miss Rey, I'm grateful—" he began.

Amethyst held up a hand. "I hope so, because I'm beyond uncomfortable about meeting you like this."

"Of course. I understand. I've made a botch of our meetings so far, especially the last. For that I most humbly apologize."

She wasn't about to say it was okay. "What did you expect to accomplish?"

He looked out over the dog park. "I knew what you're capable of. I knew what I'd heard of you. What I didn't know is what sort you are. If you were ruthless or kind, trustworthy or not. Before I spoke to you, I needed to find out."

So Jas was right. Balgaire had been testing her. "So what, exactly, are you afraid of, Mr. Balgaire?"

His head snapped around to stare at her.

She smiled a little. "You didn't think I'd take your assurances of safe conduct at face value, did you? I might be young, but I learned pretty quickly that wizards aren't to be trusted."

He sighed. "Alas, I fear you're right. So you might be willing to forgive me for my own mistrust."

She grunted, pushed off the fence and started walking along the narrow strip of park between the softball diamonds and the parking lot. "I guess that depends on your motives."

"I've told you before, I mean you no harm. But there

are others who might."

"Tell me something I don't already know." She laughed humorlessly. "Ironic, isn't it, that the same wizards whose power I returned see me as a threat."

"A threat," he said. "Or a prize."

Amethyst wheeled away, pulling magic with her.

Balgaire held up his hands. "No, no. Not me. I've no wish to hold a tiger on a leash."

She kept her distance, magic humming and crackling around her. "Then what are you talking about?"

"Stand down, lass. I can't think when you're about to blaze away at me."

"Good. Don't think. Just talk."

He lowered his hands, keeping them loose and unthreatening at his sides. That didn't mean he couldn't still wield the magic, of course, but she supposed it was meant to put her at ease. She knew better.

"There's a man in the east gathering power," he said. "He's already begun meddling in the affairs of ordinary folk. I found myself curious about his aims, and quickly discovered he'll brook no other wizard within his reach, unless it's as a servant. I've no mind to be any man's servant, so I hied me away."

She let go the magic, but didn't relax. "So what does it have to do with me?"

Although she had a sinking feeling it would eventually have to do with her.

"I've seen his like before. Their greed and ambition know no bounds, and they'll gobble all before them until they're stopped. The drake laird was one, devouring the power of every wizard with the misfortune to cross his path."

Great. Another predator. Or maybe this one was a dark lord. *Sweet Mary in Heaven*, she thought. *Save us.*

"And you—" Balgaire glanced down at her. "You're powerful enough to have vanquished the drake laird."

"Please," she said. "Please tell me you don't expect me to stop this eastern guy."

"I'd never presume so much." He bowed. "I offer you my aid, should you find yourself in need. I'll stand behind you, a staunch ally, a steadfast compatriot."

Seriously? "Look, Mr. Balgaire, to be perfectly honest, I'm not convinced of your staunchness and steadfastness." *Much less of your trustworthiness.*

"Aye," he said. "Aye, I've given you no cause to. But give me the chance to prove myself."

It wasn't a proposition, but still, it was ironic. She'd spent her adult and young adult life attracting close to zero male interest. Now these powerful men courted her.

"Where have I heard that one before?" she muttered. "If you're asking for friendly coexistence, I don't think it's out of the question. But under the circumstances, anything more isn't likely."

"The circumstances being your liaison with Mr. Harker."

She didn't bother replying to that.

He walked in silence a few steps. "I won't say he isn't formidable, but he'll not serve you in stead of another wizard, should you face that sort of threat."

Amethyst wasn't sure whether to laugh or give a

shout of triumph. "Between the two of us, I think Jas and I can handle most what we might run into."

"Perhaps," he said. "But before you dismiss me, ask yourself this—what's a man like that wanting with a lass like you?"

She felt like he'd punched her in the gut. Hadn't she just made the same observation? She walked in silence, trying to catch her breath, trying to calm down enough to make a reply.

"What business is it of yours?" she finally said.

He shrugged. "None, I suppose. But if you'll forgive me for sayin', you're young, and attention from such a quarter can be flattering."

"Do you usually insult people when you're trying to persuade them?"

"Ah, now, I mean no insult. I only urge caution. I've known a good lot of men of his sort, and they've usually a knack for attending to their own interests."

"Oh, but not you," she said sweetly.

"Aye," he said. "I'm doing no less. But you're in no doubt of it, now, are you?"

Her stomach hurt. Why had she ever agreed to talk to this man?

"No, no doubt at all. Thanks for the warning, Mr. Balgaire. Feel free to contact me if you learn anything else about your eastern wizard. But otherwise…" She turned to face him, detesting him so much at that moment she could barely keep from cursing him—literally as well as in the ordinary sense. "…best of luck in your future endeavors."

"Miss Rey—"

She turned her back on him and stalked off, only just managing to keep herself from running.

This is ridiculous, Amethyst told herself. *Why are you so upset? It's blindingly obvious he's trying to drive a wedge between you and Jas. He has been from the beginning.*

She walked fast along Eubank, head down and hands stuffed deep in her jacket pockets. Traffic moved past in an ebb and flow of noise, the rush of tires on pavement, the rumble and whine of engines.

Of course she knew what Balgaire was up to. It didn't change the fact that he'd asked exactly the same question she herself had asked Dad: *Why me?*

She swallowed the queasy feeling in her gut and forced herself to think. Did she really still believe Jas was playing a part?

No. He might be a charmer, he might be wily, but if he was playing a part, he'd have to slip up sometime. And what she'd sensed in him the more time they spent together was *more* honesty and sincerity, not less. *Unless he's deceiving himself,* a nasty little voice whispered.

She didn't have an answer for that.

"Forget about that," she muttered. "That's not what's really important here."

Not in the big picture, anyway. And the big picture was worrisome.

J as smiled when he read the thank-you card that had come in the afternoon's mail. Amethyst was glad to see it. In another minute or two, he wasn't going to be smiling.

He laid it aside and raised his mug to her. "Well done."

He'd brought home take-out from Pei Wei, which was the next best thing to P.F. Chang's. Cartons and little sauce cups and take-out trays littered the table, and the lingering aroma of Asian food filled the air. Caramela lay on the floor at her feet, sniffing hopefully.

Amethyst gave a startled laugh. "Me? You're the one who kept the little girl from being traumatized."

"Then let's say we make a good team," he said.

About that...

She smiled and blew on her tea to cool it, jasmine-scented steam swirling around her face. "Yeah, we do. So I need to tell you what I found out today."

Jas' smile disappeared. "Oh?"

She took a sip of tea and steeled herself. "I talked to Balgaire this afternoon."

"You did *what?*"

Amethyst held up a hand. "It's okay. We met at the dog park. There were a lot of people around."

Jas sat silent for a long, dreadful moment. "As you once pointed out to me," he finally said in a dangerously even voice, "with the right kind of spell, no one would see anything."

She knew him well enough by now to know when he assumed that glassy calm, he was very angry indeed.

"I know," she said, hanging onto her own calm. "But

it would take power and attention to do it, which would put him at a disadvantage."

He put his hands flat on the table. "I went to the trouble of warning the man off, and you go to meet him."

"Yes. He sent a note asking to talk to me. I figured if he was still pestering me after what you did, he wasn't going to stop."

"Did it ever occur to you to consult with me?"

She bristled. "What do you think?"

He stared at her. It took all her will to meet that chill, black gaze.

"What was I supposed to do?" she said. "Call and ask your permission?"

"This isn't about permission. It's about common sense."

"Yeah? And if I told you what I planned and why I thought it was a good idea, you would've just said okay."

"I can't tell you what I'd say, since you declined to honor me with your confidence."

"The reason I didn't," she said, "is you would've gone down there determined to put the fear of God into him and blown your cover. And since you won't even let me tell you what he told me, you don't have any idea how bad a mistake that would've been."

He gave a negligent little wave. "By all means, tell me."

She found her hands clenched around her mug and made an effort to relax them. "There's some guy back East playing dark lord—throwing his weight around with everyone from civilians to other wizards. Balgaire managed to get crossways with him. Not our problem, but he might end up making it our problem."

"Ah," Jas said. "I assume he applied to you for refuge or protection."

"Pretty much."

"'Pretty much,'" he repeated. "What did he want exactly?"

Heat crept up her neck to her face. "It doesn't matter. More Balgaire BS. But at least we know now why he was so persistent."

"Amethyst, you're learning to dissemble with the best of them."

She narrowed her eyes. "Look, don't you think I knew you'd be mad? I'm sorry if you don't agree, but I did what I thought was best under the circumstances. You're not my dad, you're not my boss, and in case you haven't noticed, this is the twenty-first century, not the nineteenth."

"You're the one who said you like me to behave like a gentleman. Do you think gentlemen only open doors and hold coats?"

"I guess they also make sure women keep quiet and out of sight, right?"

"No. They protect those they care about."

That struck her silent. She groped for an apology.

Jas stood. "I have some business in California I've put off for far too long. Since you seem to have everything under control here, I'll go home and pack."

She felt like he'd slapped her. And for what? For daring to try to solve her own problems?

"Fine." She stood and began cleaning up the remains of dinner, not looking at him.

He picked up his coat and satchel and walked out without another word.

CHAPTER 21

Boys Will Be Boys

The phone rang. Amethyst punched the mute button on the TV remote and jumped up to answer it. *Mama*, the screen read with a photo of her standing at the kitchen sink, smiling over her shoulder.

Disappointment crashed down on her. Amethyst dropped her outstretched hand and left the call to roll over to voicemail. No way could she talk to Mama now. She couldn't talk to *anyone* right now.

She dropped back onto the sofa and put her head in her hands. Caramela hopped up beside her and snuggled close, snuffling in her ear.

Amethyst put an arm around the dog. "I'm in trouble," she whispered. "I'm not supposed to feel this way. Why did I ever let it get so far?"

She could call Jas. She *should* call him.

And tell him what? Sorry for behaving like a competent adult? Sorry I hurt your manly pride and found out something you couldn't?

"The hell with that," she growled.

If that was the kind of relationship he wanted, he'd

have to find it somewhere else. *She* damn sure wasn't going to be the subservient little woman.

She straightened and sniffed, wiping her eyes with the heel of one hand. Deliberately, she turned the sound back on and sat back to continue watching her show.

What happened in it, she couldn't begin to say.

✦ ✦ ✦ ✦ ✦ ✦

A day passed, then two. Saturday came. Still nothing. Amethyst scrubbed the kitchen sink with ferocious vigor. Cleaning was something she did when she was too upset to do anything else. The house was absolutely sparkling, the carpet vacuumed to within an inch of its life, every dead leaf and weed removed from the yard, the windows gleaming with unimpeded late winter sunlight.

The simplest, most reasonable thing was to just call Jas and talk it out. How many times did she find her phone in her hand, her finger poised over the icon with his picture, to do just that?

And what then? Go back to the delicate dance they'd been doing, Amethyst allowing herself to be lured on, step by reluctant step?

What does a man like that want with a woman like you?

She turned on the water and wrung the sponge until her knuckles turned white.

She put zero faith in anything Balgaire said. But even he'd seen enough to ask the question, as insulting as it might've been. And the answer crouched black and troll-like under the shadow of her heart.

She threw the sponge into the sink, snatched up a dishtowel and dried her hands. Scooping her phone off the countertop, she tapped the text message icon.

Do you want to talk? she tapped in.

She backed out of the screen without sending the message. Did *she* want to talk?

She flicked a stray strand of hair off her face. Maybe she'd dodged a bullet. If she felt this bad now, what would happen if she let herself fall in love with him?

The phone was sweaty in her grip. Her stomach hurt. Well, that might be because she'd hardly been eating lately.

She had to do something. Resolve this one way or the other. This limbo of silence wasn't doing a damned thing.

She went back to the text message screen.

Hope your trip went well, she thumbed in. **Let me know what you want to do…**

She stopped, deleted part of the sentence.

Let me know if you want me to come into the office, she re-typed.

She pushed 'send.'

Pain exploded in her gut. Amethyst dropped her phone and doubled over, clutching her middle, her breath gone. Another lightning bolt of pain cracked across her ribs. She gasped, yanked up her shirt to see what was hurting her.

Nothing. Smooth, perfect skin. What the—?

Shit! The link!

She wasn't hurting—Jas was. Something was happening to him, and she felt it through the link between them.

Adrenaline burst through her in an icy rush. More pain struck the next instant, this time in the small ribs of her back. Caramela leapt to her feet and scrambled to Amethyst, whining. Amethyst clenched her jaw on a whine of her own and forced her wizard's senses open.

There was the link, a transparent cord that writhed and twisted through the magical ether. She wound her power around it, grabbed the magic and willed herself to the other end of the link—to Jas.

She blinked back into existence in a parking lot. And there, on the asphalt in front of her, were Jas and Balgaire, rolling around like two cats in a bag.

Amethyst stared, shocked. Balgaire was on top of Jas, Jas with one leg hooked over Balgaire's, the other driving into the bigger man's groin. They grunted, elbows pumping as each struggled to get in a good punch on the other. Jas, his teeth bared, his black hair wild, head-butted Balgaire. Balgaire roared and swung, catching Jas on the jaw.

An echo of the fireworks Jas must've felt burst in Amethyst's head. She yelled, scrabbled for the magic and sent a shock of electricity crackling over the men. They yelped and stiffened. Of course, so did Amethyst, since she got to feel *that* pain, too. Then they went back to pummeling each other.

She didn't remember moving, but she suddenly had hold of Balgaire's long hair, hauling on it for all she was worth while she kneed him in the ribs. Snarling, he knocked her away with a sweep of his arm. She hit the asphalt hard. Loose pebbles drove into her flesh and her breath went out in a whoosh.

Gasping for breath, Amethyst scrambled to her feet.

"Stop it, *STOP!*" she shouted.

That seemed to finally get through to them. Cursing, Jas gave Balgaire a shove. Balgaire shoved off of him. Jas rolled to his feet, raked a hand through his hair and began trying to put his torn, dirty clothes to rights with sharp, angry tugs.

Amethyst stood trembling with fury and reaction.

"What the *hell* do you think you're doing?" she shouted at both of them. "And you!" She glared at Balgaire. "I can damn sure see why that guy back East has it in for you. You're nothing but trouble!"

"I'm not the one who started this!" he shouted back, blood running from his nose down his chin to splotch the front of his shirt. One eye was swelling shut, too. "Here I am, mindin' me own business—"

"You know what, Balgaire?" she cut in. "I don't want to hear it. I already told you to leave my friends alone."

"As did *I,*" Jas added, slapping grit off his pants.

She glared at him. Was *that* was this was about? Oh, for—

She swung back to Balgaire. "*We* are leaving. If you have the sense God gave a sack of potatoes, you will too."

She stormed past him, giving him a look that dared him to try anything. Whatever he saw in her face made him shut his mouth and step back.

Seizing Jas by the arm, she shaped the magic and zapped them both back into her kitchen. Caramela jumped up barking.

Trembling now with the aftereffects of using a spell that powerful twice in a row—once with a passenger—Amethyst stomped out of the kitchen and down the hall. In the bathroom, she dug bandages, disinfectant, gauze pads and tape out of the medicine cabinet. She snagged a couple of clean rags out of the linen closet as she went back down the hall.

Jas stood at the kitchen sink, running water over his scraped, bruised knuckles. Caramela stood behind him, a dark line down her back and her tail wagging stiffly.

He looked a sight. His waffle Henley shirt was full of grit and oil, ripped over the elbows and stretched out over the shoulders. His lip was bleeding and a reddish lump was rising on his jaw. Her own jaw throbbed, so she knew it hurt.

"Are you crazy?" Amethyst plunked the first aid stuff on the counter. "Brawling in a parking lot like a fifteen-year-old! What's the matter with you? What if he'd used magic on you?"

"He'd've had an unpleasant surprise," Jas said.

"Gah!" She smacked her forehead. "You're supposed to be under my protection! What the *hell* are you doing picking fights?"

He gave a thin smile. "What's sauce for the goose is sauce for the gander."

"Fine. We're even. Happy now?"

She opened the freezer and rummaged for an ice pack. She also pulled out a bag of frozen peas and one of corn for good measure.

"Here." She shoved the cold bags at Jas. "Take off

your shirt. I need to look at the damage. And I don't want dirt all over my furniture."

He cast her a baleful look. "I'm perfectly capable of taking care of myself."

She crossed her arms and gave him a look back. "You can't heal your own wounds."

"I'm fine." He turned away.

She wanted to throttle him. "I beg to differ. In case it didn't occur to you, *I'm* suffering from your testosterone-fueled antics."

He gave her an appalled look. "Oh."

He began struggling to get his shirt off.

"Yeah, 'oh.'" She walked over, grabbed the hem and pulled it up. "Bend over."

He did as she ordered. She got the shirt off and dropped it on the floor. He carefully lowered himself onto one of the dining room chairs.

He had a bad case of road rash on his back. Bruises marked the pale skin over his ribs and stomach. His elbows, besides being scraped, were also bruised.

She got down a bowl from a cupboard, splashed a little disinfectant into it and filled it with warm water. Jas' breath hissed through his teeth when she set about cleaning his scrapes. Fortunately, she didn't pick up the echo of that pain. Either he'd done something to block it, or the pain had to be from something that caused real damage.

He held the icepack to his jaw. Ignoring the weakness from the two spells of transference, Amethyst knelt by his chair, closed her eyes and reached for the magic.

She could see the swirl and pulse of pain and bruising, but it mostly looked superficial. An electric quiver in one rib suggested it might be cracked. She laid gentle hands over his hurts and smoothed magic into them, easing the throb of swelling, soothing the battered tissue of bruises.

The pain referred through the link eased. She sank down onto her heels and let go the magic.

Tremors ran through her. She took a long breath then another, trying to still them, but couldn't. She sank further, put out an arm to catch herself.

"Amethyst!" Jas caught her arms and lowered her to the floor.

Caramela whined and snuffled her. Footsteps moved across the floor, then Jas was propping her up. She blinked up into his scowling face.

He held a glass to her lips. "I'm obviously not the one who's lost my mind. What are you thinking? Why did you work a healing if those transport spells drained you so much?"

She sipped orange juice. "Because I hurt, dammit!" There was no strength in her voice.

"Drink the juice."

She grunted and swallowed the rest.

"Was that the only reason you came?" he said.

The way Jas held her, she couldn't see his face without twisting around, but she could feel the tension in his arm and body.

"I came," she said, "because you were hurt! D'you think just because I'm mad at you I'll ignore it when something's happening to you?"

She was getting mad now. She struggled to push away from him.

His arm tightened around her. "What are you doing? Lie still."

"Like hell! If that's what you think of me, just leave me alone. I don't need your help."

"That's fairly obvious."

The support of his arm abruptly disappeared and he stood. She barely caught herself on her elbows.

She struggled to push herself up. When that didn't work, she rolled onto one arm, trying to get her feet under her.

Jas heaved a sigh. "For godsake, Amethyst. This is ridiculous."

He knelt again, gathered her into his arms and picked her up. He grunted, and a wave of pain overflowed into her.

"Dammit, Jas! You're hurting yourself!"

"You've lost weight," he commented between short, shallow breaths.

He carried her into the living room and deposited her on the couch. The landing was a little rough because he couldn't bend quite enough. He pushed himself awkwardly to his feet on the arm of the sofa and went back into the kitchen. A few minutes and much clattering later, he returned with a several sandwiches, a banana and a pile of peanut butter cookies.

"Eat." He eased himself down onto the edge of the coffee table, sitting unnaturally straight.

She ate the banana first, then picked up a sandwich. It was peanut butter and jelly cut in little triangles.

She eyed it and took a bite. "Thank you, Mommy."

"Amethyst, I'm angry too. Don't provoke me."

She took another bite instead of saying what came to mind. She ate the other three quarters of the sandwich, then started on the cookies.

"I don't know why you're so mad," she said to the third cookie.

"Don't you?"

She crunched the rest of the cookie. "Okay," she said. "I knew I should've told you I was going to meet Balgaire." She picked up another cookie. "But I was afraid—"

He waited, but she ate the cookie, still avoiding his eye.

"Afraid of what?" he finally said.

"I don't know! Of something like what you did today."

"And that's all."

"No, that's not all. Telling you just seemed..." She gave an angry shrug. "It seemed wrong. For a lot of reasons."

"In other words, you were working hard to justify it to yourself," he said. "How would you feel if the situation were reversed?"

"You mean like today?" she shot back.

He grinned, then winced when it pulled his cut lip. "I suppose you're right. But there was a certain amount of satisfaction to it."

"Guys are stupid. *I* went to meet Balgaire because I didn't want the problem to get worse. *You* went to see him so you could see how bad it could get."

She reached for another sandwich. He caught her hand.

"I *don't* think you came to my rescue only out of self-interest. I'm sorry I said that. I saw when you dropped on Balgaire like an infuriated sparrow hawk." He handed her a triangle of sandwich. "But after days of not hearing a word from you, I was angry."

Several responses leapt to her lips, none of them particularly gracious. She stuffed a bite of sandwich in her mouth instead, then sighed.

"I'm sorry, too. I didn't mean to hurt you." She took another bite. "But I didn't hear a word from *you*, either."

"To be perfectly honest, my reaction caught me by surprise. I don't generally get that angry." He gave a rueful laugh. "We'll have to be careful to avoid such misunderstandings. In the future, let's make sure we get to the bottom of the problem before either of us goes storming off. Deal?" He offered his hand.

A smile tugged at her lips. She put her hand in his. "Deal."

But a little worm of uneasiness crawled through her gut. How could she ever begin to address the black heart of her doubt?

CHAPTER 22

Moment of Truth

"So, are you going for the sexy-scruffy look?" Amethyst said, studying Jas. "Or are your growing your beard to match that lovely black and blue creeping across your jaw?"

They'd met for dinner at Sandiago's. She was curious to see how much her healing had progressed since yesterday. The bruise she could see didn't look any better, but Jas was moving more normally today.

"It started out as camouflage," he said. "But if you think it's sexy, I might change my mind."

"It's sexy until you start kissing. Then I'm here to tell you, beard-burn really kills the mood."

He cocked an eyebrow. "I'm sure there's a spell for that."

"Mmm," she said, trying not to follow that thought to its logical conclusion.

The restaurant's windows looked out over Albuquerque, a glittering carpet unrolling to the west. A string of jewels marked the freeway where it spilled out of Tijeras Canyon and threaded to the West Mesa.

The waiter in a bright tropical-print shirt brought chips and salsa. Amethyst dipped up a bite of pico de gallo.

"I got your text," Jas said.

Crunching a corn chip, she frowned. "I didn't—"

Crap. Yes she had. Just before she'd zapped herself into the middle of Jas and Balgaire's fight.

"Did you truly believe I might not want to see you again?" he said.

She chased a jalapeño with a piece of chip. "It seemed like it at the time."

"No," he said. "Don't ever think so."

The sincerity on his face made her heart squeeze. She ducked her head. "I'll try."

"I'm not trying to reopen a subject we've already resolved. I simply want to know you're certain on that point. I did indeed have business to take care of last week, and I expect to be tied up with more of the same for some days to come. If I'm not able to call, I don't want you to be uneasy."

If her heart had squeezed before, it positively wrenched now. How many men would stop to think how a woman would interpret their silence?

"Thank you, Jas."

"I'd like to make it up to you, though. I thought you might enjoy a Jane Austen film festival. What do you think?"

"Are you kidding? I'd love it!"

He smiled one of his special smiles. "Good. I'll call you next week and let you know when and where."

"I can't wait." And that was the literal truth.

'When' turned out to be the next Friday night. 'Where' was Jas' house in the foothills.

"Bring Caramela," he told her. "There are a lot of movies."

A little flutter of something went through her—excitement or nervousness, Amethyst couldn't say.

Not that she hadn't been to Jas' house before—she had a few times. But somehow, this felt special. Then again, it was probably just her imagination. You didn't usually bring the dog along on Special Dates.

Still, she stood in front of her closet, agonizing just as much over what to wear this time as she had on that first date. Her hand hovered over the same silk top she'd worn to Santa Fe. *No.* She shook her head. She wasn't sure why, but wearing that didn't seem right. She settled on a knit boat neck top and black cords.

Sandia Heights, where Jas lived, was one of the fancier areas of town, sandwiched between Tramway Boulevard and the Sandia Open Space. The roads, un-bordered by sidewalks, wound among bouldered slopes. Big, architectural-showcase homes sat well back from the road, screened by the native vegetation of junipers and branched cholla cactus and piñon pines.

Amethyst parked her Outback on Jas' stamped concrete driveway. Caramela hopped out when she opened the car door and immediately went sniffing. This close to the mountains, her nose was no doubt treated to a banquet of smells—rabbits, coyotes, deer, maybe even bear.

Amethyst called the dog and walked up a flagstone walk to Jas's courtyard gate. Tucking Caramela's bed under one arm, she pushed the call button on the intercom. The lock clicked and Amethyst pushed the gate open.

Its rustic boards stood in contrast to the house itself, which was all glass and stacked sandstone and sharp angles. A water feature burbled in one corner of the courtyard. Tall Mexican jars held winter-brown grasses and vines, their forms and seed heads still attractive even while dormant.

Amethyst stepped up onto the flagstone-paved porch and touched the door latch. One door, nine feet of solid birch, swung open on pivots rather than hinges. The tiled foyer was empty, as was the bit of living room she could see through the archway ahead.

"Jas?" she called.

"In here."

She followed the sound of his voice across the foyer to the living room, Caramela trotting ahead. A fascinating combination of smells met her own nose: fresh-baked bread, onions, chicken, and others less identifiable.

She stepped through the archway into the living room and stopped short.

Lit by the coppery light of sunset through the windows behind him, Jas stood near the kiva fireplace. But this wasn't the Jas Harker she knew. This man was dressed in a double-breasted coat in a deep, rich green with a high collar, wide lapels and tails. Under it he wore a green and gold paisley satin waistcoat, high-waisted trousers and...ohmigod...a cravat. Not the kind of sissy-looking rich-guy cravat like she'd seen at the party. No, this was a for-real cravat, folded, knotted and spilling in elegant ruffles over his collar.

She became aware that she stood there, opening and closing her mouth with nothing coming out. Finally, she caught her breath.

"Holy crap, Jas!" she squeaked then shut her mouth again, heat rushing into her face.

He bowed and advanced on her. "May I take your coat, Miss Rey?"

She nodded dumbly, dropped Caramela's bed and let him help her out of her coat. He offered his arm. She stammered some more and laid her hand on it. He led her to the sofa and seated her.

"Would you care for a glass of wine?"

"Um…yea—I mean, yes, please."

He poured wine from a cut crystal decanter on a table and offered her a glass. She'd never been in so much need of a glass of wine in her life.

He smoothly flipped his coattails out of the way and seated himself near her, so splendid she had trouble looking at him. She peeked anyway to be sure this gorgeous stranger really was Jas, and yes, there were the mismatched brows, the same dark eyes, the black hair brushing his high collar.

She took a sip of wine. She was no connoisseur, but she could tell this one was excellent, rich and smooth as cello music.

She felt grossly underdressed. On the other hand, an empire waist appropriate for the period would've looked like crap on her, so on the whole, she'd rather be underdressed.

Silence stretched, broken only by the crackling of the fire in the fireplace.

"Are you well, Miss Rey?" he asked.

"Other than feeling like I'm orbiting too close to the sun, yes, fine, thank you."

He laughed, and he was suddenly just Jas again. "I certainly don't mean to intimidate you."

She managed to actually look at him this time. "If you get any handsomer, I'm going to pass out."

"That won't do at all." He stretched his arm behind her and leaned close. "We have a long night ahead of us."

Her insides quivered. "You cad."

"I beg your pardon."

The sun sank below the horizon and city lights began to sparkle out. A wire crescent moon floated above the last glow of sunset. The view out Jas' windows was as spectacular as it had been from the restaurant.

She was beginning to get used to Jas dressed like a Regency gentleman. She eyed the intricate folds and knot of his cravat. "So, do those things come pre-tied?"

A teasing gleam came into his eyes. "No."

Did she really want to know? "You learned how to tie it from a YouTube video, right?"

"No," he said again.

"Oh." She bit her lip. "Does that knot have a name?"

"It was called the Cascade." He watched her. "Does it bother you?" He wasn't talking about the cravat.

What, you mean the fact that you're at least a couple hundred years older than I am? "With you sitting there looking like that, right now it's kinda cool."

"Good."

"Did you have to beat the women off with a stick then, too?"

He almost choked on his wine. "Once or twice." After a moment, he added, "I don't have any sticks at hand tonight."

She grinned.

"Shall we dine?" he said and rose, offering his arm again.

He led her through another archway into the dining room, then pulled out her chair. Amethyst could count on one hand the number of times a man had done that for her, and she had yet to get the knack of sinking into the chair just as the gentleman slid it in.

The dining room table was covered with an incredible array of dishes. Two place settings lay at one end. The linen tablecloth, actual silver silverware and china looked like meticulously preserved antiques. The china was painted with delicate, cream-colored roses.

Amethyst let out a wondering breath. She felt like Beauty at the Beast's castle. Well, okay, except the roles were reversed in this case.

Thankfully, the couple doing the catering was dressed in normal, 21st century clothes. After serving the soup, they disappeared into the kitchen.

Jas described the food, filling Amethyst's plate with her choices. The gesture seemed strangely intimate.

"I avoided some of the more exotic dishes," he said.

"I didn't think you'd appreciate calf's foot jelly and pigeon pie."

"Ick. No."

It grew quiet as they ate, the only sounds the tinkle of silverware on china, the occasional snatch of conversation between the caterers in the kitchen.

She looked at the magnificent dinner in front of her, at Jas, sitting by her in his magnificent clothes and thought, *He did all this…for me.*

She'd thought there might be something special about this date. She'd been right. But was it only what he'd said, making up for the days of angry silence? Or something more?

At the end of a leisurely dinner, they rose and Jas escorted her to his home theater, Caramela padding along behind.

He'd managed to decorate so it looked like a comfortable room and not like a church to worship the TV. Of course, an enormous flat-panel TV and speakers tucked into *nichos* dominated one wall, but the sofa and lounges and ottomans were plump and plush and upholstered in fabric in inviting dark gold and terra cotta and burnt orange. The bank of clerestory windows that ran above the TV showed black rectangles of night sky.

Amethyst studied them. "Those would look good with stained glass. Maybe a theme that ran from one window to the next. You could put spotlights behind them so you could see them at night, too."

Jas seemed unusually pleased by the idea. "Why don't you work up a design sometime, if you like?"

As he had earlier, he seated her with a bow, then sat beside her, once again flipping his tails out of the way with a practiced movement. Amethyst sank into the cushions. They were just as soft and comfy as they looked. Caramela circled on her bed and settled with a sigh.

Amethyst glanced aside at Jas. "Not that I'm eager to spoil the view or anything, but you don't have to leave the coat and cravat on for me. I wouldn't expect it if you were in a suit and tie."

Besides, he'd probably still look awesome in the waistcoat and shirt.

He heaved a sigh. "I'm forever in your debt."

He stood, took off the coat and carefully draped it over the back of a lounge. Then he began unwinding the cravat, what looked like yards of fabric. And yes, that wonderful paisley waistcoat and the full-sleeved linen shirt looked pretty damned good all by themselves.

Sitting down once more, he picked up the remote. Amethyst almost laughed at the picture that made: *Regency Gentleman with Television Remote.* The screen lit up and music swelled from the surround-sound speakers.

"Oh!" she said. "The BBC *Pride and Prejudice.* My favorite!"

Jas settled back and put his arm around her. "I thought it might be. Besides being the most historically accurate, it's also the version truest to the novel."

As much as she'd been excited by the idea of a Jane Austen film festival, it was suddenly hard to relax and enjoy the movie. She was acutely conscious of Jas beside her, his warmth, his scent, the feel of him against her, the weight of his arm around her.

She couldn't hear the caterers cleaning up after dinner, but they must be. How long would they take? Would she and Jas know when they left?

More to the point, why did it matter? That was a thought she didn't want to examine too closely.

She couldn't look at him without being obvious, but Jas seemed relaxed, content to enjoy the movie with her tucked against his side. Her awkwardness dwindled.

It was getting so hard to continue fighting herself, to fight what she wanted to feel for this man. After tonight, she didn't know if she could. Worse still, she didn't know if she wanted to. No matter how much it might hurt in the end.

Sighing, she nestled more comfortably into the couch and leaned her head on his chest. It felt surprisingly easy and natural.

His chest rose and fell with a long breath and he pressed a kiss to her hair. It seemed just as natural to turn her head to offer a kiss of her own. The cringe-worthy moments in the movie when Elizabeth Bennet's family make a spectacle of themselves at the Netherfield ball faded. There was only Jas drawing her to him, his arm curving behind her neck, his mouth capturing hers.

She breathed in the desert scent of him, tasted the lingering sweetness of the pomegranate wine they'd been sharing. Her hands slid over satin and firm muscle into the silk of his hair. He pressed her back into the yielding cushions of the couch, one hand molding her body from hip to breast, the other arm locking her tightly enough she couldn't pull back even if she wanted to. She didn't want to.

Fire sizzled through her and she raised one leg, hooking it over his hips. His hand followed the curve of her bottom to the back of her thigh, pulling her leg higher as he pushed his hips more firmly against hers. And oh, his weight on her, pinning her against the couch cushions, was indescribably delicious. Her own hands wandered down his back, over the waistband of his trousers and down.

He broke from her mouth long enough to look into her face, bent and kissed her deeply, then rose again. "Amethyst, make love to me."

Desire almost drowned her—all but for a seed of despair.

She let go a long sigh. "We might as well. Maybe you'll get it out of your system then."

Jas jerked back as if she'd slapped him. His eyes flashed.

"It isn't something to *get out of your system*." He sat up, pushed off the couch and stood, straightening his waistcoat. "You're right, Amethyst. This is never going to work."

She sat up too, pulled shaking fingers through her hair, tugged her top back into place. "You bet it won't work. Because I know what's going on here."

"What, exactly," he said in that level voice that was more ominous than any shouting, "do you think is going on?"

"Forget it. It doesn't matter." She stood, crossed the room.

He came and planted himself in front of her. "Don't tell me 'forget it.' Say what you mean. You're usually so good at that."

"Oh, so that's a fault now, is it? Well, where you're concerned, I can see how it would be."

She tried to go around him, but he stepped in front of her again.

"Don't change the subject," he said. "If you're going to accuse me of something, I expect you to have the decency to tell me what it is."

"You really want to know? Fine." Her voice shook. She ignored it. "The handsome lord of the manor descends from his marble halls to honor the dull little peasant girl with his attentions? I think we both know how *that* ends."

"Indeed I do. I'm old enough to remember that sort of thing. But there's something you apparently don't realize. The peasant girl in question would've been beautiful enough to catch the eye of one of the gentry. By your own reckoning, you aren't that. So what do you suppose I'm after?"

She clenched her fists, a flush of humiliation burning from collarbone to hairline. "Oh, come on. How dumb do you think I am? It's all about the thrill of the chase. Any woman you look at is all, 'Oh, yes, please!' But me? I'm the one to tell you no. The minute I say yes, you're done."

Something—realization or calculation—flashed across his face. He folded his arms. "You seem to think you know me quite well."

She folded her own arms, hugging herself. "I know a

rich, good-looking guy can only want one thing from somebody like me. I'd rather find out now instead of later, when—" *when I completely lose my heart to you.* She closed her mouth.

He pinned her with that dark gaze of his. "And it's my own fault you think that way, isn't it? My interest in you was too good to be true when we first met, and that's exactly how it turned out. No matter how hard we try to put that behind us, there's always that little doubt in the back of your mind—what I want. What I'm after."

She nodded once. "You got it."

"All right." He paced a step up, one back. "Do you want to know why I've pursued you ever since you decided to begin speaking to me again? Shall I tell you what I see in you?"

Her throat felt threateningly thick. She only shrugged.

He took a step closer, but still didn't touch her. "I see a woman with intelligence and talent, a woman with a sense of humor that catches me by surprise. A woman whose straightforwardness and honesty are like rain after a long drought. I see a woman who can challenge me, who keeps me on my toes, who insists on my best. A woman who understands me and can meet me on equal ground. One I can be myself around, and not rich, powerful Jas Harker, owner of Magus Corporation."

She swallowed hard. "And what about in a year, or five years, or ten? The novelty will have worn off. You'll decide I'm an uptight stick-in-the-mud, an oddball geek with the social skills of a box of Pop-Tarts and all the presence of a half-grown chicken. I'll be an embarrassment to be around."

The look he gave her was half disbelieving, half appalled. He turned aside and slashed a hand through his hair. "God *damn* it."

Amethyst flinched. Not at the curse—a lot of people used curses like seasoning. But at the fact that Jas, who never cussed in her presence, would say it.

He turned back. "I would love," he said, "to get my hands on the fellow who made you feel that way about yourself." His eyes blazed. "And thrash him to within an inch of his life."

She just stood with her mouth open.

He took her hands. "Amethyst. I'm not some young idiot led around by his libido, and you aren't a conquest— or a prize. I've been around a long time, long enough to know what I like and what I want. Do I want to go to bed with you? Of course I do, I won't lie about that. But if you truly want to get rid of me, that won't be the way to do it. The more I'm with you, the more I want to be with you. And once I've had you this way…" He raised a hand to trace her lip with his thumb, trail his fingers along her jawline and down her neck. "If you think I've pursued you doggedly before, wait until then."

At his touch, a shiver went through her. Jas was grand master of dazzling with bullshit. She might be the biggest fool west of the Pecos, but this didn't feel like bullshit. This felt like a man baring his soul. It felt like truth.

"So I suppose the question becomes," he said, "do you want to get rid of me?"

She squeezed her eyes closed and took what had to

be the biggest leap of faith in her entire life.

"No."

His grip on her hands tightened and a long breath went out of him. "Amethyst, will you let me do what I've wanted to for the last year and more?"

"You mean lure me into your evil clutches so you can have your way with me?" She meant to joke, but the unsteadiness of her voice betrayed her.

His lips curved in a wicked smile. "Exactly."

She gave a shaky laugh at that. Her insides were doing some interesting things when she thought about being in his evil clutches.

"Well…" She glanced at him from under her lashes. "Okay."

He cupped her face and kissed her, long and tenderly. "Then come with me."

CHAPTER 23

Evil Clutches

Jas took her hand and led her down a hallway that branched off from the entry foyer. Her heart beat hard enough to make her breath come short.

Amethyst had never been into this part of the house. A row of windows looked out onto the courtyard, lit here and there with soft lights. Jas opened a tall door at the end of the hall and led her into the room beyond.

Lights soft and low as candlelight illuminated a master bedroom suite. A huge bed piled with pillows stood under a sweeping bow of windows that rose from a knee wall all the way to the ceiling. Beyond the windows, the mountain rose, a dim bulk against a fringe of glittering sky.

The magic rippled, a *foomp* came, and a fire sprang to life in the fireplace on one wall, sending its red light flickering across the room.

The light sketched a reflection of her and Jas on the dark landscape outside. She saw him come up behind her, gather her hair and bend his head to kiss her neck. Then she closed her eyes and there was only sensation, the feel of his lips on her skin, the bulge of his arousal against the base of her spine, his hands gliding over her hips and up her waist, lifting her top as they went. She let him slip it off over her head then his fingers went to work, deft and smooth, on the button and zipper of her cords.

He slid them down, molding her legs with his hands as he went. She could feel his breath shake against her skin. Hers shook, too, a quiver that ran through her and wouldn't stop.

He stood again, tangled his fingers in her hair, circled her with his arm and crushed her to him, kissing her deeply, hungrily. She dug her fingers into the muscles of his shoulders. The air lay cool against her skin, the touch of his hands, his lips, his tongue spreading fire under it.

She didn't remember moving, didn't remember crossing the room, but he was suddenly pressing her down onto the bed. She reached to pull back the covers.

"No," he said. "I want to see you."

He stretched her out then stood over her, devouring her with his eyes from the crown of her head to the tips of her toes. She wriggled a little, heat climbing into her face from the heat of his gaze. His chest rose and fell quickly under the waistcoat and linen shirt and his erection strained against the tight, high-waisted trousers, and oh god, he looked so sexy like that, like some impossible romantic hero.

He sat on the edge of the bed beside her and ran his hands over her, caressing her breasts through her bra. She took hold of his arms, pulling at him.

"Shh," he said. "Lie still. Let me enjoy you like this first."

"Lie *still?*" Her voice cracked a little.

He laughed softly. "You promised to let me have my way with you."

She growled and squirmed but laid her hands back on the comforter.

His hands glided lower, over her belly. Lower, along the inside of her thighs, opening her legs. She shivered under his touch, her breath hitching. He turned back, unhooked her bra, pulled it away and lowered his mouth to her breast.

She arched into him, knotting her fingers in his hair. He gave a low growl of his own and slid his hand behind her back, lifting her, flicking her nipple against his teeth with his tongue. She gasped. There was something decadent about lying there in nothing but her panties while he bent over her fully clothed, the buttons of his waistcoat pressing against her bare skin, the satin sliding as he nuzzled and teased first one breast, then the other.

He kissed his way down her belly to the waistband of her panties, then ran his lips along the edge, his breath hot on her skin.

She giggled, half in ticklishness, half in nervous humor. "Do not tell me you're going to pull my panties down with your teeth. Just...don't."

He looked up, annoyance on his face. "Amethyst—" he began.

He stopped, grinned suddenly, then buried his face in her belly and bit at her, growling.

She squealed and doubled up, laughing, squirming to get away. He got her panties down to her knees, then off entirely, then transferred the bites to the insides of her thighs. That put an end to her fight, because it wasn't ticklish at all there.

She fell back onto the bed, groaning, clenching her fingers in the bedding as he nipped and kissed. One hand ran up her leg from calf to hip, the other teased a nipple. The sensations ran through her and all crashed together. She whimpered with need as he made his way back up her body with those same delicious little nips.

The pressure began to build when he turned his attention to her nipples once more. When he had her writhing again, he gave her neck the same treatment.

"Jas—" she gasped, pulling at him.

He sat up. "What?" he asked innocently.

"You know what." She sat up and started popping waistcoat buttons open. "Get it *off*."

He caught her fingers, kissed them, then slowly undid buttons, teasing her with his eyes. She lay back and watched him, trailing her fingers up and down his thigh.

"Did some gigs with Chippendales while you were at loose ends, huh?"

He snorted, shrugged out of the waistcoat and laid it across a chair. "Six-pack abs are a vulgar sign of vanity."

As he pulled the shirt off over his head, she had to agree. Flat, trim muscle was much more attractive. She ran her fingers down the strip of black hair on his chest. He gasped and caught her hand when it reached his waistband, then stood up out of reach and took care of those buttons, too.

The magic flickered and the lights went out, leaving

only the firelight to dance along the curves of shoulder and buttock and thigh, stroking the shadow of black hair. He pulled back the covers, slid her over and lay down beside her, slowly caressing up and down her body. Either the fire had warmed the room or he'd called warmth into the air, because she no longer noticed the coolness against her bare skin.

She stroked him in return, a little shy now that she'd had a chance to calm down. He slid his hand down her belly and into the heat between her legs, teasing and stroking. She forgot all about the shyness then. Kissing her again, he moved on top of her.

She gave a squeak when he entered her.

He stopped instantly. "All right?"

"It's…been a while," she admitted. Almost a year and a half. Since Talys.

"We'll take it slow, then."

He rocked gently against her, going deeper each time, the tightness giving way to luxurious fullness. She matched his rhythm and angled her hips until, oh! That was *nice*. She dug her fingers into his butt, pulling him closer.

He wound his fingers in her hair, nuzzling and nipping her neck, and god, how *good* that felt, the pressure of his mouth on the sensitive skin of her throat, his clever fingers teasing a nipple. Sighing, she arched and opened to him, abandoning herself to the feeling of him moving inside her, the little spangle of sensation at the end of each thrust. Heat began to build in her, a lazy, molten flow expanding outward.

Heat—and magic. It wrapped her with a tickling

warmth, like the touch of snowflakes in reverse, then gathered, swirling heavier, hotter, molding her skin with unbearable sensitivity, moving through her, in her, an ever-increasing pressure.

"Jas—" she gasped, gripping him as if to keep from being spun away. He took her face in his hands and kissed her, catching her lip in his teeth, tracing it with his tongue.

His hands moved to her bottom, lifted her so that each plunge sent a burst of heat straight to her center. She clutched him, little whimpers escaping her throat as the magic and pleasure threatened to tear her apart.

This was different. This wasn't the way she usually felt with a man.

"Let go, Amethyst," he whispered. "It's all right. Let go."

She closed her eyes and concentrated on what felt familiar. Sweet ripples of pleasure began to swell through her...

Then the magic exploded in her.

She spun together with Jas in it, waves of green and purple rising, twining, melding, surging upward. His pleasure as well as her own swept over her, more than she could hold until it burst past the edges of herself, leaving her blind in a whirl of amber-scented light, throbbing with the pulse of irresistible heat. She shuddered, every nerve quivering and exposed, the magic moving hot and wild through her. She couldn't resist it, didn't want to, helpless as it swept her along and finally plunged her into back into herself.

Jas lay atop her, panting, a slick of sweat between

them.

"Dear God, Amethyst," he murmured.

His hips still rocked against hers and his hands gripped her thighs as if he wasn't ready for it to be over. She nibbled and kissed along his shoulder to his neck, feeling exactly the same.

At last, he raised his weight off her. He held her face and kissed her slowly, deeply, again and again. Eyes closed, she smoothed his skin from shoulders to buttocks and back again, returning those leisurely kisses while the magic ebbed into caressing swells and the heat cooled.

He shifted to the side. She sighed, snuggled her head into the hollow of his shoulder and wrapped an arm around his waist as he trailed his fingers up and down her spine. Languid and content, she rested awhile.

"Was it good for you?" he teased at last, since it was abundantly obvious that it had been very good.

It seemed she should say something flip and teasing back, but she only hugged him tight, pressing her face to his shoulder. After a surprised instant, he hugged her just as tightly.

"I do love you so, Amethyst Rey," he said, his voice husky.

"What?" She pulled away a little. "Since when?"

He smoothed her hair. "Since…" He sighed. "Long before I had any right to."

"Why on earth didn't you *say* so?"

"Would you have believed me?"

She thought about it. "Maybe." She considered a little longer. "I think. Depends on when you said it."

He continued stroking her hair. "I tried hard not to love you. I didn't know if you could ever feel anything warm for me after what I did. Then I began to hope…"

She lay quiet in his arms for a moment. "After what you did," she finally said, "I tried not to, too."

"And now?"

"Now, I think I can stop trying not to love you."

He laughed. "That is the most backward declaration of love I've ever heard. But I'll take it."

CHAPTER 24

Amethyst and Jasper

Jas woke her with kisses before dawn. Through the bow of windows surrounding the bed, a vague, purple tumble of boulders rose against a slatey sky. It was like making love outside on the mountain. Only without the discomfort and inconvenience.

With Jas spooning her, one leg thrown over her hip, Amethyst slept again afterward, warm and pleasantly exhausted.

It was full light when she swam up out of sleep, comfortable in the cocoon of blankets and Jas' warmth and scent.

Outside, the sky was a flat white, white flakes whirling against the windows above her. The boulders hunched under patchy cloaks of snow, and snow clotted the saw-toothed yuccas and holly-like algerita growing between them.

"Oh!" she whispered.

Jas stirred and cracked an eye open. "It's snowing. Oh my. Whatever will we do all day?"

She pushed his leg off and wriggled out of his grasp.

"Take a shower and eat breakfast, to start with."

She pretended not to notice his gaze on her as she crossed to the bathroom.

She'd had other things on her mind last night, so she hadn't much noticed her surroundings. The bedroom was masculine with dark wood, leather and fabrics in a deep, warm grey with splashes of Jas' customary green, this one also deep and warm.

The bathroom was like stepping into an underwater grotto. Glass blocks surrounding the vanity mirrors let in a flood of pale light, and more glass blocks made one wall of the shower. The other two were tiled with glass in every shade of green, from peridot to emerald to turquoise, the same tiles spilling out of the shower and across the bathroom floor in a pattern of swirls. Under her bare feet, the tile was warm. She gave a sigh of appreciation. Jas did have very good taste.

She was puzzling over the extra faucet handles in the shower when Jas came up behind, reached past her and turned on the shower. Water came raining down from the shower ceiling.

"Oh!" she said again.

He urged her into the shower, stepped in behind her and shut the door. It was like standing in a hot downpour, utterly luxurious.

Jas took a bottle of shampoo from a niche in the wall, poured some into his palm, turned her and began massaging it into her scalp. The scents of lemon and sage curled around her. She sighed, closed her eyes and tilted her head back, ready to melt on the spot. After he rinsed the last of the suds out of her hair, she turned to repay the favor.

He pressed her back against the shower wall and planted his hands on either side of her shoulders. "*Now,* my dear, you'll never escape my clutches."

She giggled and opened her mouth to say something, maybe *Hell, no,* but he covered her mouth with his, kissing her breathless. Then they were off again, her arms wrapped around his neck and her leg hooked over his hip as he spun her higher, higher with each deep, strong thrust.

She came back to earth, slid down the shower wall into a heap on the floor. The water pattered on her head and ran in bright rivulets down her breasts. Jas slumped against the opposite wall, head back, eyes closed, his chest heaving.

"You're trying to kill me, Jas," she panted. "It must take a year off my life every time you do that."

He opened his eyes. "On the contrary. Why do you think wizards live so long?"

"Because they have insanely amazing sex?"

He laughed and tugged her to her feet. "Because we immerse ourselves in the magic. And never more deeply than when we do *this.*"

Cupping her bottom with both hands, he pulled her to him and kissed her again. She gave a little moan.

He broke free, grinning wickedly. "Come on. The hot water will run out eventually."

He wrapped her in a thick, decadently soft towel, then gathered her hair and pulled his hands through it.

Magic crackled at her scalp and a cloud of steam sighed into the air around her. And *poof*, just like that, dry hair. No hair dryer needed

He patted her butt through the towel. "Get dressed. I'll make breakfast."

He took a couple of strides toward the door, then stopped. "That reminds me." He opened a drawer in the vanity. "Toothbrush." He set a new one in the package on the countertop and beckoned her.

Still wrapped in the towel, she followed.

He moved around the bedroom, opening dresser drawers and closet doors. "Underthings, change of clothes, nightgown."

She inspected the clothes. Boy shorts in black and deep purple satin. Lace-edged camis. A cashmere sweater in deepest garnet and soft corduroy slacks in dark charcoal. She held up a chemise of amethyst silk, not at all frilly, but sheer and very short, no doubt leaving little to the imagination. Which was probably the point.

"You presumptuous—!"

"I prefer to think of it as optimistic," he interrupted.

She gave him a narrow look. "What, were you planning a kidnapping? When did you get all this?"

His eyes glinted and he gave a slow, one-sided smile. "I'm taking the Fifth on that."

It would've been truly dastardly in reality, but imagining him carrying her off to his mountain stronghold to ravish her at his leisure made her hot all over again.

This was ridiculous.

She deliberately didn't let her eyes linger on his

muscular back and bottom when he flipped off his towel and stepped into his boxers, instead pretending interest in the selection of clothes he'd provided. Enough for three or four days. She raised a brow at that. *Really?*

Even after what they'd been doing for much of the last twelve hours, she couldn't match his nonchalance in dressing. Getting dressed in front of somebody was a little different than pouncing on them in the heat of passion.

Jas seemed to have a taste for touchable fabrics. She settled on camel-colored microsuede leggings and a cream silk cami under a long Southwestern pattern cardigan sweater in cream, sage green and dusky violet. Green and purple again. *Subtle much, Jas?* she thought.

The clothes were far sexier than anything in her wardrobe at home. She didn't wear sexy clothes because there wasn't much point. It wasn't like she had anything to flaunt. But wearing these, oddly enough she *felt* sexy. After she'd followed the smell of bacon into the kitchen, she felt even sexier.

Jas turned and gave her a slow up and down. "Mmmm."

Heat immediately flared through her again. "You have *got* to stop that."

He gripped her hips and pulled her close. "Now why should I do that?"

"Because for one thing, your bacon will burn. Then all your smoke alarms will start screaming, the pan will catch on fire and whatever spells you have in place for the possibility will kick in, or your home security system will send out a call to the fire department and in either case, the results will really kill the mood."

He tilted his head as if thinking, then sighed. "I suppose you're right."

She told herself she wasn't disappointed when he let her go.

Jas' kitchen didn't have a breakfast bar—it had a breakfast island. She climbed onto a tall Mexican chair of dark, carved wood and watched him move around the kitchen, as smooth and competent there as with everything else. Soon, he set a plate of bacon, some kind of egg casserole and blue corn and piñon pancakes in front of her.

"Wow," she said around a mouthful of pancakes drenched in butter and real maple syrup. "You cook pretty well for a bachelor."

He took a seat beside her. "Thank you. There have been times I've had to, if I wanted to eat well."

She ate a few more bites, savoring the herbs and cheese in the casserole. "It's nice when someone else does the cooking sometimes."

His hand found its way onto her thigh. "Then I'll cook for you every day, my dear."

The way he said 'my dear' sent a shiver through her. He must've felt it, because he glanced aside at her. She cleared her throat and put her hand on his, enjoying it there but suspecting it would lead to other things in fairly short order.

"I'd like to take Caramela for a walk," she said. "See the neighborhood."

This time the sideways glance was skeptical. "It's still

snowing, Amethyst."

"So?" She leaned a shoulder against his. "It'll be so *romantic.*"

He snorted a laugh. "How can I resist?"

Amethyst would usually put on Caramela's coat if she took her out on a day like this. Since Caramela's coat was at home, she set a spell to keep her warm and dry. She slipped into her own coat, took Jas' gloved hand and stepped out into the fast-falling snow.

Snowfall in the desert was always a study of contrasts: clumps of snow clinging between the spines of tall, jointed cholla cactus and the pads of prickly pear cactus, outlining the long, toothed leaves of yuccas. Snow softened the lines of stuccoed courtyard and parapet walls, the sweep of gravel between dryland plantings, the gritty, hunched shoulders of granite boulders.

They walked in absolute silence. Tracks in the street showed that cars had driven there, but no purr of motors or whoosh of tires marred the silence now. The mountain, normally looming some five thousand feet over these foothills, disappeared into a soft veil of white.

Jas swung their linked hands, his breath puffing white between snowflakes. "You're right. This is nice. It's been a long time since I walked in the snow."

"Remember, you promised me a Jane Austen film festival, too. And I've only seen a couple of episodes of *Pride and Prejudice.*"

"Don't tell me you're disappointed in the way we spent the evening."

"Now you're just fishing for compliments."

"Not at all. I only want to hear how you can't bear to spend another night without me."

The funny thing was, she really was starting to feel that way.

"I don't hear you protesting," he said.

"I'm thinking."

He slid an arm around her waist. "Good. I have two more nights to convince you." He bent his head and said in her ear, *"My dear."*

Dammit! He knew what that did to her. "That," she said, "is not fair."

He only smiled.

She was chilly by the time they got back to his house. It was still snowing, so Jas took her and Caramela through a side gate and into a mud room where they shook off their coats and hats and stamped off their shoes. Caramela, of course, trotted in perfectly dry and comfortable.

Jas hung up their coats and led the way into the living room. With a glance and a flick of magic, he ignited a fire in the kiva fireplace. Amethyst moved to stand in front of it, holding her hands to the blaze. Jas followed, took her hands in his and called warmth around them. The painful cold drained from her fingers in a burst of prickles. He cupped her chilled face and did the same.

She sighed. "I love it when you use magic on me."

He looked startled, almost taken aback, then caught her in his arms and squeezed her tight.

"What?" she said into his shoulder.

He loosened his hold, but kept her in his embrace. "You have a trusting, generous spirit, Amethyst. By all rights, you should recoil when I use magic on you."

That took *her* aback. When had she finally forgiven him for that binding?

"Maybe I should've added 'now.'"

He chuckled. "I suspect so."

Enfolded in Jas' arms, she stood in front of the fire a few minutes, savoring both his and the fire's warmth.

"I've had fantasies about this," he murmured, brushing his lips over her hair.

She spluttered a laugh. "About *me?*"

"Oh, yes. I've carried you off here—"

"Jas! That's terrible!" she said, despite her thoughts along the same lines only a couple of hours ago. She narrowed her eyes at him. "Just how much experience do you have carrying off women?"

"I have a great deal more *fending* them off. My experience with you was a novel one."

"See, I told you it was all about the thrill of the chase. So you've carried me off. Then what? I cuss you up one side and down the other then blast you, your house, and the nearest chunk of mountain into the middle of next week?"

His hands began to drift up and down, from the sides of her breasts to her hips. The silk of the camisole slid caressingly over her skin.

"Then I seduce you—"

She didn't let herself turn so that his hand slid over her breast. "And exactly how do you manage to get close enough to do that?"

"You've been secretly desiring me despite your best

efforts to resist."

"Guys are *such* egotists. Do you want me to tell you how I really thought about you during the time you would've had to carry me off?"

"Better not. I suspect it will utterly ruin my fantasy."

"You suspect right. So you seduce me without me turning you into your constituent atoms. And?"

"And you beg me to take you."

Ignoring the liquid heat that poured through her, she put her hands on his shoulders, lowered her eyelids to half-mast and said in a deliberately throaty voice, "Take me, Jas. Right here. Right now."

His eyes flared wide and he stiffened. She tried to decide whether to laugh or jump on him or torment him some more, because tormenting him really was a lot of fun.

He had her sweater off and her cami over her head so quickly she was sure he must've used magic. Then there was nothing left to decide.

By the time Amethyst became aware of anything beyond Jas, the snow had stopped and was piled deeper than the last time she looked outside. She lay tangled with him on the rug in front of the fireplace, ironed flat by sex and magic. Or maybe it was magical sex. Or sex magic. Whatever it was, judging from the slack weight of his arms and legs, it affected Jas the same way.

Around them, the magic coiled and caressed like a cat

purring in the sun. Working it usually left her drained and hungry and too sensitive. She was certainly drained, every nerve quivering, but not in the same way. It almost felt like….the magic *approved*, doing its best to inspire more of the same. Was that why she couldn't seem to get enough of Jas? She shifted, unsettled.

"Mmm," Jas purred in her ear. "Are you cold?"

The murmur of his voice and the small circles he traced over her ribs made her forget her unease. She certainly hadn't noticed before, but the fire had burned down to embers.

"A little."

A wave of heat suddenly unfurled from the fireplace. She craned her neck to see green and purple flames dancing there.

"There." He brushed his lips over her ear. "That should help until I can warm you up again."

She wrinkled her nose. "Shower first."

His fingers tracked the curve of one rib toward her breastbone. "Oh, yes."

Seemed he couldn't get enough of her, either. Did that make it all better?

She pulled back enough to frown at him. "You have an awful lot of energy for an old guy."

He stood, pulled her up and drew her close again, his hands traveling along the contours of her back to her hips. "I'm making up for all the time I've had to restrain myself."

The shower was just as nice as this morning. She'd be taking a lot of showers, if they were all like this. It was still hard to get dressed in front of him, especially since Jas lay propped on one elbow on the bed, watching her.

She frowned again. "Do you plan to do that every time I get dressed?"

"Indeed I do. Every time you get *un*dressed, too."

Oh, come on, she told her body when it reacted.

"I have four words for you." She counted them off on her fingers. "Jane. Austen. Film. Festival."

He laughed and rolled off the bed, making a fine view of his own as he crossed to the dresser for a pair of shorts.

This time they settled on one of the lounges in the home theater. He picked up the remote and resumed *Pride and Prejudice*.

Amethyst was amazed at how comfortable it felt to lie back against Jas' chest in the circle of his arms. What a relief it was to finally stop struggling against him. She'd wondered what it would be like to be with him. She hadn't thought it would be like this. Being happy, content, sharing something she enjoyed with him.

"It's funny to think that Jane Austen wrote these stories two hundred years ago," she said. "Her teenagers act like teenagers now, and men and women still hoped to find love and happiness with someone."

"True. But she was writing romance no less idealized than any romance you might read today. The social constraints of the time made finding such happiness difficult. Respectable men and women were expected to marry and have children, and the pool of potential mates was often very small. Like Charlotte Lucas…" He nodded at the TV screen. "…most people were forced to take what they could get."

"I'm sure you had a terrible time finding a suitable wife," she teased.

"No," he said. "But I learned early to be suspicious of the smiles and attention I received."

She turned in his arms, surprised. "You mean there are downsides to being rich and handsome?"

She said it as if teasing again, but he didn't smile.

"More than you know," he said. "It becomes tiresome to be viewed only as a prize. Now you understand why I find you so appealing. Even in the beginning, there was no avarice in you. Only doubt that you should be the object of my interest."

"You mean in two hundred years nobody ever played hard-to-get?"

"Oh, yes. They *played*." He traced her lips with a thumb. "But you—you weren't playing."

"Jas. Don't tell me you never found someone honest and loving in all that time."

"I did, once or twice." He sighed. "And then she would grow old, and die."

He looked past her, at the TV, where people spoke and dressed as he once had.

"After I lost my son," he said, "the one with a wizard's power, the one who should've lived through the centuries with me..." He fell silent a moment. "After that, there were no more wives, no more children."

Her heart turned over and she laid a hand on his cheek. "Oh, Jas."

How long? she wanted to ask. At least a hundred years,

from what he'd said before. Maybe more. How terrible must it be to love someone…and know with absolute certainty that they'd be gone in a few short years.

"When Talys was killed," she said, very low, "I wanted to die, too."

"I know."

"I hated waking up every morning, because the moment I did, I'd think, 'Oh, god. He's gone. I'll never see him again,' and it would feel like somebody was trying to carve out my guts with a dull knife."

"Yes." He closed his eyes.

She pulled herself up and kissed him gently. "I'm sorry. I'm sorry your son wasn't one of the wizards who came back."

Jas put his hand over hers. "He might yet be. If he was, he'd be looking for me back East. I'm watching, just in case."

She hesitated. It was still hard to think about, harder still to talk about it. "And I don't think I ever thanked you for being there for me after what happened to Talys."

"Don't thank me for that, Amethyst." He said sharply, then made an abrupt, dismissive gesture, as if to wave away the words. "It was hard seeing you in such pain and knowing there was nothing I could do to ease it. I was—am—grateful you allowed me to help. Especially given the way you felt about me then."

"Jas, I always liked you. I was just really, really mad and hurt for a long time."

"I know." He traced the line of her hair. "You don't know how many times I cursed myself for that binding.

We could've been here two years ago if not for that."

"Maybe not," she said. "I still would've run the other way once I found out you're a wizard."

She turned and settled back against him again. On the TV, Lydia Bennet flirted shamelessly with Wickham and the other army officers.

Amethyst thought about the century or so that Jas had gone unmarried. There would've been hookers, of course, but she somehow didn't see Jas as the type to make use of prostitutes' services. Then what? Mistresses? Things would've gotten a lot easier by the 20th century. But what about before that?

"It must've been hard to have flings back then," she said. "Seems like any woman who did was ruined."

"Not as hard as you think. As you noted, people are people, no matter what century. If they're attracted, they usually find a way to act on that attraction. It simply wasn't polite to talk about it. There were always *arrangements*." He made air quotes. "People would generally look the other way as long as they were carried out discreetly." He nodded at the screen. "Wickham's mistake was making his affair with Lydia so obvious. Even though she was a gentleman's daughter, both of them might've gotten away with a brief indiscretion as long as it was kept out of sight. It was the very public elopement, along with Lydia's crowing about it, that caused the trouble."

It was strange, listening to him talk so familiarly of past centuries. The age difference between them should have been freaky. But Jas looked somewhere between thirty-five and forty, and usually acted no more than ten years older than she, so instead it was like talking to someone from a foreign country. Or her very own human time machine.

Already, questions popped into her mind. She shook them away and concentrated on the movie. She'd have plenty of time to ask him what things had been like.

"You notice," Jas said during the closing credits, "Elizabeth fell in love with Darcy only after she sees his estate at Pemberley."

She smacked his leg. "That's exactly the mistake everyone makes."

"She tells Jane so herself," he argued.

"And she's *joking*," Amethyst said. "Jane tells her to be serious and tell the truth because she knows Lizzy isn't the kind of woman to marry a man because of his money. Hell, Darcy had the same money when she refused his first proposal."

He turned off the TV. "Not many women will turn down a man if he has money."

"I guess it depends on the man," she said cautiously. She had a pretty good idea where this was going. Leave it to Jas to turn even Jane Austen to his advantage

"Or as in *Pride and Prejudice*, how he behaves."

She didn't say a word.

"Shall I ask if you still feel the way you did a few months ago?" he said.

It was what Darcy had asked Elizabeth in the movie.

She swallowed. "If you did, I guess…I'd have to say no."

He was quiet a moment. "Am I allowed to ask

another question now?"

She turned so she could see him, folding her legs over his. It felt like somebody was playing pinball in her stomach. "Jas—"

"Let me try."

He reached to the table beside the lounge, pulled open a small drawer and took something out. It was the ring he'd tried to give her the first time he proposed: an amethyst as deep and rich as a desert twilight surrounded by a spray of diamonds.

The magic quivered as Jas shaped a spell, one he'd used with her a time or two in the past. She tensed. It was a spell that resonated to truth.

"Amethyst Maria Rey, will you marry me? Will you be the light of my nights, the face I wake up to each morning? Will you brighten my days with thoughts of you? Will you be my most trusted friend, my partner, my lover, the mother of my children?"

The spell hummed like a bell with truth. Tears pushed into her eyes.

He wasn't finished yet. "Will you honor me with your love, trust me with your heart, share your life with me for the next three or four hundred years?"

She sniffed and turned to wipe her cheek on her shoulder. "I was going to say yes until you said that."

He grinned and leaned forward to brush away her tears with a thumb. "Let's start with a shorter term, then. How about forty or fifty years. We can renew the contract then."

She pressed his hand where it rested on her cheek.

"Okay. I think I can handle that."

"'Okay'?" he repeated. "*Okay?*"

She rolled her eyes. "You're determined to embarrass me. Fine." She took a breath, trying to ignore the sense that she was stepping off the edge of a cliff. "*Yes*, Jas. I'll marry you. But you'd better plan on a long engagement. It's never a good idea to marry someone you've dated only a few weeks."

He smiled, slid the ring onto her finger and kissed her hand. "We'll see."

Which was Jas-speak for *It'll happen sooner than that.*

CHAPTER 25

Down on the Ranch

How did everything change so quickly?

The Gwyneth Paltrow *Emma* was playing, but Amethyst couldn't keep her mind on the movie.

She loved Jas. After fighting it for so long, it was hard to get used to the idea, much less what it actually meant for the future. She touched the ring on her finger. That idea was even harder to get used to.

On the TV, the credits were already rolling. She blinked, surprised. Jas picked up the remote and the TV went dark.

"Ready for bed?" The way he said it made a shiver go through her.

No matter how overwhelming everything else was, that was one thing she could be sure about.

She cocked her head as if thinking. "Okay," she said casually. "But only if you can catch me."

Surprise chased puzzlement across his face in the instant before she grabbed the magic and zapped herself into his bedroom.

She leapt for the dresser, yanked open a drawer,

snatched out the purple chemise.

"Amethyst!" Jas' voice came from across the house. "What…?" She couldn't make out the rest.

"Trying to maintain some privacy!" she shouted back.

Even with that warning, it wouldn't take him long. The magic still swirled from her spell of transference, but he seemed to be coming the ordinary way.

She darted into his walk-in closet, stripped off her clothes and dropped the chemise over her head. She glanced down. *Holy….*

It was—*short*. Even shorter than she'd thought. The neckline plunged below her breastbone.

This time his voice came from the doorway. "If you're that shy, you only have to say—"

She stepped out of the closet, trying to ignore the fact that the chemise's full skirt barely covered her crotch and her headlights showed through the sheer silk.

Jas blinked, then his eyes did a quick up-and-down.

"Ah," was all that came out.

She walked toward him. "'Ah'? That's it?"

His gaze still didn't rise to her face. "It…looks…" He finally met her eyes. "Good God, Amethyst."

She swallowed a giggle. "I don't know why you're so surprised. You're the one who bought it. And you've already seen what's underneath."

He reached for her as if in a trance. "That's an entirely different matter."

His hands molded her body through the silk. He closed his eyes and let out a shaky breath. "Amethyst, you're beautiful."

She opened her mouth to argue.

"No," he said first. "To me, you are beautiful. Can you believe that?"

She turned her face away, shy now. "Right now I do."

His thumbs traced circles around her nipples. They peaked against the fabric, sending ripples of sensation straight to her middle.

"Never think for a moment that I don't like what I see." He slipped his hands inside her panties, then slid them down. "Because I like it very much." His hands returned, warm and caressing, cupping her bare bottom under the chemise's short skirt. He pulled her to him. "Very much indeed."

Through his pants, his erection pushed against her groin. That was the thing about Jas—give him half a chance, and he could convince you of anything.

❖·❖·❖·❖·❖·❖

Amethyst woke early, Jas' breath warm against her neck, his arm heavy across her. She lay quiet a few minutes, content and pleasantly achy. The echoes of last night's pleasures seemed stamped into her body, reminding her of every touch, every stroke, every kiss.

Lazy heat unfurled through her. She could turn in Jas' arms, kiss and caress him awake. But he looked so sweet sleeping there, his lashes a dark fan against his cheek, the shadow of a day's growth of beard on his jaw, his black hair irresistibly tousled. She began easing from under his arm.

"Amethyst?" he murmured, his eyelids flickering.

She kissed his nose. "Go back to sleep."

He mumbled something and snuggled into the covers. She grinned. It had been a long night.

She slipped into a robe and padded barefoot along the heated tile floors, Caramela trotting behind. It was strange how comfortable she felt here in Jas' house, as if she belonged here.

There was still a lot of snow on the ground from yesterday. Caramela stopped at the open patio door, eyeing the scene outside with head down and ears drooping.

"I'm sorry," Amethyst said. "You have to go out."

Once she wrapped a spell of warmth around her, Caramela relented.

Jas had some kind of fancy, high-end coffeemaker that ground its own beans, but Amethyst had paid attention when he'd used it and managed to get a pot started. She let Caramela back in and got her breakfast ready.

While Caramela ate, Amethyst sat at the breakfast island sipping a cup of hot chocolate. Early morning sunlight slanted through the windows and washed across her, striking every color of purple from the ring Jas had given her, from lilac to deepest violet.

Her chest squeezed and her stomach made a strange lurch, as if she'd missed a step in the dark. It still didn't seem real, like she'd taken an irrevocable step out of the life she'd known and was feeling her way across an utterly unfamiliar landscape. Abruptly, she slid off the stool and walked to the windows, breathing deep to calm the sudden pounding of her heart.

She managed to get herself settled down again by the time Jas padded into the kitchen.

Slipping his arms around her from behind, he kissed her neck. "Cheater. Sneaking out of bed on me."

She relaxed into him. "I did think about waking you up, but I know old guys need their sleep."

He squeezed her hard and growled into her neck. Suddenly ticklish, she laughed and squirmed in his arms.

He let her go. "It's just as well, I suppose. There's something I want to show you today. Let's get dressed and we'll go for breakfast."

They stopped for breakfast at a little bakery tucked into a strip mall on Tramway then got back into Jas' Range Rover and headed west. Amethyst forbore asking questions until it became clear that Uptown was their destination.

"We're going to work?"

"Not today."

But sure enough, he pulled into the Magus lot and into his reserved spot. Mystified, she got out of the car.

The parking lot wasn't as empty as she'd expect on a Sunday, although the lobby was deserted except for the security guards on duty. Walking with Jas to the elevators, her fingers twined with his, she felt a surprising spurt of guilt as she passed Talys' fountain.

Jas must've noticed something, because he paused. "All right?"

She looked from the glossy black boulder to the concern on Jas' face, from something that could never be again to what was now.

She put on a smile and shrugged. "I'm okay."

He studied her a moment more, then nodded. She raised a single glance to the fountain as the elevator doors closed.

The building used biometric security, so she assumed a retinal scan let Jas activate a usually locked button on the elevator's panel. The elevator hummed up, and up, past the executive floor on the twenty-fifth story. The doors slid open on brilliant sunlight and the unmistakable pulsing whine of a helicopter's idling engine. She gave Jas a surprised, questioning look.

He urged her out onto the roof. "Come on."

The chopper was sleek and black with the Magus logo displayed discreetly on the door. She'd been vaguely aware that there was a company helicopter, but it wasn't really the sort of thing that crossed her radar. Now it hit her: it wasn't just the company's. It was *Jas'* helicopter.

He handed her in and she settled into a leather seat in a cabin that looked more like the inside of a luxury car than any kind of aircraft. They buckled in and the pilot secured the door. A moment later, his voice came over the intercom advising them of takeoff, the blades sped up and they were lifting away from the roof.

"Wow," she said faintly.

The southern fringes of Albuquerque slid past below, then the dirt roads and unidentifiable structures of Kirtland Airforce Base, then finally the native desert of the Isleta Pueblo reservation.

"Where are we going?" she said.

"You'll see," Jas said.

The chopper swung east. The Manzano Mountains, white with snow, passed the windows on the left. Snow still whitened the high plains on the east side of the mountains, a good thousand feet or so higher than the Rio Grande Valley. Rumpled hills dotted dark with vegetation stretched away in a line ahead.

"Do you see that mesa?" He pointed through the window at the flat-topped hill. "Mesa Viento. That's where we're going."

The pilot's voice came over the intercom again: *We'll be landing in five minutes, Mr. Harker.*

The mesa's steep sides swept past and they were over the mesa itself, a snowy island rising from the surrounding plains. The chopper descended on a helipad cleared of snow, touching down with scarcely a bump.

"Thanks, Richard," Jas said to the pilot when they stepped out. "Make yourself comfortable at the bunkhouse. We'll be heading back this evening."

Amethyst blinked. And just like that, they had a helicopter ride home again.

A slight man wearing a heavy Western jacket and shoulder-length hair met them at the helipad. His face was weather-lined and freckles sprinkled his nose.

"Rusty," Jas greeted the man, "this is my fiancée, Amethyst Rey. I thought I'd give her a tour of the ranch."

At the word *fiancée,* a wave of dizziness rolled over her and her mouth went dry.

Rusty looked at her with new interest. "Well, we're glad to have you here, ma'am. Let's get you to the house and out of this cold. Watch your step. It's a mite icy."

A walkway of native sandstone swept clean of snow led toward a huge northern New Mexico-style house. An entry roofed with beautifully timbered trusses led into a spectacular Southwestern interior. The house must've been sited at the edge of the mesa, because the tall windows of the living room ahead looked out on a view that went on forever, sparkling white and blue and gold in the bright winter sunshine.

It made the house on the bosque, where she and Jas had attended that party, look humble. Everything was New Mexico style without being over the top, a tasteful sense of place in every room, from the *viga* and *latilla* ceilings to the *nichos* in the walls to the kiva fireplaces in several rooms.

Amethyst looked around, as dumbstruck as when she'd seen Jas dressed in all his 19th century glory.

"I use this place primarily for business meetings," he said, guiding her from room to room. "It's large enough to accommodate as many guests as I'm likely to invite, and it's private. I also occasionally come out here to get away."

If she'd felt like her life had wandered into unfamiliar territory before, she'd been positively dropped into another world now. She tried not to goggle at Navajo rugs and Pueblo pottery, each piece no doubt worth thousands of dollars. At original Bev Dolittle and R.C. Gorman paintings.

She'd known Jas had money, of course, but had always assumed it extended as far as nice cars, fine restaurants and a fancy home in the foothills. All out of her reach, but nothing that far out of the ordinary.

This—*this* was a whole different level.

She must've been quiet too long.

He glanced at her. "What do you think?"

"It's...awesome." Literally.

They'd made their way back to the living room. Rusty, reading on his phone, waited there in a square, Navajo rug-patterned chair.

"Would you like to ride out and see the ranch?" Jas said then turned to Rusty. "Can we get boots and a heavier coat for her?"

"It sounds like a lot of trouble—" Amethyst began.

Rusty got to his feet. "No trouble, ma'am. It's what we do here. Pat's left some coffee in the kitchen for you in the meanwhile."

"Thank you," Jas said. "You can put the clothes in my bedroom. We'll change there."

"How much have you ridden?" Rusty asked Amethyst.

She shrugged. "Not a lot. I rode a friend's horse a few times when I was a kid. Maybe only two or three times since."

"Diego would be a good choice for her, if he's still here," Jas said to Rusty.

"Yessir, he would, and he is," Rusty said. "I'll have Jaime saddle him up."

A cup of coffee and a trip upstairs to the master suite later, and Amethyst was dressed in flannel-lined jeans, cowboy boots with insulated socks and a quilted down jacket. Jas wore much the same. She'd seen him in Western wear once before and had been surprised by how well he wore it. Now she knew why.

They walked back outside, once more following the sandstone walkway to a stable a few hundred yards off.

"Rusty manages the ranch." Jas pointed out a house in the same style as the main house. It would've been large in her neighborhood, but here, it was dwarfed by the main house. "He and his wife, Pat, live there. The wranglers and cowboys stay in the bunkhouse, there."

The bunkhouse looked like an upscale apartment building. Each apartment had its own entry porch. Piñon-scented smoke furled from a chimney—maybe Richard, the helicopter pilot, making himself comfortable.

Rusty and a young Mexican man waited with two horses, one a buckskin and the other the deep, rich red of cherry wood. Jas greeted the bay horse with a pat on the cheek then turned to check the buckskin's girth and stirrups. He gave a satisfied nod and held the reins while Amethyst mounted. She didn't scramble too much, but she wasn't particularly graceful, either. She'd forgotten how big horses are.

Jas, on the other hand, swung up into the bay's saddle with practiced ease. She was surprised for only an instant. Of course he'd know his way around horses. Cars hadn't existed for much of his life.

The Mexican man—Jaime, she supposed—opened a metal gate and they rode out.

Her horse walked calmly alongside Jas' without pulling at the bit or throwing his head, as smooth and rolling as a carousel horse. Between the snow and the length of time since she'd been on a horse's back, she was content to just ride along and let the horse take the lead.

The mesa stretched ahead, nearly flat except for the slight tuck and roll of drainages. Piñon pines and junipers rose in dark clumps from the snow. The voices of the men back in the stable yard fell behind and after a few minutes, the only sounds were the muffled clump of the horses' hooves in the snow, the whuff of their breaths, the creak of saddle leather.

Jas let out a breath that plumed white in the cold, still air. "This is why I come out here even when I don't have guests."

She rode along beside him, thinking about it. "It's like going home."

"A little, I suppose. Although I wouldn't trade modern plumbing and electricity for more than two or three days' worth of quiet."

She made a face. "Chamber pots and baths once a week had to suck."

"Once a week…if you were well-off enough for servants."

"Ick."

A piñon jay screeched and swooped in a flash of blue from a tree, scolding them for disturbing his own privacy.

"This is a working ranch," Jas said. "We raise longhorns and bison, and train horses as well. Ranch-trained horses are in high demand by serious horsemen."

"Somehow, I never pictured you as a ranch owner." She slanted him a look. "A dude, maybe."

He barked a surprised laugh. "*Dude!* Them's fightin' words," he drawled with a southern New Mexico twang.

"City slicker?"

"Just remember who can ride here—and who's on the gentlest horse in the stable."

She didn't have a good reply to that.

"I bought the place from Rusty's father in the 1950s," Jas said. "It was during a severe drought, and most of the ranchers in the area had to sell off entire herds. It's hard enough to keep a ranch solvent, but under those circumstances, it became impossible."

"Wait a minute. You knew Rusty's father in the Fifties. How does that work? You must look the same now as you did then. Don't you?"

"I do. And it can be problematic when you know someone over a long period of time," he said. "There are several ways to handle it—I'll have to teach you. You look a young twenty. You'll be able to get away with that for another five years, ten at the most, before people start wondering why you look so young."

"So what do you do? Illusion to make yourself appear to age?"

"Or mind-magic." He glanced aside at her. "If I'm dealing with someone who's known me a while and the subject comes up, I make them believe I was much younger before. Or make myself appear the way they expect. In Rusty's case, he thinks it was my father he remembers when his own father was managing the ranch."

She frowned.

"I know you don't approve of that sort of thing," he said. "But in time, you'll need to decide how you want to deal with the problem. I doubt you'll want to start a new life every ten years or so."

"No," she admitted.

"With the people who know you're a wizard—Melodie and your family—you can always appear as you are."

She tried to wrap her head around it. How you'd make it work for people who'd known you for twenty or thirty years—and those who'd known you only five or ten. Or people you'd known ten years ago and suddenly met again one day.

"Ugh," she said. "When the time comes, maybe I'll just say I dye my hair and had a facelift."

They rode in silence a while. It was indeed soothing out here, away from the bustle and noise and demands of everyday life. It occurred to her that the whole weekend had been like this. She didn't want to think about tomorrow, when she had to return to the real world.

Jas suddenly reined over, close enough to bump knees. He slid his arm around her and kissed her.

He gave her one of his special smiles. "I'm glad you're here with me."

Love for him swept over her in a warm rush, so strong it took her breath away.

She leaned over and kissed him back. "Me too."

Why was it so hard to tell him what she felt?

"Look," Jas said, pointing. "Bison."

She hadn't been paying much attention to the various dark lumps dotting the snowy landscape. Now she saw that some of those lumps were lower and darker than the others—and were staring at them intently.

"Oh!" she said.

Jas reached for her reins to stop her the same moment she pulled on them.

"They are, for all intents and purposes, wild animals," he said. "They'll be fine as long as we keep our distance. Otherwise, we'd better be ready with a barrier spell."

She sat still, watching the animals while her placid horse rolled the bit in his mouth. "Do you have pronghorns here, too?"

He nodded. "Also elk and deer, and the occasional bear. We saw mountain lion tracks up here some years ago, but you're more likely to find cougars down in the canyons, where the cover is better."

She sighed. "I'd love to see them."

He reached out a gloved hand and squeezed hers where they held the reins. "You will."

She didn't understand the tremor that went through her at that.

"Are you ready to turn around?" he said. "I think I can safely promise you an excellent steak dinner in front of a warm fire when we get back."

"And a helicopter ride over the city lights?"

"Mmm. And fireworks after we get home, my dear."

There he went with the *my dear* again!

Amethyst smacked her thigh. "You have *got* to stop doing that."

CHAPTER 26

Foreboding

Amethyst woke again before Jas did, but this morning, she lay staring up at the section of indigo sky visible through the windows behind the bed.

An uneasy feeling coiled in her middle. She searched herself, trying to pin down the problem, the sense of formless fear.

She must've moved, because Jas stirred and opened his eyes.

"Good morning," he murmured sleepily.

She slid her arms around him and hugged him tight, desperate love squeezing her heart. A stirring against her thigh told her he was waking up quickly. He made a pleased noise and began to caress her. She shivered, sighing, raised her mouth to his and lost herself in him once more.

After a shower, he wrapped his towel around her, pulled her close and kissed her. He felt good against her, warm and solid and still damp from the shower.

"Now *this* is a very good reason to get up early," he

said, smiling down at her. "I regret the thought of going to work."

She leaned her head on his shoulder and closed her eyes, breathing in the scent of clean skin and sage soap. The warm tingle from their lovemaking still rippled through her. "Yes."

"Will you be here tonight?"

That uneasiness curdled in her gut again. She withdrew a little.

"I don't know, Jas. I should take care of my own house sometime."

He sighed. It was a very small sigh, one she didn't think he'd meant her to hear.

"At least have dinner with me."

She smiled and put a hand to his cheek, the stubble rough under her palm. "Okay. I can do that."

While he got ready for work, she discovered the appeal of watching someone dress. There was something alluring in the way his clever fingers worked the buttons of his dress shirt and tied one of his usual green silk ties, the way he shrugged into the suit jacket, transforming from the Jas she'd grown comfortable with to formidable CEO. He caught her at it.

"If you keep doing that," he said, "I'll have to take it all off again. Then we'll never get to work."

Yesterday, she would've said something smart or suggestive. Today, she only smiled.

If he noticed the difference, he didn't show it.

❖ ❖ ❖ ❖ ❖ ❖

It felt odd seeing him off for work, almost dislocating. Like it wasn't her, but someone she didn't know. Amethyst paced across the kitchen, suddenly out of place when she'd felt so at home only yesterday. She breathed deeply, slowly, groping within for the source of—what? Dread? Dismay? —that gripped her.

She cleaned up the breakfast dishes then sat on the floor, petting Caramela to calm herself.

At last, she got up, pulled her fingers through her hair and took another long breath.

Okay. Time to stop brooding and get back to business. Start with checking the phone. She wandered back into the bedroom for her purse.

Five missed calls, two from Melodie. Damn. She forgot she'd turned off the ringer Friday night. And her phone had been more or less the last thing on her mind after that.

She dialed Melodie.

"I was getting worried," Melodie said. "It's not like you not to return calls."

Amethyst took a long breath. "I've been at Jas'."

A heavy silence on the other end of the line. "All weekend?"

"Um…yes."

More silence. "How did it go?"

It was suddenly hard to get a breath. "Oh god, Mel."

"That good, or that bad?"

"Both," she said, her voice coming out strangled.

"Tell me what— No, wait. Listen, I'll take an early lunch. Why don't you meet me at Fuddruckers. The one along I-25."

"Okay. Give me about an hour. I have to take Caramela home, first."

Amethyst arrived first and scouted for a moderately private table. Well before the lunch rush, Melodie slid into the booth across from her, sleek and professional in slacks and heels and a silky champagne-colored blouse.

She studied Amethyst. "Somehow it seems like you should look happier. Where do you want to start?"

"So. Okay." Amethyst struggled to gather frayed strands of sense. "Jas invites me over for a Jane Austen film festival. When I get there he's dressed like Mr. Darcy—coat, waistcoat, cravat, the whole bit—and what woman except Lizzie Bennet can resist Mr. Darcy?"

"Oh, shit," Melodie said.

"Right. So a couple of episodes through *Pride and Prejudice*, the one with Colin Firth, in the part with Mr. Collins, which is about the most annoying part of the whole show anyway—"

"Okay, okay, I get it. You end up going to bed with Jas."

Amethyst nodded.

Melodie looked worried. "What, does he have a Red Room of Pain? Did he want you to do weird, kinky billionaire stuff?"

Amethyst laughed in spite of herself. "No, nothing like that. He was gentle and considerate. And…it was amazing."

"Amazing sex. That's always good. But then after he got what he wanted, he told you he'll call you next week or something like that, right?"

"No, he asked me to marry him again."

Understanding sympathy washed across Melodie's face. "And you told him no, so the whole thing's gone off the rails in a hideous, fiery crash."

"No." Amethyst's voice quavered threateningly. "I said yes." She put her head in her hands.

"I'm not following here," Melodie said. You're upset because you told him you'd marry him?"

Amethyst nodded again.

"And you don't love him?"

Amethyst slumped. "Heaven help me, I do. No matter how much I didn't want to, I do."

"So then you think he doesn't love you. You still think he's after something."

"I did think so. I told him so, too." She swallowed hard. "And he told me all the reasons he wants to be with me. And he…he…he told me he loves me."

"But you don't believe him."

"I do. I can't believe I believe it, but I do."

Melodie was looking more and more perplexed. "So…you're worried you won't be happy with him?"

"That's the craziest thing of all. I *am* happy with him. I look forward to being with him. He's kind and thoughtful and dependable and patient and fun in an aggravating sort of way…" Her voice squeezed into silence.

Melodie sat back, drumming her fingers on the table. "Okay, let's look at this logically." She started ticking off points on her fingers. "You love him, and he loves you. He makes you happy and you enjoy your time with him. And don't think I didn't notice, even though you didn't mention it—he buys you clothes, for godsake, since I know *you're* not gonna plunk down a couple hundred bucks for a cashmere sweater. The physical side of things is great, but he doesn't want you only for your body."

"Please," Amethyst said.

"He's bent over backwards to show you," Melodie went on as if she hadn't spoken, "*and* your friends and family that he isn't the complete bastard we all thought he was. So what's the problem?"

"If I'm married to him, everything will be different!"

"Well, yeah. That's what usually happens when you marry somebody."

"You don't understand. *Way* different. It'll be like living on another planet." She found herself breathing hard. "Do you have any idea how he lives?"

"A guy who owns a company like Magus? I can guess. It's not like he's trying to separate you from your own people." Melodie frowned. "Is he?"

"No. But…" She waved her hands. "I'll stop being *me!*"

"Oh, for godsake, Wiz. Listen to yourself. You're panicking. Why are you panicking?"

"I don't know! Everything's just the way it should be. What more could I ask for? I know I'm being stupid. I keep trying to figure out what my problem is…but I can't."

Melodie studied her for a long moment. "Maybe the problem is you just don't want to marry him."

Amethyst only rubbed her forehead.

"If that's the way you feel, you have to tell him."

"That's easy for you to say!" Amethyst flared. "You haven't liked him for a long time."

"You think that's what's going on? Gee, thanks a lot," Melodie fired back. "It's nice to know my best friend thinks I have ulterior motives." She steamed a minute. "Excuse me, but wasn't I the one who told you he's worth it?"

Amethyst folded her arms and looked away.

"I never thought I'd be saying this," Melodie went on, still hot, "but it isn't fair to Jas to keep dragging it on, letting him think he has a chance if he really never did. If you've gotten cold feet or can't commit or whatever the hell the problem is, you need to quit tormenting him and end it. If you don't, if you force yourself to go on, both of you will end up miserable. Go ahead and make that choice for yourself, if that's what floats your boat, but you don't have the right to do it to somebody else."

Amethyst put her head in her hands again. "I know. I'm sorry. You're right. It's just that I kept thinking…" She gritted her teeth, trying to keep the tears in check.

Melodie sighed. "You kept thinking it's not reasonable to feel that way, so you shouldn't."

Tears spilled down Amethyst's face.

Melodie took one of her hands, prying it away from her face. "It might not be reasonable. It might not make any sense at all. But if it's the way you feel, it's not like you can help it. But you have to be honest with yourself and care enough about Jas to face it. As hard and painful as it is to do it."

Amethyst stared down at her plate, at the food mostly untouched and gone cold. After a long moment, she nodded.

✦ ✦ ✦ ✦ ✦ ✦

Caramela knew something was wrong as soon as Amethyst came home. She hovered close, casting worried looks up at her.

There was plenty of work to do, but Amethyst ended up in the living room in the corner of the sofa, her feet tucked under her and staring out the window.

She thought of Jas in the chair in old jeans and a flannel shirt, his socked feet up on the ottoman, a glass of wine at his elbow. Jas at the dining room table behind his laptop, giving her that cocky smile of his. Jas putting dishes in the dishwasher, throwing the ball for Caramela, riding along on horseback beside her. Jas dressed in Regency magnificence, the lights of 21st century Albuquerque glittering through the tall windows behind him. The tenderness in his dark eyes as they made love.

Amethyst wouldn't trade any of it for anything. So why did the thought of marrying him strike her with cold fear?

She got ready for dinner with him blindly. Caramela kept glancing at her even as she ate her supper, then left her bowl half-full. Great. She could manage to make even her dog miserable. Amethyst left the remainder of the food down for her, filled her water dish and got into the car to go meet her fate.

Jas, looking as good as ever in jeans and a sport coat, was waiting for her at the top of the stairs at Sandiago's, at the base of the Sandia Peak Tramway. He leaned on the railing, watching the lights of the tram cars glide up and down the mountainside. As she walked toward the restaurant, he raised a hand in greeting. Amethyst's heart beat so fast she could hardly gulp air.

He gave her a kiss when she reached him then led her to the left—not into the restaurant, but toward the tram terminal.

Her confusion must've shown on her face, because he explained, "We're having dinner at High Finance."

Her stomach dipped. High Finance, at ten thousand-plus feet at the top of Sandia Crest, was one of the more expensive restaurants in town.

She must've acted more or less normal. Either that or even worse, Jas might've been too happy to realize if she *wasn't* acting normal. She was grateful when they boarded the tram for the ride up to the top of the Crest. She could look out the windows and pretend to be absorbed in the view of the city lights spread out below, the jeweled necklace of I-40 strung to the west, the gently glowing green pyramid of the Magus Building at Uptown growing smaller and smaller as they climbed higher.

It was hard to concentrate on the menu. After that it was pure torture, the need to keep up the conversation, smiling when appropriate. Jas ordered wine. An appetizer arrived, a spinach-artichoke dip that she managed to force down a few bites of.

"You seem distracted tonight," Jas said. "Is everything all right?"

She'd already taken some sips of wine for strength, the alcohol fuming on her palate and down her throat to seethe in her belly. She'd just lifted her glass for another. She put it down and pushed it to one side.

She made herself meet his gaze. "I've been thinking." Her voice came out amazingly steady. "About the future."

He grew very still.

She swallowed on a dry throat and twisted the ring he'd given her. "I thought about how it would be to continue my life the way it has been, on my own. I've been independent a long time, taking care of myself, making my own choices. It's not easy to give that up, to get used to including somebody else. And, you know, we're so different. We live completely different lives, we have different ideas…"

With every word, his gaze grew cooler, more distant.

Amethyst put a hand to her head. "Oh, god. I'm making a mess of this."

Jas just sat across from her, his eyes black and expressionless.

"What I'm trying to say is that I spent a lot of time thinking this afternoon. What it would be like with you in my life—or not. And I decided…"

She put her hands in her lap and squeezed one inside the other. He sat as still as he'd been cursed to stone.

"I decided that I *do* want to share my life with you," she said. "Even though it scares me."

He was instantly out of his chair and on one knee

beside hers, straining her to him so tightly she could barely breathe.

"Jas—" she said, glancing at the startled faces at nearby tables and struggling to free an arm to hug him back.

He shifted his grip—and it was a *grip*—tangled his fingers in her hair and kissed her. And kissed her. And kissed her. Amethyst became dimly aware of scattered applause and a couple of enthusiastic whistles.

At last, he let her up for air, stroking her hair back from her face. "Don't be afraid, my dearest Amethyst. I'll never give you cause to regret it."

The naked joy and relief on his face almost broke her heart. Sometimes it was so hard to reconcile the true, faithful Jas Harker she'd come to know with the smooth charmer she'd learned to be on her guard against. And this man on his knees beside her had been steeling himself for his own heartbreak a minute ago.

She swallowed the threatening lump in her throat. "Well, don't over-promise."

He took her hands, kissed the knuckles of one, then the other. His eyes glinted, suspiciously bright. "If nothing else, I can promise you'll never be bored."

She cupped his cheek, the weight of doubt and anxiety that had been suffocating her all day evaporating. "I bet I won't."

EPILOGUE

O f course, Jas wanted to make the official announcement.

"You already ruined your credibility on that front," Amethyst told him. "I'd better tell my friends. You can tell yours."

He sat across the table from her, tapping his fingers against his wine glass and looking very much like a thwarted wizard should. "I'm not the least bit happy about it. But I suppose you're right."

"Of course I am," she said, leaned across the table and kissed him.

She met Dad and Mama the next day at the Cowgirl Café in Santa Fe. After a few moments of stunned silence, Mama was just as delighted as she had been after Jas had made his prank call a few months ago. Walking back out to their cars after lunch, she was in raptures.

"Oh, *mija!* So rich! So handsome! Such a lucky, lucky girl!"

It was word for word what she'd said after Jas' call.

Dad took her elbow and pulled her aside before he climbed into their Highlander.

"Thistle," he said. "Are you sure?"

Amethyst sighed. It was a sad omen of what to expect from everyone who knew her.

◇◇◇◇◇◇

Amethyst sat at her worktable, running the final lines of solder on the fall aspens window. Tomorrow she'd patina it, then she could turn it over to the client's carpenter for installation in a door.

Her phone rang with a fast techno beat, vibrating across her desk. Jas' smiling face, that one quirked brow raised suggestively, looked up from the screen.

Her heart beat quicker and something inside her fluttered like a bird leaping into the air. How long would a simple phone call have that effect?

She grabbed the phone, tapped the speakerphone button and set it on the worktable, safely out of the way of the soldering iron's cord.

"Hey, Jas. What's happening up there in CEO Land?"

"Amethyst." He drawled her name in a way that made her put the soldering iron in its stand before she burned herself. "What are you doing?"

She almost laughed. She hadn't had this kind of phone conversation with a guy since she was nineteen or twenty.

"Soldering a window." She put her chin in her hand. "What are you doing?"

"Thinking of you. What are you wearing?"

Amethyst raised a brow at the phone. "What do you think I'm wearing while I'm wielding a hot soldering iron?"

"I can't stop thinking of you in that purple chemise," he said. "Next time I have you in it, I will—"

"No, Jas," she broke in. "I am not having phone sex with you."

"Why not?"

She gusted a sigh. "Because it's distracting and frustrating."

"Then come to my office and we'll have the real thing."

"*What?*" Good thing she'd put down that soldering iron.

"Just think of it. A view of the mountains rising on one side, the city spilling out below us on the other. It'll be spectacular. I have a big, sturdy cherry wood desk perfect for the purpose. There's even a lavatory convenient for afterwards."

"Uh-huh. And tell me. Just how much action has this desk already seen?"

"Ah…"

"That's what I thought," she said. "No."

"But never with my fiancée."

"Never with your *wife*, either."

"Never is a long time, my dear."

When he said 'my dear' with that dark lord purr, she had serious second thoughts about the desk idea.

"You're going to spend the next three or four hundred years talking me into things, aren't you?"

Even over the phone, she could hear the smile in his voice. "Absolutely."

Also by Kathlena L. Contreras:

The Land of Enchantment

Familiar Magic

Do You Believe in Magic (short story)

Crooked Magic

This Magic Moment (short story)

Could It Be Magic

Fated Magic – a Land of Enchantment novel

Also…
Shadowbound

Kathlena L. Contreras writing as
K. Lynn Bay:

Blackthorne

ChanceShaper

Springtime in Hades

For reading samples and book descriptions,
go to FlyingTigerPress.com

To hear about new releases by Kathlena L. Contreras and K. Lynn Bay, you can sign up for my mailing list at FlyingTigerPress.com. I promise I won't spam you, and I'll never share your information with anyone.

If you enjoyed this book, please take a moment to write a review on your favorite site. Your opinion can help other readers decide to try a book by an author new to them.

Thank you for reading!

Check my Flying Tiger Press page on Pinterest for images from *Could It Be Magic*.

About the Author

Kathlena Contreras has been writing since the age of eight, when while hanging out at her dad's office one summer, she typed out a story about a saber-toothed tiger that encounters a time machine. The story was three paragraphs long.

Many years and many paragraphs later and here she is, still writing about weird things. In between writing, Kathlena has been the owner of a successful small business, an assistant medical librarian, a database manager and a pusher of paper in countless offices. She's also been a copy editor for three nationally distributed rodeo magazines and the editor of a local literary magazine.

She currently lives with her husband, five dogs and assorted livestock on the edge of the woods above the valley east of Albuquerque, New Mexico, USA, the Land of Enchantment, a place where the view goes on forever.

Kathlena L. Contreras also writes as K. Lynn Bay.

Stop by and say hi at FlyingTigerPress.com

To hear about new releases, you can sign up on my website. I promise I won't spam you, and I'll never share your information with anyone.

Email at kathys.wizards@gmail.com
Flying Tiger Press on Pinterest
Kathlena L. Contreras on Facebook
K. Lynn Bay on Google+